Praise for

JENNIFER RYAN and the
WILDES OF WYOMING

By Jennifer Ryan

Stand-Alone Novels
THE ONE YOU WANT • LOST AND FOUND FAMILY
SISTERS AND SECRETS • THE ME I USED TO BE

The Wyoming Wilde Series
MAX WILDE'S COWBOY HEART
SURRENDERING TO HUNT • CHASE WILDE COMES HOME

The McGrath Series
TRUE LOVE COWBOY • LOVE OF A COWBOY
WAITING ON A COWBOY

Wild Rose Ranch Series
TOUGH TALKING COWBOY
RESTLESS RANCHER • DIRTY LITTLE SECRET

Montana Heat Series
TEMPTED BY LOVE • TRUE TO YOU
ESCAPE TO YOU • PROTECTED BY LOVE

Montana Men Series
HIS COWBOY HEART • HER RENEGADE RANCHER
STONE COLD COWBOY • HER LUCKY COWBOY
WHEN IT'S RIGHT • AT WOLF RANCH

The McBrides Series
DYLAN'S REDEMPTION • FALLING FOR OWEN
THE RETURN OF BRODY MCBRIDE

The Hunted Series
EVERYTHING SHE WANTED • CHASING MORGAN
THE RIGHT BRIDE • LUCKY LIKE US • SAVED BY THE RANCHER

Short Stories
"Close to Perfect" (appears in SNOWBOUND AT CHRISTMAS)
"Can't Wait" (appears in ALL I WANT FOR CHRISTMAS IS A COWBOY)
"Waiting for You" (appears in CONFESSIONS OF A SECRET ADMIRER)

Max Wilde's Cowboy Heart

A Wyoming Wilde Novel

JENNIFER RYAN

AVONBOOKS

An Imprint of HarperCollinsPublishers

MAX WILDE'S COWBOY HEART. Copyright © 2023 by Jennifer Ryan. All rights reserved. Printed in the United States of America. No part of this book may be used or reproduced in any manner whatsoever without written permission except in the case of brief quotations embodied in critical articles and reviews. For information, address HarperCollins Publishers, 195 Broadway, New York, NY 10007.

First Avon Books mass market printing: March 2023

Print Edition ISBN: 978-0-06-311144-8
Digital Edition ISBN: 978-0-06-309466-6

Cover design by Nadine Badalaty
Cover photograph © Rob Lang (couple)
Cover images © iStock/Getty Images; © Shutterstock

Avon, Avon & logo, and Avon Books & logo are registered trademarks of HarperCollins Publishers in the United States of America and other countries.

HarperCollins is a registered trademark of HarperCollins Publishers in the United States of America and other countries.

FIRST EDITION

23 24 25 26 27 BVGM 10 9 8 7 6 5 4 3 2 1

*For all those who believe in true
love and second chances.
This one is for you.*

Max Wilde's Cowboy Heart

Chapter One

KENNA HAD barely walked into her apartment after a hard day teaching math to a bunch of rowdy teens when someone pounded on her door. She jumped, startled by the aggressive banging. They didn't stop until she yelled, "Who's there?"

"It's me. Open up."

The hummingbird beat of her heart slowed as relief swept through her.

She lived alone. Her brother ought to know better than to scare the crap out of her.

She unlocked and opened the door, but stood her ground. "I thought you were some maniac trying to murder me."

Kyle rolled his eyes. "So I knocked first?"

"Okay, so it doesn't make a whole lot of sense. Neither does your urgency to see me."

Kyle pushed past her. "Close the door. Lock it again." Paranoia filled his voice.

That didn't ease her mind, so she locked up, then

turned to him, one brow raised as high as her suspicions that something wasn't right. "What's going on?"

Kyle raked his fingers over his head, sending his blond waves into even more disarray. "I have to go away for a while." Kyle went to her slider and peeked through the long hanging blinds. "I don't think they followed me, but . . ."

That jacked her heart rate back up. "Why would someone follow you?"

"It's a long story."

Kenna leaned back against the door and crossed her arms over her chest. "Start at the beginning. *Who* are *they*? And what do *they* want?"

He looked away. "The less you know, the better."

"Kyle." She said it with all the exasperation she used to get her students to participate when they didn't want to.

"No time." He blew her off. "I just came by to see you in person and say goodbye. And I didn't have anything at my place, so maybe you can give me some snacks for the road. It's a long drive."

She rolled her eyes. Her brother was always waiting to the last minute to hit the grocery store and then running out of food. "Where are you going?"

He peeked between the blinds again. His body vibrating with energy. "Better if you don't know."

She sighed. "Kyle, this isn't like you. Just tell me what's going on. Maybe I can help." She feared some sort of mental breakdown. Too many video games, or long hours coding, coupled with no sleep maybe. Stress.

A breakup she didn't know about. Something had turned her mild-mannered brother paranoid.

Drugs?

He didn't seem high.

"You can't help." He pressed his lips tight. "As soon as I'm settled, I'll call and tell you what I can."

She released her arms, went to her pantry, pulled out a plastic shopping bag and filled it with a bag of chips, peanut butter cracker packs, a couple granola bars and three bottles of water. What little she had, she'd gladly give to Kyle, if for no other reason than to reassure him he could count on her. Maybe then he'd open up and tell her what was going on.

"Do Mom and Dad know you're leaving?"

"No. They're out of town. One of Dad's veterinary conferences in Arizona."

Kenna hadn't heard they were going, but whatever. She didn't tell her parents everything she did. Not that she ever went anywhere. Not on her teacher's salary.

"What about your job?" she asked, turning back to him with the bag in her hand.

Kyle stood by her bookcase, hands behind his back, his face a mask of feigned, nothing-to-see-here.

She held back a grin and looked at the menagerie of cat figurines on the shelf, noting the new black-and-white addition.

Kyle joked all the time that she had lived alone so long she was turning into the old lady in number 13. All she needed was a bunch of cats. She'd love one, but she was allergic. She didn't take offense. Kyle really wanted her to find someone who made her happy, because after her last breakup, she'd shut down and shut men out of her life.

Until recently, when she had finally gotten tired of her own company and started dating again.

But over the last few years, Kyle had reminded her about what she was turning into by surreptitiously leaving the little ceramic critters on the shelf when she wasn't looking every time he stopped by. The number of cats staring back at her reminded her of just how much time had passed her by the last few years, how many days, weeks, months vanished and she still wasn't even close to happy. Not the way she used to be.

She scrunched up one side of her mouth. "You know I'm seeing someone now."

Kyle shrugged. "How is Marcus?"

"Good. We have a dinner date, in . . ." She checked the time on the microwave. "Ten minutes. Which I need to get ready for."

Kyle eyed her. "You're not in love with him."

The gut reaction she had to that told her a lot about what she felt. And didn't. "How do you know?"

"I know you. It's been weeks. Aside from telling me you started seeing him, I've barely heard anything else about him. There's no excitement in it for you."

"It's new."

"You need to either tell *him* the truth and see where that takes you, or let *him* go and really move on."

Kenna knew they weren't talking about Marcus but her ex, Max Wilde. "That ship has not only sailed, it sank."

Kyle shook his head. "Stubborn. I wish I had the time to tell you all the ways you're wrong right now, but I've got to go." He put his hand out for the bag.

She placed the handle of it in his palm but didn't let it go.

He gave it a tug. "Seriously, I have to go."

"I don't like this, Kyle. You're acting strange, not telling me the truth, and it seems like you're running away from something. That's not like you."

He tilted his head. "You're doing it with Max."

"He's moved on. In fact, he's moved on so many times since me, I bet he doesn't even remember what we shared." She waved that away as habitually as she stuffed her true feelings down deep. "Whatever it is that's got you scared, let me help."

"You can't. Not with this. The last thing I want is for you to get involved. I'll handle it."

She waited a beat, holding his gaze, hoping he would change his mind. When the silence stretched, she relented and released the snack bag.

"Thank you." He pulled her into a rare hug and held her tight.

She wrapped her arms around him, feeling his need for her to hold on to him.

He bent his head and whispered, "Remember when we were kids, we used to play with all those codes?"

She smiled, her heart lightening at the reminder of

how close they'd always been. "We had a lot of fun with that. I was better than you at it."

"Math nerd." The affection in his voice matched the hold he had on her. He suddenly released her and held her by the shoulders, the bag bumping her side. "If I can't contact you by phone or email, I'll send a code." He rushed for the door before she could stop him and ask why he'd resort to childish games.

"Kyle," she called out, but he slammed the door behind him, leaving her with a whole lot of questions and worries about why he had to leave town so abruptly. "And I thought teenagers were dramatic."

Still, what would send Kyle on the run and have him resort to code breaking to communicate with her?

Chapter Two

Kenna scrambled to get ready for her date and ulti- mately decided to stay in the slacks and blouse she'd worn to work. She touched up her makeup, brushed her teeth, and called it done, just as Marcus arrived. Right on time.

Kenna spent the whole car ride to the restaurant thinking about Kyle and imagining a number of sce- narios that would send him fleeing from town for god knows how long.

What was she supposed to tell their parents?

When they got to the restaurant, she sat across from Marcus. Not beside him. She didn't even think about sliding in next to him. Not like she used to do with Max.

She really needed to stop thinking about him.

If only.

She blamed Kyle for bringing him up.

Marcus lowered his menu and stared at her. "Are you okay?"

No. Because I can't stop thinking about what Kyle said about letting go of Max.

"Um. Yeah. I'm fine."

"Are you sure?" Marcus raised a brow and patiently waited.

She hadn't even opened her menu yet. She didn't feel like eating. Worse, she didn't really want to be here.

Her gut soured. This wasn't fair to Marcus at all. He'd planned a wonderful night out, and she simply couldn't be present for it.

She looked at his earnest face and thought about the last six weeks they'd spent dating and getting to know each other better.

Before Kyle showed up at her place, she wondered if tonight was the night they got naked. Now she wondered what she was doing here. With Marcus.

They'd agreed to take things slow because they worked together. She felt a little like a cliché. The teacher and the vice principal working to better the minds of their students, when sparks fly, and they fall for each other.

It sounded like a nice story.

But the spark between them seemed to have grown in Marcus, while in her, it remained a flicker of hope that she'd eventually feel something more than the deep friendship they shared.

It was the same thing that had happened with the last three guys she'd dated. A couple others hadn't gotten past the first date.

Either she sucked at this, or finding love just wasn't in the cards for her.

Not again. She had it once and lost it.

But maybe she needed to change tactics and think of

this more scientifically, instead of mathematically, because the odds seemed wholly not in her favor. If she wanted to connect and bond with someone, then she needed to form an attachment. What better way than sex?

She liked sex. She missed sex.

She missed feeling wanted and desired by a man.

Marcus made it clear that he wanted more in the kisses they shared.

Maybe it was time to stop holding back and take another step into a deeper kind of relationship with Marcus.

If she couldn't have all of what she wanted, then maybe she needed to settle for the kind of friendship and connection she could have with him.

She'd had the amazing, all-encompassing passion kind of love once. It was her fault she'd lost it.

She needed to move on before her brother filled not just one shelf, but the whole damn bookcase with cat figurines.

"Kenna. Are you okay?" Marcus asked again.

No. Damnit.

Marcus deserved what she'd had with Max. He didn't deserve a woman who settled for him. He didn't deserve for her to use him as an experiment to find a connection that wasn't there.

He deserved to be loved.

And while she thought of him as a dear friend, that's all they'd ever be, even if they took this further.

"I'm so sorry, Marcus. I'm just not feeling up to this. Would you mind taking me home?" She'd talk to him there in private and let him down easy.

"Of course." He left a few dollars on the table to tip the waitress for bringing them water, which she found sweet, since they hadn't even ordered anything yet.

She smiled at Marcus when he stood and walked out of the restaurant with her to his car.

They didn't even hold hands.

That made her sad. The little things mattered.

Marcus did hold her car door open for her. "Your brother suddenly leaving really upset you."

She took her seat in the car. "It's just not like him."

Marcus closed her door, went around the car, and took his seat beside her. "It is strange the way he left today. But I'm sure everything is fine." His reassurance didn't help, because he didn't sound so sure.

She nodded at him anyway.

Marcus drove to her place. They chitchatted about the weather getting colder, the possibility of more snow this December and Marcus's hectic schedule coaching basketball again this year.

It felt like they were an old married couple on date night.

Not like two young people hot for each other in the beginning of a relationship.

He didn't steal a kiss before he helped her into the car or even put his hand on her thigh.

The signs that she was right about breaking things off to preserve their friendship kept adding up.

As they approached her door, she stopped short and turned to him. "Marcus." Just the way she said his name, tipped him off.

"You want to end this." He sighed and looked her in the eye. "I could tell my feelings had grown faster and deeper than yours. I just hoped, given time . . ."

"I'm so sorry. The last thing I want to do is hurt you."

He took her hand, squeezed it, then let it go. "Never be sorry for the way you feel."

"We are such good friends."

"And that won't change," he assured her, not taking her words as a bad thing.

Her heart felt lighter because of it.

"I can't say I'm not disappointed. But I agree. We both have to have our hearts in it for this to work." He was such a grown-up, facing this head-on.

While she'd avoided ever having the conversation she should have had with Max when she found out the truth. Two years ago. "Thank you for understanding. I don't know what's wrong with me. You're the perfect guy. A great catch."

"Just not for you," he added, a slight, self-deprecating grin on his handsome face. "And there's nothing wrong with you. You're sweet and kind and beautiful. Some lucky guy, who appreciates that and more, like I do, will come along and sweep you off your feet."

"You're sweet, too. Thank you for saying that." It made her feel better and worse about ending things.

"Then I'll see you at school tomorrow."

She was about to return the sentiment when something heavy dropped inside her apartment, drawing both their attention.

She turned and walked toward her door and saw

the splintered wood, the door ajar. She pushed it open. "What the fuck?" The whole place had been trashed.

Someone broke in, she thought inanely.

Fear burst through her that someone might have taken her most treasured possession.

A man dressed in black jeans, a black leather jacket, gloves, and a ski mask stepped out of her bedroom, his bulk filling the short hallway. He rushed her, grabbed her by the arms, dragged her inside, and shook her. "Where is it?"

Stunned, she simply stared at him, confused and dumbfounded.

Marcus brushed past her, hooked his hands on one of the guy's arms, and tried to pull the man off her.

The intruder stood at least four inches taller than Marcus and had about twenty pounds of muscle on him. He released one hand from her, planted it on Marcus's chest, and shoved him away. Marcus landed on his back on her coffee table so hard the legs on one side broke out from under it, sending Marcus up into a sitting position, his ass on the floor now.

The guy grabbed the front of her blouse, picked her up off her feet, and shoved her into the wall. Her head cracked on a hanging picture of her and her family. The glass cracked, the wood frame broke into a sharp point that cut her scalp. Blood oozed down the back of her head and neck.

The guy got right in her face. "Tell me where you hid it."

Marcus scrambled up and grabbed the guy by the shoulders again. "Let her go."

The guy released her.

She dropped back to her feet, the wood cutting her head even more, the bottom of the frame scraping and bruising her back. She put her hand to the back of her scalp and felt the warm wetness as she reached into her purse with her other hand, trying to find her phone.

Marcus and the guy grappled with each other, crunching and smashing all the things that had been dumped on her floor under their feet. The guy shoved Marcus back.

Nine-one-one answered her call, but before she could spit out any words, the guy looked over and made a grab for the phone. She dropped it, her purse fell off her arm, and she screamed when he planted his hand on her chest and shoved her back into the wall with a thump. She used the wall as leverage and shoved the guy away from her. He slipped and stumbled on a magazine that slid on the floor under his foot.

Marcus bent low, rushed him, and shoved his shoulder into the guy's midsection. Out of nowhere the guy pulled a knife. He held it up, ready to plunge it into Marcus.

Adrenaline sent her leaping forward onto his back, her arms around his neck, but she couldn't stop him from stabbing Marcus in the back. Once. Twice. Three times.

Marcus dropped to his belly on the floor and didn't move.

Kenna screamed his name.

The guy shoved her back into the wall so hard her teeth rattled, his body pushing against hers. She saw stars and lost her grip on him, but came away with the mask he'd had over his head as he pulled his body away from hers. Her legs gave out and she landed on her ass on the floor, her knees bent.

Someone yelled her name from outside. It sounded like her neighbor Carolyn, but it was hard to hear with the sirens so close, her head pounding, and her heartbeat echoing in her ears.

The guy snatched the mask back, pulled it on, then got right up in her face. "Fucking bitch. I know you. Now you know me. This isn't over." He rushed out of her place, leaving her on her knees beside Marcus, crying, her phone forgotten on the floor as she pressed her hands to Marcus's back, trying to stop the blood.

She leaned down to his ear, saying over and over again, "You're going to be okay."

She didn't know how long it took for the cops to arrive and find her hunched over Marcus, her cheek pressed to his. "Wake up. Wake up. Wake up," she pleaded with him, knowing he was gone.

Someone touched her shoulder. "Kenna. Kenna, honey, look at me."

She knew that voice. It was so close to the Wilde she'd lost. But not the same at all. Through her blurry vision she looked up and saw Hunt. Officer Wilde. Max's brother.

His eyes filled with concern and compassion.

"He won't wake up." Fresh tears spilled down her cheeks. She hugged Marcus harder, hoping this wasn't real. It wasn't true. This never happened. "Wake up," she pleaded again.

Hunt put his hands on her shoulders and gently pulled her upright. "Kenna, honey, I need you to let him go and come with me."

She stared down at Marcus's bloody back and the blood all over her hands. "He won't wake up."

"No, honey, he's gone. Let me take you out of here."

"He tried to save me."

"He did save you," Hunt assured her.

She leaned over and kissed Marcus's head. "I'm sorry." So sorry she hadn't loved him the way he deserved to be loved. Sorry she'd approached her apartment without thinking someone could still be in there. Sorry that their last moments together were about her not trying to be more for him.

Hunt pulled her back again. "How bad are you hurt? Can you stand up?"

She couldn't really feel anything but deep, overwhelming grief and regret. So she shifted her weight, planted one foot, and let Hunt help her to her feet. The room spun and she tilted off her axis and would have gone down if Hunt hadn't wrapped an arm around her shoulders to hold her up. He scooped her into his arms and walked her out the door, just as two paramedics showed up with a gurney.

"I'm okay."

"No, you're not," Hunt grumbled. "You're bleeding like crazy." He set her on the gurney and she caught a glimpse of the blood all over his shirt before the paramedic pressed a gauze pad to her head. She closed her eyes and winced at the lightning bolt of pain shooting through her scalp. "Ouch."

"Take her to the hospital. Get her checked out." Hunt squatted beside her. "I'll be there after I check out your apartment to talk to you about what happened tonight."

She could barely focus on him, let alone nod.

"Do you want me to call someone for you?"

She frowned, another wave of tears coming. "Kyle left town. Mom and Dad are . . ." She couldn't quite remember where they'd gone, only that they were away for a week or something. "I don't have anybody to call." She covered her eyes with her hands, not caring that the paramedic was trying to take her blood pressure, and let out a fresh wave of tears.

Hunt's hand settled on her shoulder. "I'll come and see you as soon as the doctor checks you out, okay?"

"'K." That's about all she could manage to say, then her mind went back to Marcus. "You have to call his family. Oh God. His family. He's gone." Her mind still didn't want to believe it, but her heart felt the pain sharply.

"Take her now." The urgency in Hunt's voice set off an alarm in her that maybe she wasn't really all right.

God, that voice. So close. But not his. Not the one she desperately wanted to hear right now. Not the man she wished she'd never lost.

Poor Marcus.

Why would someone kill him? Who was that man? And what did he want from her?

Chapter Three

MAX WAS lying in bed. Alone. Not sleeping—again—but listening to the achingly quiet night, feeling every empty centimeter of space beside him, doing another mental deep dive on his so-called life.

It seemed that every night before his brother Chase went home to his wife and daughter, he took a second to ask Max, "How are you?" leaving a pregnant pause, while Chase waited to see if Max would say something other than, "Fine."

Max didn't think he'd actually been fine in a long time. Overworked, tired, restless, bored, angry, lonely—those were all things he'd been and more lately. The last one really got to him, especially as he'd watched his two brothers fall in love and live the kind of happy he used to have before everything went to shit with Kenna.

His brothers had been on his case for a while now to stop all the late-night drinking at the bar and using women to pretend he wasn't really alone.

Without those distractions, all he really had left was the ranch and his regrets.

His older brother Chase had been the golden child. The one who would succeed their dad and run the ranch, but Chase ran off to join the military several years back in order to save the failing ranch with an influx of cash from Chase's signing bonus. Max took over the ranch and ran things just fine for all those years. Thank you very much.

But Chase came back broken and different.

He finally got his shit together this past year and now they ran the ranch together, but Max took the lead role because he'd earned it.

Chase was a good partner. He didn't mind following Max's lead. Chase had his wife Shelby and daughter Eliza to fill the nonwork hours of the day.

Max had work and recently traded his late nights at the bar for sunset rides and time to think about what he wanted for his future. He thought he'd have what his brothers found with their wives. In fact, there was a time he'd thought he'd be the first of them to get married even though he was the youngest.

But that all fell apart.

No good deed goes unpunished.

He'd learned that the hard way and lost Kenna and the trust and love he thought they'd shared until she called him a liar.

He rubbed the heels of his hands into his tired eyes and wondered why he still couldn't let it go and get past it.

His phone rang on the bedside table. He wanted to ignore it. He had no desire to talk to whoever it was, probably one of the many women he'd had a fling with, who wanted to see him tonight.

The phone went quiet, then immediately rang again.

Someone really wanted him to answer. In case it was an emergency, he picked up the phone and checked caller ID.

He swiped the screen and picked up Hunt's call. "Everything okay?" His police officer brother was nearly always on the job and anything could happen. Max worried about him a lot.

"No. I wanted you to hear this from me." The urgency in Hunt's voice scared him.

Max sat up. "Are you hurt?" He immediately went to the worst-case scenario and imagined Hunt shot and bleeding out.

"I'm fine. It's Kenna."

His heart dropped and his stomach went tight. The thought of her hurt, or worse, dead, made it hard to breathe. "What's happened?"

Hunt explained the situation, then said, "I'm on the way to the hospital to see her now. Last I saw her at her place, she was bleeding pretty bad and was disoriented."

That didn't sound good at all. "Is she going to be all right?"

"I think so. Best I can piece together, she was thrown up against a wall, hit her head on a picture frame, busted it up, and cut the back of her head severely."

"Who hurt her?" Max wanted a name. A target.

"No idea. She was too distraught to get anything out of her when I arrived on scene."

"What the fuck happened?"

"She called 911 but wasn't able to communicate. The operator heard a commotion and her scream. Two neighbors called in, too, said there was a fight at her place. They thought she got into it with her boyfriend. But one neighbor reported a masked man leaving her place." Hunt paused. "And then we discovered that her boyfriend is dead. Stabbed three times."

He felt sorry for the guy, but remained focused on Kenna, fear stirring up an urgency to get as many details as possible. He needed to know that she'd be all right. "Was she stabbed?"

"No. At least, the only injury I saw was to her head. She's being checked out at the ER right now."

Max jumped out of bed and grabbed a pair of jeans. "I'll meet you there." He hung up on Hunt, got dressed, pulled on his boots, grabbed his wallet, phone, and keys, and rushed out of his room. Once he was down the stairs, he called out to his dad in the kitchen, "Kenna is hurt and in the hospital. I'll be back later." He ran out of the ranch house and straight for his truck.

He climbed behind the wheel and headed to town, desperate to see Kenna and make sure she was okay and whoever had hurt her wasn't a threat anymore.

Because, although they weren't together, protecting her seemed as natural as loving her.

Chapter Four

Max found Hunt parked right outside the Emergency Department in a space reserved for the police. Hunt was at the back of his car unbuttoning his bloody uniform shirt.

Max surveyed all the blood covering the long sleeve. His stomach pitched and heart sank that the blood belonged to Kenna. That urgency riding him amped up again. "Have you seen her yet?"

Hunt shook his head. "I didn't want to walk in there looking like this and frighten people."

The sight of all that blood nearly made him panic. "But she was okay last you saw her?"

Hunt dropped the soiled shirt in the back, pulled out a clean one, and put it on. "She was awake, but not really alert and coherent. In shock from watching her boyfriend being murdered on top of the head injury she suffered. I'm not sure if she had any other injuries or if she had more of an altercation with whoever trashed her place."

"Let's go find out." Max needed Hunt to get him in to

see Kenna. He wasn't family. He wasn't anything to her anymore, except a lying, cheating ex.

At least, that's what she thought. His word hadn't meant shit. And it still stung.

Hunt tucked in the shirt and wrapped his gun belt around his waist again.

Max was already headed toward the hospital door by the time Hunt slammed the hatch closed and rushed after him.

They were greeted by a receptionist at the desk in the small lobby area. Emergency only consisted of five cubicles, so Kenna had to be close.

"How can I help you, Officer Wilde?"

"I'm looking for Kenna Baker."

"The doctor is in with her. Cubicle two. Drapes open. You can go over."

Max followed Hunt to the partially opened drape. He spotted Kenna immediately, wearing a hospital gown, a sheet covering her legs up to her waist. She was lying on her side, her head propped up on two pillows, her bloody blond hair partially covering her way too pale face. The doctor sat behind her, sewing a four-inch gash closed.

The need to go to her and comfort her was so strong, he barely contained it. The relief he felt, seeing her awake and alive, nearly sent him to his knees.

Hunt approached her slowly. "Kenna, honey, do you feel up to talking to me?"

"Don't move," the doctor warned Kenna as he sank the curved needle into her skin again.

"Is he really—" Choked up, she couldn't finish the statement. Her voice sounded so desperate and anguished.

It cut Max deep to see and hear her like this.

Hunt grabbed a rolling stool like the one the doctor used, shifted it next to the bed, sat, and put his hand on Kenna's forearm, avoiding the IV line going into her hand.

Max wanted to be the one that close to her. He wanted to be the one who comforted her.

He wanted to go back to the way things used to be.

But that was never going to happen.

So he stood back, just out of her sight. There, but unable to do anything other than appease his need to see for himself that she was okay. Alive. Well. In this world, where, every once in a while, he got a glimpse of her and it made him feel better to know she was still here.

"I'm sorry we keep meeting like this."

"Me, too," Kenna said weakly.

It took Max a moment to remember why Hunt would have seen Kenna recently, and then it hit him. A couple of months ago Max had seen Kenna and Sean, the guy she'd been seeing then, leaving the diner. Not even an hour later, Sean died in a car accident after dropping Kenna at work. Hunt made the notification to Kenna, because everyone in town, including him, had heard that they'd recently started dating.

And then it was over.

Max hated why it ended, but he was also glad he didn't have to see her with someone he knew either.

Hunt cleared his throat. "Can you tell me what happened?" Hunt whispered, trying to keep things calm.

"I . . . I don't know. It happened so fast." Her bottom lip trembled.

The doctor put in another stitch and began knotting it.

Hunt tried again. "Why was Marcus there? Did he come to pick you up? Was he dropping you off?"

A single tear slid down Kenna's cheek. "We went out to dinner."

"Okay. Did you have a good time?"

Why the hell was Hunt asking that? Max didn't want to hear about her out with some other guy.

"We didn't even order. I asked him to take me home."

"Why? Were you sick or something?"

"Because it wasn't right."

Hunt raised a brow. "How so?"

Kenna closed her watery eyes for a second, tears slipping past her lashes and rolling over her nose and cheek. "We were saying good-night."

Max caught what she didn't say. Marcus wasn't going inside with her. She ended the date before they ate, and she hadn't planned to spend the night with him in her bed.

His little green monster settled down for a nap.

Not that he had any right to be jealous. Still. He couldn't help it.

Kenna had been his. She would still be his if she'd believed in him.

"Then what happened?" Hunt asked, his words soft and gentle.

"I turned to the door and saw the broken frame. I didn't think." She raised her fisted hand and pounded it against the side of her head three times.

Hunt caught her wrist. "Stop. You'll hurt yourself more."

Max had never seen her so distressed.

The doctor held the needle and thread away from her to be sure she'd settled again.

Kenna squeezed her eyes shut. "It's my fault."

Hunt sighed, turned, and stared at Max.

He didn't have an answer for why she'd say that, why she'd even think it. She was a good person. She'd never hurt anyone.

Well, she hurt him. But she never set out to do that.

"It was so stupid to think about the watch and not that someone could get hurt."

Max's heart triple-timed in his chest.

"There must be something really special about that watch," Hunt blurted out.

Max didn't want to hear that answer. He knew it already.

"It's stupid to hold on to something so hard that isn't yours. But I can't let it go." The words spilled out of Kenna like a confession and a tide she couldn't stop. "I keep it by my bed and hold it when I go to sleep. And it's like time stops and I'm back there. With him. When we were happy." Kenna seemed to catch herself. She gasped and pressed her lips tightly closed. "Don't tell him." She gripped Hunt's hand. "Please. You can't tell him."

"I won't," Hunt assured her, catching on that she was talking about something of his. The watch he'd always worn and left at her place and never went back for after they split.

It took Kenna another minute to continue. "I didn't care about the rest of the stuff. None of it mattered."

He couldn't believe something of his still meant so much to her.

What did that mean?

"I didn't hear anyone . . . but then he came out of my room and . . ."

"And what?" Hunt prompted her.

"He came right at me. He was huge. Six-two. Built like a tank. All in black. A leather jacket with some kind of patches on it."

"Did you get a look at his face?"

She paled considerably. "I . . ."

"Take your time."

"I d-did." Her lips trembled. She lifted her head a bit.

"Hold still, Kenna," the doctor warned, working on another stitch.

How damn many was he putting in her?

Kenna settled again. "He asked me where it was."

Hunt leaned in. "What?"

"I have no idea."

"But it seemed like he was looking for something specific?" Hunt's gaze narrowed with suspicions.

"I guess. Unless he just meant my money or something." She looked up at Hunt. "Why didn't he just take what he wanted and leave?"

"You said you cut the date short. You surprised him."

Kenna's eyes went wide. "He was followed."

"Who?"

That's what Max wanted to know.

"Kyle stopped by to say goodbye right before I left."

"Why would someone follow Kyle to your place?" Hunt asked.

"I don't know." She sounded exasperated Hunt would even ask.

Hunt scrunched his lips, then tried to get Kenna back on track. "What happened next?"

"He grabbed me by my blouse at my chest and shoved me up against the wall. Even in my heels, I couldn't touch the floor. I thought he was going to kill me. But Marcus pulled him away. The guy shoved Marcus off him. Marcus landed on the coffee table and broke it."

When she didn't go on, Hunt tapped her arm with his finger. "Then what?"

"I . . . um . . . I grabbed my phone and tried to call 911. I sent the call through but I didn't have time to say anything."

Hunt nodded. "Your neighbors called, too. I was on duty. When they told me it was you, I rushed over to help."

"Thank you. That's nice, considering."

Hunt glanced over at Max, as shocked as he was that Kenna thought a Wilde wouldn't help her because they broke up. It punched him right in the gut that she believed that.

"What happened before the police arrived?" Hunt nudged her to continue.

"The guy was coming after me again, but Marcus slammed his shoulder into the guy's midsection. But the guy . . . he . . . he pulled a knife. I jumped on the guy's back and tried to stop him."

Max swore under his breath and thought of all the terrible things that could have happened to her.

"It happened so fast. *Bam, bam, bam.* He stabbed him. He just . . . stabbed him again and again like it was nothing. He slammed me back into the wall. I hit my head again and let go of him and somehow pulled off his mask. Marcus dropped to the floor. The guy . . . he called me a bitch, then . . ."

"What?" Hunt leaned in.

"I could hear the sirens and someone outside calling my name."

Probably one of her neighbors, Max thought.

"He said, 'I know you. Now you know me. This isn't over.' And then he pulled the mask back on and ran."

Hunt swore.

Fear filled her eyes. "He's coming back for me, isn't he?"

"You can ID him as Marcus's murderer." Hunt's bluntness made Kenna pale even more.

Her eyes widened with terror.

Max, and especially Kenna, could have done without Hunt's candor.

Hunt squeezed her arm. "I have the basic description. Can you give me more details about his face and hair?"

"Dirty blond. I didn't realize it until I pulled the mask off, but it was long and straight, tied into a bun. His face was . . . I don't know. Rugged. Lines at the corners of his eyes. His nose looked like it had been broken. There was a bump on the bridge of his nose. He had a close beard, darker than his hair, but not brown. His front upper tooth had a tiny chip out of the corner."

The guy got close enough for her to see all those details.

Max seethed.

"That's good," Hunt praised. "Any other distinguishing marks? A tattoo maybe?"

She rubbed the heel of her hand roughly against her forehead a couple of times. With her head injury, she probably had a killer headache to go with the long gash. "He was mostly covered." She squinted her eyes. "Except, I did see something peeking out of his collar, like a swirl or point of a tattoo going up from his shoulders and halfway up the back of his neck. I don't know what it was, except a black curve of something." She shook her head.

Luckily, it appeared the doctor had finished sewing her up.

"I'm sorry I can't tell you more. I just wanted to get to Marcus to see if he was all right. But he wasn't." She met Hunt's gaze. "He wouldn't wake up."

"No, honey, he didn't. But I think he saved you."

"It should have been me."

Hunt squeezed her arm again. "I'm glad it wasn't you."

Kenna closed her eyes as more tears fell.

Max had a hard time standing by, witnessing all this, listening to her anguished voice recounting seeing her boyfriend die right in front of her and being helpless to do anything about it.

He felt like a jackass just standing there, not doing anything.

But it wasn't his place. He didn't even know why he came, except that he had to see for himself that she was going to be okay, or he'd simply go insane worrying about her.

She didn't look like it right now, but he knew Kenna. She was strong and resilient and she'd get through this.

The doctor stood and pushed the tray of implements he'd used to work on Kenna out of the way. "You're all stitched up. The numbing will wear off in an hour or so."

Hunt glanced over at the doctor. "Are you releasing her tonight?"

"I'll have her discharge papers in a few minutes." The doctor directed his next words to Kenna. "You'll need to keep those stitches dry. I understand you'll want to shower and wash your hair. Just be sure to dry your scalp really well so it will heal. I'll send you home with some antibiotic ointment. You have a very mild concussion that should resolve in the next day or so, so don't drive. There's some bruising and swelling on your head that will probably hurt for a few days. Over-the-counter pain meds should help with that." The doctor picked up the paper bag from the counter and held it out to Hunt. "We bagged her clothes for evidence just in case."

Hunt took the bag. "Thank you." To Kenna he said, "I brought you something comfortable to wear."

The doctor came around the bed to Hunt's side to address Kenna directly. "Is there someone we can call to pick you up?"

Kenna didn't meet his gaze, just stared off into space.

"My brother left town. My parents are away, too. I guess . . . I'll just go home."

"You can't," Hunt quickly spoke up. "Your apartment is a wreck and a crime scene. I'll take you to the ranch tonight."

Max breathed a sigh of relief that Hunt stepped up to take Kenna to his place.

"We've got plenty of empty beds in the big house," Hunt tacked on.

Max swore under his breath.

Hunt didn't look at him at all, the asshole.

"I can't stay there." Kenna said it like it scared her.

He didn't like that. He understood if she simply didn't want to be anywhere near him, but to be afraid . . .

Hunt pushed. "Your family isn't here to help. You need someplace to sleep. Plus, I'll put an officer outside."

Max caught on, that Hunt wasn't only setting him up, but also that he didn't want to bring Kenna to his place, where Cyn and the baby were, and put them at risk. If this guy came after Kenna, Max, his dad, a cop outside were better equipped to keep her safe without worrying about Cyn and the baby.

"I'll be by in the morning to update you about the case."

"But . . ."

Hunt shook his head. "It's okay, Kenna. Max won't mind helping out an old friend."

She frowned, tears gathered in her eyes. "He hates me."

Max couldn't let that stand and pushed open the curtain. "No, I don't."

Kenna stopped breathing for a second, then sighed

and turned her head just enough to face him. "What are you doing here?"

He didn't know. More accurately, he didn't want to admit why he'd come. To her. To himself. It hurt just looking at her. And at the same time, he yearned for something that used to be, but would never be again. "Hunt called to tell me what happened. I was worried."

"You don't have to do this. I can go to a motel, or something."

"He's here. He can drive you home," Hunt announced like it was a done deal.

Max didn't acknowledge the flutter of whatever the hell it was inside him at the notion that the ranch was Kenna's home.

It should have been.

But it never was.

It wouldn't be.

But yes, he could help out an old friend, even if they weren't even that anymore.

"I'm ready whenever you are." He never lied to Kenna, but that felt awful close to one, given that he was so not ready to be this close to her again.

It took an hour for the IV to finish and the doctor to finally discharge her. Hunt had left her clothes. A nurse helped Kenna change and rolled her out to the parking lot in a wheelchair. He pulled the truck up front and got out to help her in, but she did that all on her own, avoiding him touching her, even though he could see she was sore and tired.

He wondered how badly that guy roughed her up, but

didn't ask. He didn't want to bring what happened to the forefront of her mind again.

He drove her home with the music turned low, letting it be a distraction and something that filled the quiet between them.

Truthfully, he didn't know what to say to her.

It had been too long and not long enough, it seemed, for both of them.

She had enough to deal with tonight, so he left the past in the past and focused on getting her home.

By the time he pulled into the driveway and shut off the engine, she seemed wound tight and ready to unravel all at once.

"I'll put you up in the guest room."

She stared out the window at the house. "You didn't have to do this."

"Yes. I did." Once he knew what happened to her, there was no turning back. He had to help her. He didn't owe her anything. He chalked it up to respecting their past and what they shared, which was a hell of a lot more good than the one bad thing that happened. Because of that, he felt like this was the least he could do for someone who'd loved him so perfectly, at least for a little while.

That's more than some people ever experienced.

He wouldn't give up those memories for anything.

He wouldn't let the woman who'd made those memories with him suffer alone.

He'd put a roof over her head, settle her in a warm bed, feed her, then let her go tomorrow again, knowing it would probably be just as hard to watch her leave as it was the last time.

A patrol car pulled up behind them and parked.

"You'll be safe here." He could give her that peace of mind, too.

"I was always safe with you," she whispered, then opened the truck door and slipped out.

Maybe this wasn't such a good idea. It brought back too many memories for both of them.

He climbed out and followed her up to the house. He had to take her arm at the porch steps to steady her. "You okay?" He rolled his eyes at asking such a stupid question.

"Tired. My whole body hurts."

Yeah. That guy slammed her around good.

Max hoped the guy got what he deserved. Soon.

Watching Kenna struggle up four steps tied his gut in knots. So when he escorted her into the house and looked up the staircase to the second floor, his mind said, *Nope.* He scooped her up in his arms and carried her up.

Three steps in and she protested. "Put me down. You don't have to do this."

"I do, actually. I can't stand to watch you hurting."

"I'm fine."

"We promised to never lie to each other," he reminded her. He didn't have to look to know the tears streamed down her cheeks again.

He figured the best thing to do was get her settled for the night and give her some space. So he walked into the guest room across from his, set her on her feet, but kept his arm around her to steady her, pulled back the covers on the bed, and nudged her to climb in. She did without a word and seemed to sink into the mattress like a puddle, all her energy spent.

"I'll get your ointment from the truck and grab you a couple ibuprofen and water. Need anything else?"

She barely shook her head.

He carried out those tasks and walked back into her room. She was in the exact same spot, staring at the closet doors across from her. He set the water on the nightstand and held out the ibuprofen. "Come on, you need to take these. They'll help."

She struggled to sit up and do as he asked. Once she downed the pills, she settled back on the pillow, her vacant gaze straight ahead.

"I'm sure you remember, but the bathroom is one door down on the right. If you need anything, I'm across the hall. Just call out. I'll hear you."

The tears came again.

He wanted to wipe them away, hold her until they stopped, take away her pain and grief. But that wasn't his place anymore.

They were finally in the same room together again, yet they were still as far apart as they'd been when they split.

He still hated it.

He still wished it hadn't happened.

He wanted it to be different.

But it couldn't. It wouldn't. And it still made him angry.

So he left her and went back to his bed, the same thoughts he'd had earlier about the state of his life circling his head. The same loneliness he felt without her.

And in his heart, a spark of hope that maybe, somehow, she'd believe again that he wasn't what she accused him of so long ago, but the same man she'd loved so well he couldn't get over her.

Chapter Five

KENNA SAT in the rocking chair in the living room by the window overlooking the wide front porch and the barn. She and Max had avoided each other all day.

It hurt that he couldn't look at her, that he hated having her around. But she still secretly loved being here, because Max had always been her safe place. And even if he didn't want her anymore, she still felt secure here.

He'd done the decent thing, taking her in, in her time of need, because he was a decent man.

She refused to let herself believe anything different, to even hope there was something more to his actions, because that would lead to utter disappointment. And she simply couldn't take anything more right now.

She thought of what her brother said before he left, about telling Max the truth.

She'd wanted to for a long time.

What difference would it make now?

Which made her wonder why he showed up at the hospital last night at all.

Except that maybe, if Max had been attacked and

hurt, she'd need to see with her own eyes that he was alive and well. Because once they were everything to each other. Maybe that, on a basic level, never went away even if it had all crumbled to pieces. That piece still remained, even if the whole of what it used to be had shattered, it still connected them.

She couldn't sit here all day, thinking about Max, hoping to catch another glimpse of him, only to run up to the guest room the second he headed back to the house.

She couldn't stomach anything right now. Not when she felt so sad about Marcus. It seemed she couldn't erase the images of him fighting off their attacker or him bleeding on her floor. She could still hear herself begging him to wake up.

The whole thing seemed like a nightmare and all too real at the same time.

Her body started trembling again. Her eyes teared up, even though she spent most of the night waking from one bad dream after another and crying all over again.

She needed to get out of here and find a way to block it all out.

She grabbed her phone to call Hunt again. He hadn't answered her earlier call or returned it after she left him a message. They had to have finished processing her house by now.

The officer who showed up last night to watch the house, had been replaced by a new one today. She'd gone out to his car earlier to ask if he knew when she could leave. He told her to talk to Hunt.

She tapped the screen and sent the call through.

"You've reached Hunt Wilde. Leave a message."

"Hunt, it's Kenna. Again. Please call me back. I need to go home." She hung up and set her chin on her knees as she sat curled up in the chair. She didn't actually want to go home, she just needed to get away from here and there was nowhere else to go.

She feared she'd never escape her own mind and heartache.

She'd called into work, told them what happened, and asked for a couple of days off. But once she felt a little better, she decided that getting back to her students, doing something productive, would help her cope.

"Are you okay?"

Startled, she gasped and turned her head to Mr. Wilde, who stood in the archway between the front door entryway and the living room. The bruised and battered muscles in her back and shoulders tensed, sending a wave of pain through her body.

Mr. Wilde held up his hand to let her know he meant no harm. "Sorry. I was just watching you watch Max. You look so lost and alone. It looks like you miss him a lot."

She wondered how her life turned into this, when at one time she'd pictured her life so differently and every scene included Max.

What she wouldn't give to have that kind of steady and ordinary and special back.

Maybe she was cursed after doing what she did to Max. He was the one person she never wanted to cause pain, and she'd done it in spades.

Maybe she deserved this kind of loss and pain.

She wiped at the fresh tears. "I was just . . ." She didn't know how to describe the remorse and grief she carried.

She'd hurt Max.

Two men she'd been seeing had their lives cut short. For what? Why?

Mr. Wilde sighed. "I remember you and Max and how really happy you were together."

Tears filled her eyes. "Yeah. But I killed that happiness."

He cocked his head. "I don't believe you meant to."

"Doesn't matter. I did it."

Mr. Wilde pressed his lips tight. "I haven't had a chance to tell you how sorry I am about your friend."

She hadn't been in any condition to talk to anyone last night or today. "Thank you. I miss him." She swallowed the lump in her throat and held back more tears.

"Had you been together long?"

She shook her head, but stilled because it made her ache even more. "Not really. We went on a dozen or so dates over the last six weeks." The memory of them almost made her smile. "It was new. He was becoming more of a friend than a coworker. I thought we were getting closer. I hoped things . . ." She let that go, because what she'd hoped was that she'd eventually feel for Marcus the way she'd felt when she was with Max.

And last night she'd realized her heart still belonged to him, and that wasn't fair to Marcus.

And wasn't that pathetic and stupid. She was never

going to have with anyone else what she had with Max. You just didn't find that every day, or even once in a lifetime for some. She'd had it and destroyed it.

"It doesn't matter. It's over now." Guilt swamped the sadness soaking her insides. She couldn't believe his last moments were spent getting dumped by her, even if he had taken it well. And then he tried to save her life.

She pressed her fingers to her aching forehead and tried not to fall into another fit of tears.

"For what it's worth, Max couldn't get out of here and down to the hospital fast enough last night to see you."

Yeah. She hadn't expected that at all. "I don't know why he'd do that."

"Because he cares."

A short burst of sardonic laughter escaped her. "He's just a good guy, who did something nice for someone he used to know, even though he, rightfully so, doesn't like me anymore."

Mr. Wilde held her gaze for a long moment. "I think you're wrong about that."

"He told me himself, he just needed to see that I was okay. I am. So we're right back to where we landed after the breakup."

Mr. Wilde glanced out the window at the barn where Max had gone. "People say a lot of things. But their actions . . . That shows you exactly what you need to know."

Maybe he had a point. But Max's actions last night didn't change their reality today.

Mr. Wilde went on. "I don't know exactly what

happened between you two, but I know the kind of feelings he had for you back then . . . They don't just go away."

"Trust me. Whatever he felt for me once upon a time, a long, long time ago, those feelings are dead, burned, and buried now."

She and Max certainly hadn't gotten the happy-ever-after fairy-tale ending they thought they'd live.

Her life was shaping up to be some kind of tragic drama.

For a long time after she and Max broke up, she'd purposely remained alone. Until even her own company became too lonely to bear.

And watching Max go through women, one after another, broke her battered heart into pieces, because she desperately wanted to be the only woman in his life again.

But he'd never take her back, so she'd tried to find a glimmer of the happiness she had with him with someone else.

It hadn't worked so far. Because the guys she dated didn't make it to serious relationship status because they weren't a good fit. She feared she'd forever be disappointed by a man simply because he wasn't Max.

The man himself walked in the front door, boots off, his jeans outlining his long legs, while his T-shirt stretched across his wide chest and around his thick arms. He held his jacket in one hand.

He barely spared her a glance and addressed his father. "I'll get cleaned up and be down for dinner in a minute." He took the stairs up like an agile cat, quick and efficient.

She gave Mr. Wilde a "see" look.

Max didn't want anything to do with her.

A buzzer went off in the kitchen.

Mr. Wilde waved her forward. "Come on. Dinner's ready."

"I'm not hungry. But thank you."

"You barely touched your breakfast. You skipped lunch."

She wasn't the only one. Max hadn't come in for lunch either.

"You need to eat." He stepped to the side and waved his arm out. "Now let's go."

She didn't want to be rude when she'd been welcomed into his home in her time of need. So she stood and proved how little she'd eaten that day and swayed on her feet before she caught herself.

Mr. Wilde took her by the arm to steady her. "I know you're in a bad way right now, but you need to take care of yourself."

She gave him a half-hearted grin. "I can't seem to do anything right, right now."

Mr. Wilde nudged her to start walking. "I'll fix you a plate. You'll eat. You'll feel better." As orders went, his were delivered with a gentle but firm command.

A few minutes later she found herself seated at the table with a plate of food in front of her. It looked amazing. Pork chops with caramelized onions and apples on top, rice pilaf, and steamed fresh green beans.

The cinnamon on the apples smelled like heaven. But her stomach knotted anyway at the thought of eating anything.

Mr. Wilde set a glass of milk in front of her, then stared at her until she picked up her fork and took a bite of the chicken and garlic flavored rice pilaf.

Satisfied, Mr. Wilde went back to retrieve the other two plates and brought them to the table.

Max walked in and took the seat furthest away from her. He smelled of soap and hay. He said a gruff, "Thank you," to Mr. Wilde for handing him his dinner plate. He waited for Mr. Wilde to sit and begin eating, then put his head down and did the same.

Kenna didn't look directly at him. She couldn't. She'd start crying all over again.

Mr. Wilde engaged him in conversation, asking about his day and how things went with moving some cattle this morning.

Max kept his answers short in between eating two chops, a mountain of rice, and all his green beans. He packed it away, finished off his iced tea, then stood and took his plate and cutlery to the sink. He rinsed them and put them in the dishwasher. "I'm headed out." There was a long pause, then he added, "Maybe she'll eat and not just move the food around her plate if I'm not here." With that grumble, he walked out of the house again.

Mr. Wilde sighed.

She couldn't help herself and looked out the window to see if he was getting in his truck to go meet . . . someone besides her.

"Max traded his late nights at the bar for sunset rides a few months ago. He spends too much time alone now."

"He'd rather be out there, than anywhere near me." She stood. "Thank you for dinner. I'm sorry, I just can't eat anything more." She'd barely been able to choke down the few bites she did eat with her stomach knotted. Her heart was so heavy she couldn't bear Max's complete dismissal of her along with the loss of Marcus. "If you'll excuse me. I think I need to lie down."

"I'll put your plate in the fridge. You can come down and eat it later."

"Thank you. For everything. Being kind. Letting me stay here."

"It's no trouble. I'm happy to help."

"I appreciate it." She glanced out the window. Max walked a saddled horse out of the barn, mounted, and off they went into the sunset washed pasture. "I'm sorry I've made him unhappy again and reminded him of our past. I'll be gone as soon as I can get back into my place and he can forget me again."

Mr. Wilde's blue eyes met hers. "Some women you never forget."

She appreciated the sentiment. It touched her. "Maybe. But the fact is, he'd like to." About to cry again, she turned and walked out, knowing she was right and feeling those broken pieces of her heart shatter once more.

She needed to get out of here before she made things worse.

Chapter Six

MAX FINISHED brushing down his horse and settling Ziggy in his stall for the night when he turned and found his dad standing at the gate. "What's up?"

"You tell me."

Max shrugged like he didn't know what his dad meant. "I'm headed in to take a shower. You going out or something?"

His dad put his hands on the top of the gate. "Are you going to ignore her the whole time she's here?"

"You can thank Hunt and his damn meddling for her being here."

His dad grinned. "You think Hunt set this up to get you two back together?"

"That's never going to happen. And yes, Hunt invited her, when he damn well could have taken her home with him." He knew that wasn't a viable option, but it didn't mean he couldn't stay mad at Hunt for it.

"They have a new baby in the house."

"And a perfectly good guest room where she could stay and cry all fucking night and wake up screaming from her nightmares." He'd barely slept. He'd been tormented listening to her last night, feeling her pain and wanting to do something for her. Hold her. But he couldn't open that door because it was too damn hard to see her, let alone be that close to her.

She thought the worst of him.

She ended things.

"She was attacked."

He'd seen the aftermath of that and still cringed when he thought about watching the doctor stitch her head wound closed.

"She watched the man she was seeing be murdered right in front of her." His dad unnecessarily laid it on thick.

Max held his hands out and let them drop, unable to do anything about that. "I know. And still, I'm the last person she wants to say a bunch of stuff to that won't matter to her anyway because there's no changing what happened."

"You could be her friend."

"After what happened, she made it clear we can't even be that. Why do you think I'm so fucking mad about it?"

His dad shook his head and gave him a sad half frown. "You want to be mad. The thing is, you're hurt."

"You're damn right. And for good reason." He'd been accused, and then refused even the benefit of the doubt or a chance to defend himself.

His dad pushed. "And still you went to the hospital last night."

"I never said I didn't care if she was hurt or in trouble. I didn't squash Hunt's offer for her to stay here until she can go home."

"Why not?"

He didn't want to answer, but the words came out anyway. "Because I need her to be okay."

"She's not."

"I see that," he snapped, not upset with his dad but with the situation. "I hoped she'd feel safe here and get some sleep and know that . . ."

"What?"

"She wasn't alone," he admitted. "Her brother left town. Her parents are away. She didn't have anywhere or anyone to go to. She was in no shape to make a decision last night, so Hunt made it for her." And Max planned to give his brother hell for putting him on the spot like that.

What the hell had Hunt been thinking?

Kenna didn't want to be here. In fact, it seemed to be making her worse. She couldn't even eat with him in the room.

"I'm worried about her."

Join the club.

His dad gave him that look he got when he wanted Max to do something Max didn't want to do. "I want you to go up and talk to her. I'm afraid she might be a danger to herself."

He didn't want to believe it was that bad. "She's not going to open up to me."

"You know her best. You'll be able to tell if I'm right. I hope I'm not. But I don't want to be wrong."

Neither did Max, even if he thought his dad was setting him up. Just like Hunt.

"Fine. I'll go check on her."

His dad grinned. "Thank you, son."

Max felt played, but walked back up to the house with his dad anyway. After seeing her when he returned to the house before dinner—the dark circles under her bloodshot eyes, the haunted look in them, the fact that she still looked on the verge of tears every moment—he needed to know that this was just the grief and trauma, not something more dire. Because he couldn't live in a world where Kenna wasn't in it.

He parted ways with his dad at the stairs and headed up to her room. He knocked and waited. "It's me. Max." Like she didn't already know. But he was the last Wilde she'd probably like to see right now.

Her lack of response made his gut tighten with dread. What if his dad had been right and she'd done something desperate? He knocked again. "Open up. Now." Fear clawed at him.

She opened the door wearing the same Metallica T-shirt, baggy black sweatpants, and snow cone print socks Hunt had delivered to her last night at the hospital.

Hunt should not be in charge of packing a bag for a woman ever again. But it had been thoughtful of him to do, given the situation and Kenna's clothes ending up as evidence and not being suitable to wear ever again.

She'd pulled her long hair into a messy topknot. Most of it was coming loose. The doctor had done an adequate job of rinsing out the blood from the golden strands.

It dawned on him that she hadn't showered or changed

today at all. Because Hunt had only brought her one set
of clothes, the dumbass.

She shifted from one foot to the other, waiting. When
he didn't say anything, she said, "Hi," breaking the ice.

He looked her up and down and back again, still
frowning that she'd never looked worse. Or better. It had
been a long time since he'd been this close to her.

Except for the long drive home last night when she'd
sat as far away from him in the truck cab as she could
get and stared blankly out the window, saying absolutely
nothing until they got to the ranch. Given her traumatic
experience, he'd let her be.

He couldn't do that now.

For some reason, he looked her up and down again
and finally realized what kept hanging up his brain.
"Hey, that's my shirt."

She'd stolen a lot of his shirts over the years they
dated. She loved having a piece of him close. He always
thought she looked so damn good in them.

She still did.

Tears filled her eyes. "You want it?" She ripped the
shirt off over her head. He got a glimpse of her perfect
breasts before she flung it right in his face. "Take it."

Then she slammed the door and burst into tears behind it.

Instinct told him to open the door and do what he
came here to do—make sure she was okay. Common
sense said he already had his answer. She was far from it.

And just like he feared he would, he'd made it worse.

Would it always be this way between them now?

Chapter Seven

SOMEONE KNOCKED softly on the door. Kenna had been lying in bed most of the night crying on and off, overwhelmed by the nightmare of how her date with Marcus ended and how badly things were going with Max.

She cried because Marcus wasn't here and she'd used him to try to get over Max.

She cried because the life she thought she'd have with Max was gone. She'd lost her best friend and the only man who had ever loved her the way she deserved to be loved. And it was all her fault.

Worse, there was no fixing it, because she'd made Max hate her.

She saw it in his eyes last night. Just looking at her made him angry. Maybe it even hurt him to see her.

Well, she could do something about that. She'd make sure he never had to see her again. She'd get out of his life for good.

She rolled out of bed on a mission and went to the door, knowing he was on the other side. She opened it and stared at the plate he held out to her.

"Breakfast. Please eat it. My dad's really concerned. It's not good for his heart," he added, making her feel terrible for stressing the poor man out after he'd had some heart issues a while back.

She took the plate, then the thermal mug he held up. The smell of coffee perked her up.

"You found the shirt."

"I did. I'll return it once I have something else to wear." As much as he'd wanted it back, he must have remembered at some point last night that she didn't have anything else to wear and left it hanging on the outside doorknob. She got up to pee last night, hoping neither he nor his father saw her with her arms over her breasts sneaking down the hall to the bathroom.

He opened his mouth to say something, then thought better of it, closed it, and turned to go.

"Hunt texted me this morning. He'll be here in an hour to get me."

Max slowly turned and met her gaze, his narrowed. "You shouldn't be alone."

"I'm used to it," she lied.

He pressed his lips tight. "Maybe it's for the best. Maybe you'll feel better sleeping in your own bed."

In the apartment where Marcus died? Not likely.

She wasn't sure she could ever go back there. It wasn't optimal, but she'd go to her parents' house until she figured out what to do next. She had no idea when they'd be home from their trip. Yesterday, she'd left her mom a simple message to call her back, but she kept it low-key and not urgent, so it wasn't a surprise she hadn't heard from her. She didn't want to leave all the details in a message and freak her mom out.

She thought about going to Kyle's place, but remembered that he may be tied to what happened to Marcus. Until she knew for sure, best to avoid his apartment.

But she couldn't stay here and continue to make Max this uncomfortable in his own home. She needed to find the courage to do what needed to be done. "I'll be fine." She said it to him, needing to hear it herself. "Thank you for letting me stay."

"Sure."

"Okay, then."

"Okay, then." Max hesitated a beat, then walked away.

She closed the door, happy to have that awkward exchange finished.

Hunt couldn't get here fast enough.

To kill time, and to make sure she didn't upset Mr. Wilde, she sat on the edge of the bed and ate as much of the breakfast as she could without upsetting her sore stomach. Too much crying and too many nightmares were making her stomach clench and left her feeling sick.

She probably looked sick, too, when Max came to her door. Not that he cared what she looked like anymore.

Or ever really. He'd always been sweet about telling her she looked great to him no matter what.

She missed that, having someone who saw the best in her.

She managed to eat all the fluffy scrambled eggs, one of the four pieces of bacon, and half the crispy fried potatoes. The coffee, she downed.

She left the plate on the dresser, feeling full and semialert, thanks to the caffeine kick. She walked down to the bathroom and gasped at the sight of herself in the mirror.

No wonder Mr. Wilde was worried. If she'd looked half as bad yesterday as she did right now, he'd probably think she needed a tranquilizer and her head examined.

She didn't have a lot of time, so she finger brushed her teeth with Max's toothpaste, washed her face, finger combed out her long hair, and, using the hair band she'd found at the bottom of her purse, gathered all her hair in a ponytail low on the back of her head. She left it loose, so it didn't pull her stitches, but she still looked somewhat improved.

She found the ibuprofen in the medicine cabinet and took two. That, with the caffeine, should help ease her headache and sore muscles.

She couldn't do anything about her outfit. Or the fact that she didn't have a bra or underwear. Hunt obviously didn't have experience packing for a woman, though he'd at least brought her comfortable clothes.

Feeling refreshed and not like death warmed over, she headed back to her room, grabbed her dishes, and walked to the stairs.

"What do you mean she can't go home? She needs to go home." Max's emphatic voice stopped her cold.

Hunt stood in the entryway with Max, Mr. Wilde, and a man she didn't know.

"Kenna." Just her name from Hunt had Max spinning around to stare up at her.

He folded his arms over his chest. "Did you eat?"

She tilted her plate enough for him to see. "Most of it." She looked at Mr. Wilde. "Thank you for breakfast." She continued down the stairs.

Mr. Wilde shrugged. "Don't thank me. Max made it for you."

She snapped her head back to Max.

He didn't look the least remorseful for lying to her. Well, he didn't say Mr. Wilde made it, only that she should eat it so that Mr. Wilde didn't worry about her.

"You look better," Mr. Wilde said, being kind.

She did not look better, just less frazzled.

She focused on Hunt. "You said you were coming to take me back to my apartment?"

Hunt shook his head. "Actually, I texted that I'd be here in an hour."

She narrowed her gaze. "The rest was implied."

Hunt looked amused. "Um. No. It wasn't."

Her anxiety amped up again. "Then please explain."

"You're in danger and you can't go home," the man she didn't know said bluntly.

She looked him up and down, wondering if she should know this person. "I'm sorry. Who are you?"

He pulled out his credentials and flashed her his FBI badge and ID. "Assistant Special Agent in Charge Nick Gunn."

That made her heart stutter with dread. "Why is the

FBI interested in a local crime?" She looked to Hunt, but the agent answered.

"Because your brother took something, possibly hid it in your apartment, and put a target on your back."

Her stomach dropped and pitched. She thought she might lose the breakfast Max had been kind enough to make her.

Mr. Wilde took the dishes from her and walked back toward the kitchen.

She swallowed hard and tried to think. "What did he take, Agent Gunn?"

"A prototype. One worth a lot of money, designed to do one thing, but capable of doing a lot of harm in the wrong hands."

Since the FBI was involved, she made an educated guess. "I take it this prototype came from a government contract."

Agent Gunn remained silent on that one.

She played the scenario out. "But the company under contract decided they could make more money off it using it in a different way."

Agent Gunn's eyes filled with admiration. "Actually, the director in charge of the project stole it by transferring it to a secure server in a country that doesn't have an extradition treaty. Your brother stole it from him and a server that is supposedly unhackable. We need it back."

She swore under her breath. "Well, I don't have it."

Agent Gunn eyed her. "Are you sure? Because I have it on good authority that the man who attacked you and killed your boyfriend followed your brother to your place earlier that day and went back to find what he suspects your brother left with you."

She beamed, excited that one thing could be done to get justice for Marcus and take the target off her back. "Great. Then you know who killed Marcus. Is he in custody?"

"No," Hunt grumbled.

She deflated, her hopes dashed.

Mr. Wilde rejoined them.

Hunt gave her more bad news. "The feds are hoping he leads them to the director and your brother."

She gasped. "You mean when he goes after Kyle to get back the prototype and kill him?"

Agent Gunn shrugged. "Your brother put himself in this position. He got back what didn't belong to the director who took it. But Kyle didn't return it to us."

She gave her muddled mind a second to process and fill in the blanks in that announcement. "Kyle is . . . experienced at getting into things he shouldn't," she said diplomatically because her brother loved hacking into things just to see if he could do it.

"Yes, he is," the agent confirmed.

Kyle was . . . Kyle. Quiet. Introverted. Lost in his electronic world. A gamer. A hacker, sure. But a thief? No. She didn't want to believe it. It didn't fit.

Agent Gunn held her gaze. "I need your help to get to your brother before the man who is after him gets to him first."

"Kyle didn't tell me where he was going or when he'd be back." And it frustrated the hell out of her. It scared her, too, because she didn't want anything to happen to him, even if this was his fault.

He had to have a good reason.

She just needed to talk to him and find out why and how they could end this.

A thought popped into her head. "Shit."

Everyone stared at her, expecting her to say more. Instead, she pulled out her phone from her sweatpants' pocket and called Kyle with everyone staring at her.

She put the phone to her ear, knowing she'd get Kyle's voice mail. Once she heard the message, she knew everything the agent was telling her was the truth.

Agent Gunn stepped closer to her. "Why would he leave that message on his voice mail?" He'd obviously already listened to it.

"He taunts me for not using my aptitude for math doing something more lucrative."

Agent Gunn's intense stare didn't waver. "Like what?"

He already knows. "Cryptography."

Agent Gunn nodded. "Code breaking."

"Basically. Yes. Those were the kinds of games we played together as kids and teens." They'd been competitive. She'd always wanted to best him. Most of the time, she did.

And because the agent knew something about that, she surmised that whatever he was trying to get back, this something the government wanted, was some kind of code breaking program. Which fit right into why Kyle wouldn't want just anyone to have it. For national security purposes, it would be a coup for the U.S. If another country, or terrorist organization had it, it could be disastrous.

Agent Gunn eyed her. "So . . . What does the message mean? 'The password is, apple pie for two.'"

"It's a code."

"Meant only for you?" Agent Gunn asked.

"Yes. Unless he taught someone else the silly game we used to play as kids to make each other figure out a code to enter our room or get something from the other we wanted, like a toy or candy. It was just for fun."

"So you can crack it?"

All the men, Mr. Wilde, Max, Hunt, and the agent formed a semicircle in front of her, collectively waiting with anticipation.

She felt like she was opening a huge can of worms. She hated worms. "Sure. I need some paper and a pen."

Max went into the office off the living room and came back with a notebook and pen.

"Thank you."

"You're welcome." He held his arm out to the dining room. "Use the table."

Everyone followed her there. She stood at the corner of the table, too nervous to sit, with Max beside her on one side, Agent Gunn on the other. Mr. Wilde and Hunt took a spot opposite each other next to the other two men.

She felt Max's nearness through her whole body and tried to ignore it and focus on the task. She wrote the message on a blank page. Apple pie 4 2

She thought about the steps and which order to do them in. She should remember because this was a common one they'd used. But it had been a long time.

She explained as she went. "You use the number of each letter in the alphabet for the word apple and pie. A is the first letter, *P* the 16th. And so on." She put the numbers under the letters. "That gives us this." She pointed to the page. 1–16–16–12–5–16–9–5. "Now the last part he said 'for two,' meaning the number 4 and 2. So every number divisible by four, we do the math. *P* is number 16 and *L* is 12, so those numbers in the line change to 4s and a 3, giving us this." 1–4–4–3–5–4–9–5. "Now the 2 part of the password refers to double letters. They get multiplied by 2. So those double *P*'s in apple change from 4 to 8." She wrote down the new sequence. 1–8–8–3–5–4–9–5. "Then the last step is to change each number, except for the double letter *P* back into letters, giving us . . ."

She worked it out on the page.

"What the hell does A88CEDIE mean?" The agent looked very concerned. "And is he trying to say someone is going to die?"

Her anxiety amped up. "I hope not. I think that's an unfortunate coincidence in this case. We used to love it when a code came up with words we didn't expect."

"So that's the password," Hunt said. "What do you use it for if you can't call him?"

"Is it to a website or something?" Max asked, interested like all the rest of them.

"No. When he doesn't answer his phone, usually because he's deep into gaming or coding, I video chat him to get his attention because that pops up on his screen."

"Can you do that now?" Agent Gunn's anxious voice made butterflies flutter in her belly.

"I'll try. But I can't promise he'll answer." She wasn't sure she wanted him to take the call. If he didn't answer, perhaps he'd spare himself some repercussions.

"Just do it." The agent was running out of patience.

She couldn't blame him. She wanted answers, too. She tapped the icon on her phone and waited, but she got a message that her brother's user name didn't exist anymore.

"He's cut that line of communication," she told them, then thought about her brother's message again. "Maybe the password prompt is also the username." She typed in applepie42 and got nothing. She tried it another way, remembering how they used to feel so smart back in the day that they knew pi. She changed the username to apple31442.

"I thought that might work," Max said, looking over as she typed.

"Let's try this." She typed apple314for2.

"You found him," Max said excitedly. "Impressive."

She soaked in that praise. One kind word shouldn't mean so much to her, but from Max, it did. Especially right now when she was feeling so sad and afraid and a little swept away by all the drama happening in her life. "We still need to see if it's him."

Agent Gunn made a call on his cell. "Give me a second to set up a trace on that account." The agent stepped away and spoke softly, doing whatever needed to be done to find her brother.

Hunt picked up on her distress and put his arm over her shoulders and pulled her close for a short hug. "Whatever charges your brother is facing are nothing compared to the fact that Marcus is dead and you could be on that hit list now that they didn't get what this guy wants from you."

"Is that supposed to make me feel better?"

"Back off," Max warned.

Hunt pulled his arm free and stepped back, his hands up, a grin for Max, who simply glared back at his brother.

Hunt refocused on her. "You know this is the right thing to do."

"Doesn't make it any easier. He's my brother. I don't want him locked up for the rest of his life."

"What if you save his life by getting him to turn himself in before he or someone else gets killed?"

"I'll try. But you suck at making me feel any better about this."

Hunt gave her a half grin. "Sorry. I'd rather give you the truth and let you know you're on the right side of this, even if your brother has crossed the line."

Agent Gunn walked over. "We're all set on our end. Send the request and password, but don't tell him you're working with us. Just see if you can get him to come back."

She sent a request to connect to the user. She held her breath waiting for a response. Her head wanted one. Her heart was on the fence because she didn't want to do anything that put her brother in jeopardy.

But this call wasn't going to be what put him in a cell. He'd already broken the law.

She just didn't want to be the one who helped the cops and not her brother. It felt disloyal, even though she knew he was probably safer in the cops' hands than out there on the run from whoever was after him. And apparently her.

The request went through and a chat window popped up with one line.

What's the password, freak?

She actually found a smile. A short laugh burst out of her.

"What's so funny?" the agent asked.

"He used to call me that all the time when we were kids because I was freakishly good at doing math in my head." She typed in the code she'd worked out.

A88CEDIE Geek!

About time. You alone?

She didn't want to lie, so she asked her own question.

What's going on? Why aren't you answering your phone?

Long story. You OK?

No. Marcus was murdered. In my apartment, where I was attacked.

WTF When?

Last night.

Are you okay?

She typed fast, letting some anger out in how hard she hit the screen.

NO! Marcus is dead! I have eighteen stitches in my head! You need to come home. NOW!

I'm sorry. I can't. Too dangerous.

Why?

The FBI is after me too.

She glanced at Agent Gunn.

"I was able to speak to him briefly yesterday before he gave us the slip. He knows what he needs to do."

She pressed her lips tight and typed out another message.

The FBI can help.

She hoped she was right about that.

They want what I have. Too dangerous for the world.

She eyed Agent Gunn.

"He's not wrong."

Another message from her brother popped up.

You need to leave. Now. It's not safe.

I can't just leave. I have school. My kids need me.

They'll come after you again. Please. Leave now. Go anywhere, just don't stay there.

Let me help you. Come over. We'll talk about it.

It's my fault. But I'll fix it. I'll contact you when it's safe.
Until then, disappear for a while. Don't tell anyone where
you're going. Please.

Kyle, I'm begging you, let the FBI help you.

GO NOW BEFORE THEY GET YOU TOO!!!

The chat ended.

Whatever the person on the other end of the line on Agent
Gunn's phone said to him, he didn't like. "He's bouncing
from one IP address to the next all over the globe."

She should have known her brother was too smart and
too paranoid at this point to make it easy to find him.

Hence the secret password and new user ID on the
chat app.

"What now?" she asked, because she was obviously
a target.

"Protective custody," Hunt said adamantly.

Agent Gunn nodded. "We'll put you in a hotel with a
couple agents until we find your brother and arrest the
man who killed Marcus and is looking for you."

"You know who he is. Arrest him now, and leave her
out of it," Max suggested the obvious.

"If it's not him, it will be someone else. Right now, I have someone on him. I'm hoping he leads me not just to her brother, but also the director who stole government property before Kyle stole it from him."

Kenna was finally seeing the bigger picture. "I'm guessing this top secret prototype is related to espionage."

"You should stop guessing and get ready to leave," the agent warned.

"I can't just leave. I have a job, responsibilities to my students. Marcus's funeral. I have a life here." Not that it had been so great the last several years. But she'd made a vow to herself to change all that and focus on herself and go after what she wanted.

She'd tried to kick-start a relationship, first with Sean, then Marcus, that would take her into the next chapter of her life.

How's that working out for you?

Shitty, thank you very much, she answered that annoying voice in her head.

"Why do I have to give up my life for days, weeks, months, however long this takes?"

"To keep you alive. That's why," Max snapped.

Right. She needed some sleep to clear her head. But this was going way too fast. It felt like her life was out of control. "I don't have what they want."

"Are you sure?" Agent Gunn pinned her in his gaze.

She remembered Kyle's odd behavior last night. "Do you know exactly what it is?"

Agent Gunn narrowed his gaze and thought for a moment before he spoke, obviously trusting her with more information to get what he ultimately wanted. "Kyle wouldn't want to store it on a server. The prototype would fill multiple hard drives. Our information says that Kyle put those in a secure vault that only he can access with a key, which is actually a thumb drive, and a password."

She grinned. Maybe she could end all this. "I think I know where it is."

Agent Gunn perked up. "Great. Tell me where, and I'll go get it."

"My place was trashed. I have no idea if it's still there, or exactly where you'll find it in all the mess. Plus, I could be wrong. Who knows? Maybe that thug found it and took it."

"I don't think so," Hunt chimed in again. "Or he wouldn't have said it's not over. He didn't finish his job. And he left a loose end."

Max swore under his breath. "Find this thing for them, so they can arrest this guy," he ordered her.

Agent Gunn frowned. "Come on, let's go."

She sighed and spelled out the piece Max forgot. "Even if I find it for you, I'm still going into protective custody indefinitely until this guy leads you to the other, right?"

"Yes." When she frowned and huffed out her frustration, he added, "But it's more than that. You could be used as a means to get to your brother. Do you understand?"

Her throat went tight and her breath stopped. "Yes."

"What if she stayed here?" Hunt blurted out. "It's a

big spread. Lots of men working here to keep an eye on her and the place. Anyone who doesn't belong would be spotted immediately. She'd have some freedom here, instead of being locked in a cramped room for god knows how long." The whole time Hunt spoke, he kept his gaze locked with Max's.

Max clenched his jaw, but didn't say anything.

"I couldn't possibly impose on the Wilde family," she said diplomatically and emphatically.

"I can put a couple men on the ranch to watch over her." Agent Gunn actually considered it.

"You mean to use her as bait," Max bit out. "If the guy who vowed, 'This isn't over,' doesn't come for her, maybe her brother will feel like it's safer to approach her here than at some hotel." Max was trying to protect her.

She appreciated it. She hadn't thought of any of that. Like she hadn't considered that she'd be used as a pawn to get to Kyle.

She also agreed with Max. Staying here was not a good idea. For reasons that had nothing to do with her brother at all and everything to do with sparing Max any more upset.

"She'd be protected," Agent Gunn assured everyone.

Max eyed Hunt. "You're going to let this happen?"

"I think it's the best solution on many levels." Hunt didn't even try to hide the grin that he was poking at Max for some reason.

"Then you'll accept full responsibility, too," Max warned.

Hunt grinned wider. "Oh, I take full credit for putting the two of you back together."

Max's jaw cracked. "And if she gets hurt because of it."

Hunt eased up. "If she's here, you, me, *Chase*," Hunt emphasized, because he was ex-military, a trained soldier, "the feds, the ranch hands, we can all keep an eye on her. She'll have some freedom here. In a hotel room, she'll have four walls, three meals a day, and that's it."

It sounded like fancy jail.

She had no doubt it would be boring as hell. She'd go stir-crazy in a matter of days.

The ranch was the better option as far as her comfort and preference, but not at the expense of making Max angry, uncomfortable, and possibly hate being at his own home because she was here. Not to mention the jeopardy it put him and everyone else in. "The hotel is fine. I'll go grab my shoes upstairs and we can leave." She left the room and headed upstairs.

"Hasn't she been through enough?" She wasn't sure who Mr. Wilde asked that question of, but no one answered, and she knew why.

Max probably thought she deserved all she got.

Didn't matter. She was right back where she'd always been since they broke up. Alone and on her own.

What she needed to focus on was finding the thumb drive her brother left with her. Then she could go back to her life and leave Max to his, just the way he wanted it.

Chapter Eight

❧

MAX FELT trapped in a nightmare of his own making.

Hunt took advantage. "You know you want her here."

"She didn't have anywhere to go. You insisted it be here and not your place. I thought it would be one night. Maybe two. Not indefinitely." He'd go mad having her this close and not being able to do anything for her.

"You're welcome," Hunt teased.

"This is not what I wanted."

"Are you sure about that? Because the second I told you she'd been hurt and was in the hospital, you couldn't get to her side fast enough."

Denying it would only make him look stupid.

Hunt went on like this wasn't a disaster in the making. "You had to see for yourself if she was okay. I get it. Believe me, I do. I feel the same way about Cyn. But how are you going to feel, day in and day out when she's in protective custody, *somewhere*, for however long it takes, and you don't know *where* she is, or *how* she is? I won't know. No one but the FBI will know."

"And we won't tell." Agent Gunn got in on the action.

Max swore and shifted his weight, knowing Hunt was pushing because he thought his heart was in the right place by putting Max and Kenna both on the spot when things were already over and done between them.

"You'll hardly ever see her. You'll be out working sunup to sundown. Dad and Chase can babysit her while the feds they assign can watch the property and her, too."

Max could feel her in the house and smell her in the room. He heard her crying at night and screaming out during a nightmare.

She was already everywhere.

She was always with him, in his memories and his dreams.

Having her this close would make it near impossible to avoid her, let alone put her out of his mind the way he tried to do all the time and failed miserably.

He got in his truck this morning to run an errand and smelled her. When they broke up, he smelled her on his clothes, in the truck, he found things like hair ties and lip balms, a pair of earrings. Little reminders of her everywhere. It took weeks before he stopped finding things or seeing things that reminded him of her twenty times a day.

He didn't want to go through that again.

Kenna walked back into the room still wearing his T-shirt, the one she tossed in his face last night, leaving him with the scent of her bare skin and the image of her two perfect breasts and all that creamy skin he dreamed of touching again. "I'm ready to go."

Reality hit him hard.

He wasn't ready for her to leave. He couldn't not know where she was and if she was really safe. "I'll drive you to your place. You can pack your stuff and I'll bring you back. That way Hunt can finish work without having to drive out here and back to town again."

She stared at him with a blank look, like she didn't understand a word he'd said.

"Then it's settled," his dad said. "She's staying."

Kenna looked even more stunned.

His dad patted her shoulder. "If you're not back for lunch, I'll see you for dinner tonight."

Kenna seemed to shake herself out of her stupor. "Oh no. I don't want to impose. I'm happy to go to the hotel."

"No you're not," Max snapped, annoyed she said the opposite of what she wanted because of him. "You hate cramped spaces. While you love watching TV, two days of nothing but that and you'll go insane."

"I won't put you and your family in harm's way. I'll go."

He planted his hands on his hips. "You're staying. For your sanity and mine." Max headed for the door.

Hunt had to get another word in. "Maybe we'll all find what we're looking for."

Max wanted to punch Hunt in the mouth. He knew exactly what Hunt hoped Max would find. A way back to Kenna.

If only.

But also not in the cards.

He climbed into his truck.

Kenna walked around the front and opened the passenger door. "It doesn't have to be this way."

"It is what it is. Accept that this is how it's going to be while they search for your brother and the other guy who stole the FBI's shit, and let's move on to the next step."

"You obviously don't want me here."

"I want you to get in the truck, so we can get this done, and I can bring you back here where you'll be safe." He'd make sure of it.

She climbed in, closed the door, and buckled herself in, then folded her hands in her lap and stared out the side window as his horse Ziggy trotted in the nearby pasture. "Thank you."

He barely heard her. "You're welcome."

If they were any more polite to each other, he might hit something.

He ended up following Hunt and the fed to her place. Not like his truck didn't know the route as well as he did.

They didn't speak.

He didn't know what to say.

She looked too tired to do more than sit and stare out the window.

But the moment he pulled into the parking area outside her apartment, he noticed the way she clenched her hands tight. Her breathing changed. Everything about her tensed and went on alert.

He'd been so busy thinking about how they were going to spend the next days, weeks, maybe even months on the ranch together and not make things worse between them, that he hadn't thought about bringing her back to the place where someone attacked her and her boyfriend was killed right in front of her.

He parked the truck, turned it off, then just sat there for a moment, giving her a minute to settle.

She just wound herself up more tightly, sweat breaking out on her upper lip and forehead.

"You tell me what I'm looking for, I'll go in there and find it for you. I'll pack up your clothes, grab whatever you want, and you don't have to get out of the truck at all."

"I can't stop seeing it." She looked down at her hands. "There was so much blood." She swiped one hand over the other, like she saw it plain as day and couldn't get it off. "I couldn't stop it. He just . . . He wouldn't wake up."

"It wasn't your fault."

She swiped at her tears. "It was. He should have just dropped me off and left."

"Then you'd be dead." The thought chilled him to the bone. "And he should have walked you to your door for exactly the reason he did. To keep you safe."

She grunted. "I ruined the last moments of his life, just like I ruin everything with men. I broke up with him."

What? Max's mind did not compute that.

She opened the truck door and slipped out.

He rushed to catch up to her.

She walked with her head down, eyes on the pavement all the way to her place, which was the last unit on the end. He loved her place because it had a little courtyard with a bench out front. They used to sit out there, talk, have a beer together, and look at the stars.

Hunt and Agent Gunn were waiting outside.

Max stopped beside Kenna, hoping that having him

close eased her anxiety a little. If she broke down, or whatever, he'd be there to help her.

"Why haven't you gone in?" he asked, wondering why they were standing out here.

Hunt turned to Kenna. "Someone broke the police tape seal and went inside, since I was last here."

Kenna finally looked up and at her front door. "The frame's been fixed."

"I came back the other night after I saw you at the hospital and waited while the maintenance guy fixed it," Hunt said.

"Who else besides you has a key to your apartment?" the agent asked.

"Kyle. My parents. My landlord, of course." She paused. "And Max did back in the day."

That raised an eyebrow. The agent looked at him. "Hunt filled me in on your relationship and breakup on the way here."

Max kept his mouth shut. Being here reminded him of her and how often they spent time together here alone, just the two of them hanging out, making love, making memories.

Now the place had been tainted, but his memories weren't.

"Can we get on with this," Kenna snapped, getting more anxious by the second.

He could practically feel her holding herself back from running for it.

"Maybe Kyle came back to retrieve what he left?" the agent guessed.

"Wait here." Hunt pulled his gun. "I'll go in and clear the place first, make sure there are no surprises."

Kenna wrapped her arms around her middle and hugged herself tight, the memory of the other night still so fresh in her mind that the horror was written on her face. Max could practically feel her fear echo through him.

He wanted to wrap his arm around her and offer her what comfort he could, but he didn't, afraid that even cracking the door into something more than the nothing they shared now would utterly destroy him. He knew she thought the worst of him, and he reminded himself again that his place was not beside her any longer.

Hunt filled the doorway. "All clear." He holstered his weapon. "It's not easy to tell if something was taken or not."

Kenna marched right up to Hunt and shoved right past him, a woman on a mission. Or more likely, a woman hell-bent on getting this done and over with so she could leave.

Hunt stepped aside.

Max walked in, completely unprepared to see all the damage. Kenna's once tidy little place had been wrecked. The living room and kitchen were completely torn apart, drawers and cabinets opened, contents strewn everywhere.

In the bedroom, the mattress had been pulled off the frame, the bedding dragged off the bed and draping onto the floor.

Kenna stood in the midst of the chaos and stared

at the only empty spot on the floor between the living room and short hallway to her room.

Hunt came up beside Max. "While the door was being fixed last night, I used the cleaning supplies I found under the kitchen sink and cleaned up."

Max heard what Hunt didn't spell out. He'd cleaned up the blood. He clamped his hand on Hunt's shoulder and squeezed, letting him know Max appreciated that he'd spared Kenna that added horror.

Agent Gunn joined them, looking around the room. "Kenna. Can you find what we're looking for?"

She didn't move. She didn't say a word. A silent stream of tears ran down her cheeks and landed on her chest.

He couldn't take it anymore. He stepped in front of her, put his hand at the back of her neck, and pressed her face into his shoulder.

She went perfectly still. She didn't reach for him. She didn't say anything.

It felt like time stopped.

He whispered in her ear. "It's over. You're safe."

A tremble went through her body and into his.

"Let's find the thing, so we can leave. You don't need to come back here ever again if you don't want to."

She didn't move.

He cupped her face and made her look at him. "You can do this." He couldn't help it. He brushed her tears away with his thumbs, her soft skin under his, reminding him of a time when he could touch every inch of her and she'd welcome it.

Now she was too distraught to even care.

"Find the thing." He released her, hoping she'd get to it so he could take her to the ranch, where he could put some distance between them.

She shook herself out of the trance she'd been in and turned to the bookcases that flanked the TV stand. She went to the one on the left, closest to the slider, and looked through the contents that had been shoved around and spilled onto the floor. She squatted and sifted through the broken shards of cat figurines and a broken pot, the plant's long pointed leaves so bent and broken it probably wouldn't survive.

Kenna scooped up the bits of plant and roots and stared at it, her eyes watery again. She raised her hands up and out. The pathetic plant dropped back to the floor. She picked up one cat figurine after another and threw them at the wall in utter frustration and anger. "It's not fucking here!" She stood, her arms rigid at her sides, hands fisted, and stamped a foot. "Aaaaah!"

Hunt looked at Max, one eyebrow raised.

Max had never seen her this pissed.

"He came here pretending to say goodbye, because he was scared someone was following him. But that was just a ruse to hide something here. And what he really did was lead them right to me. He got Marcus killed. He stole something everyone wants back. He stole my safety and my life right out from under me. And now I'm just supposed to sit and do nothing while he's out there hiding because he doesn't want to give back what he took."

She stood with her back to all of them, not really talking to them, but herself and the wall in front of her, where a painting she'd loved and bought with him at a flea market hung off-kilter, the canvas torn, looking like the guy who broke in punched his fist through it.

He mourned the loss of the painting and the memory it brought back of happier times he shared with her. He wondered if she did the same, looking at it now.

So many of the things in her apartment they'd picked out together.

He didn't wonder if she looked at them and remembered him. How could she not?

But it was the pain of their breakup they both lived with now.

They'd both moved on, even if they still held on to the memories of the good times.

Agent Gunn stepped forward. "How do you know it's not here? We've barely gone through the place."

Kenna turned to him and snagged one of the cat figurines from the bookcase that hadn't been tossed to the floor. "He brings these to me. It's a joke between us. I'm the spinster of Apartment 13. Unlucky in love. And life, apparently." She looked at the destroyed remnants of her place. "All I need is a bunch of cats to complete the cliché, but I'm allergic. He adds to my collection to show the passage of time, a reminder of how long I've been alone."

Agent Gunn looked at all the little cats. "That's a lot of poking at you."

Hunt shifted from one foot to the other. "If you were seeing Marcus, why give you another cat?"

Kenna sighed. "Because he knew, even though I didn't want to admit it until last night, that Marcus and I . . . We were never going to be more than friends." Her gaze fell to the empty, clean space on the floor again. "I thought Kyle gave me the cat because he wanted me to tell the truth."

"About what?" Agent Gunn asked.

Her gaze shot to Max, then over to Agent Gunn. "Nothing. It doesn't matter anymore. Everything is ruined." Kenna walked to the dining room table and grabbed an empty delivery box. "I'll go pack." She left all of them and went into her room.

Max and Hunt shared a look that said the same thing. *She is not okay.*

Hunt walked past him. "Since we're here, I'll clean up the kitchen."

Max followed to find a broom and dustpan to clean up the dirt and broken knickknacks and glass in the living room. He spotted the busted and bloody frame and glass in the trash that Kenna hurt her head on the other night. It sent a cold shiver through him because this wasn't over.

Hunt held a candy bar. "This wasn't here last night."

Max eyed it. "Are you sure?"

Hunt turned it around to show him the word *Sorry* written on it. "I think I would have remembered this. Kenna," he called out.

She walked back into the room carrying the same box, only this time it was full. She stopped short of Max. "You wanted your stuff back. Here you go." She shoved the box into his gut.

He grabbed hold of it and stared down at several of his old shirts, a leather bracelet she bought him at the fair, the bottle opener he'd bought because the beer he liked to keep in her fridge didn't have a twist-off cap, the jar of change she'd put on his side of the bed, so that every time he emptied his pockets he'd drop it inside. They planned to put the money toward their honeymoon. The one they were never going to take. And right on top was the watch she'd been so desperate to find hadn't been stolen. The only possession that mattered to her in her entire place.

Kenna dismissed him and turned to Hunt. "What?"

He held up the candy bar.

She swore. "It's from Kyle. He must not have gone far last night and came back right after our chat this morning and left that to let me know he'd been here. When one of us hurt or did something to the other, we'd buy the other our favorite candy bar to make up. That's the rule. Apologies come with chocolate."

Agent Gunn eyed her. "You and your brother like to play a lot of games."

"It's our thing." She snagged the bar from Hunt's hand. "Like I said, the thing he left is gone. I'll go finish packing." She left the room again.

Hunt eyed the box in Max's hands. "It's been three years and she still has all your stuff?"

"Shut up," Max shot back, and took the box to his truck. When he got back to the apartment, Kenna had two suitcases and a duffel bag packed and ready to go by the door. He took them out to the truck, too. When he got back again, Agent Gunn was on his phone, sitting on the bench outside the apartment. Hunt had the kitchen in decent order.

Kenna was on her knees in the living room trying to save a plant. She picked up the root ball, dirt spilling onto the floor. The green and white pointy leaves were mostly bent and smashed. "Look at you, spider plant, all broken and battered."

Kind of like Kenna, Max thought.

She shook her head, filled a mug with loose dirt from the floor, broke off one of the baby spider offshoots, and buried its tiny roots into the dirt, then took it to the sink and watered it.

"Do you think it will survive?" Max asked.

"Probably. They're easy to grow and propagate this way." She stared at the other three plants on the floor. "The oak leaf ivy got trampled. Every leaf on the African violet is broken." It had landed upside down. The leaves were now badly wilted. "But my sweet little Columnea with its cute goldfish-shaped orange blooms can definitely be saved." It lay on its side but looked mostly intact, though the pot had a huge crack in it.

Max picked it up and handed it to her. "You could put this in the kitchen window at the ranch."

"Too much light. I'll keep all my stuff in the room you let me borrow and out of your way. I'll do my best to make it seem like I'm not even there."

"You can have the run of the house and ranch, so long as you stay in sight of everyone protecting you."

She took the pot from him and turned her back. "It'll

be better that way, and easier for everyone." She tamped down the soil in the pot, then watered the plant and set it next to the only other one that could be saved.

He went to the closet, found the broom and dustpan, and swept the entire living, dining, and kitchen floors, while she straightened up the pillows, cushions, and debris, then disappeared into her room one last time.

Max waited in the kitchen, while Hunt and Agent Gunn conversed in low tones outside.

Kenna came out a few minutes later with a large tote bag over one shoulder, her laptop bag on the other. "I'm ready."

"Let me take those."

She stepped back when he reached for one of the bags. "I've got it."

He frowned, then picked up the two plants from the counter. "Lock up." He walked out and stopped in front of the agent and Hunt. "Did you get everything set up?"

Agent Gunn nodded. "Two agents will cover the ranch at all times. One will be assigned to her, the other canvassing the property around the house. Three sets. They'll be taking shifts. They've been briefed on the situation."

Hunt filled in where the agent left off. "Willow Fork PD, along with the sheriff's office, will increase patrols around the ranch." Hunt looked past him at Kenna, who'd finished locking up her place. For the last time, he guessed. "You need to stay at the ranch. Anything you need, we'll get it for you from this point forward, until the threat is over."

"What about going to Marcus's funeral?"

Hunt shook his head. "I'm sorry, Kenna, but that's simply too dangerous."

It looked like she knew that, but hoped to be able to say her goodbye in person anyway.

Agent Gunn held his arm out toward the parking lot. "I'll follow you back to the ranch, make sure you get there safely and check in with my guys to be sure they have everything they need. Then, we wait. If your brother contacts you again, you need to let me know immediately. If he asks to meet you—"

"I know what I need to do." With that, Kenna walked away, headed to his truck with her heavy load, and he didn't mean just the bags weighing her down.

"Give her a few days. She'll be better, more settled," Hunt said.

Max didn't think that was going to happen anytime soon. Not so long as this was all hanging over her head and she had to stay at the ranch. With him. Which was probably the last place she wanted to be right now.

He pinned Agent Gunn in his gaze. "You better end this soon."

"She's the key. If her brother won't come in to keep her safe, she's the only one who might be able to convince him to do it, or find him."

"Yeah, well, in the meantime, nothing better happen to her."

"If it does, I have a feeling her brother will go after this guy again. And he does not want to lose anything else to her brother."

"That is only mildly reassuring, when the guy he sent after Kyle threatened her because he fucked up and killed Marcus." Hunt hooked his thumbs on his gun belt.

Agent Gunn had a really great poker face. "She'll be protected."

"She better be," Max warned, knowing it did little good when the man after her needed her out of the picture and was desperate enough to try to get to her no matter what.

And somehow, Max had to survive having her at the ranch, in his house, and way too close for comfort.

THAT NIGHT, FOR reasons he did not want to look at too closely, he snuck into Kenna's room while she was in the bathroom getting ready for bed and set the watch she'd held on to all this time on the nightstand.

If it gave her comfort, the way he couldn't anymore, then she needed it a hell of a lot more than he did.

And maybe it made him feel good to know that something of his still meant something to her.

Chapter Nine

꘎

KENNA SPOTTED the watch the second she walked into the room. She'd turned and stared at Max's closed bedroom door, tears in her eyes. Her heart filled with love for the man who didn't want her here but knew that single object still held a significant sentimental value to her beyond anything else.

He couldn't give her back what she wanted most, but he did give her that small piece of their past.

She didn't dare think it meant anything more. She knew better.

Still, the sweet gesture was just so Max, it brought on a wave of missing him even more.

She appreciated what he'd done so much, she'd whispered, "Thank you," to him, even if he didn't want the words and couldn't hear her. She went to bed with the watch in her hands, held close to her heart.

She still hadn't slept much, but each time she woke, the watch brought back good memories. She focused on them and fell back to sleep with something good to think about and to wash away the bad.

For a little while anyway.

She woke up this morning to her new reality living on the ranch. The second she opened her bedroom door, she spotted the agent, Mike, sitting on the top step of the stairs, gun holstered at his side, along with his badge. He gave her a nod but that was about it, since she turned and headed for the bathroom.

She'd waited until she heard Max leave the house before venturing out. She'd silently vowed yesterday to be the most unobtrusive and most inconspicuous guest she could be. She'd do her best to give Max his space.

And make things easy on her FBI shadows.

She showered and put on clean clothes, including underwear and a bra, since she got to pack her things this time and not Hunt, before she headed down for some food. Max hadn't said anything about the box of stuff she'd given back to him. He hadn't said much of anything yesterday after bringing her home and helping the agent—that one had introduced himself as Ray—carry her stuff up to her room.

She ate the plate of eggs and bacon someone, probably Max again, left in the fridge for her, then returned to her room.

Mike took his seat on the stairs again.

She should probably say something to him. *Hi. Thank you.* But she didn't feel like talking to anyone.

Except she needed to call the principal at school about her not coming back to teach for . . . a while. She felt badly she couldn't give Patrice a definite date for her return. Given the circumstances, she hoped the principal understood and didn't fire her.

She sat on the edge of her bed and reluctantly made the call.

"Willow Fork High School, this is Patrice. How may I help you?"

"Hi. It's Kenna."

"I hoped I'd hear from you today. How are you? Better, I hope." The sincerity touched Kenna.

She couldn't really remember what she'd said yesterday morning when she called in to give a brief description about what happened to her and Marcus and that she needed a couple days off. "I'm . . . um . . . doing as well as can be expected, I suppose." Sure. Let's call barely eating or sleeping when she wasn't crying the best she could do right now. Not to mention the anxiety and weariness riding her hard.

"It's all anyone is talking about on campus. Everyone has seen the news reports." Patrice paused. "And, of course, the students are gossiping about you and Marcus seeing each other."

"Marcus and I disclosed our personal relationship to you." She wanted to make it clear they hadn't been hiding anything. "But there is something else you should know."

"Go on." Patrice sounded anxious and excited to learn something others didn't know. Patrice loved gossip.

"Originally it was thought that the break-in was random. I learned yesterday that I was targeted." She left it vague, because she didn't want to get mired in the details.

Patrice made a short humming sound, then said, "I see."

"The police and FBI are looking into the matter."

"The FBI." Patrice sounded absolutely intrigued. In a small town where nothing much happened, the FBI getting involved in a case was big news.

Willow Fork had very little crime. Murders were few and far between.

"I am cooperating with the investigation. Which means, due to the fact I'm a target, I'll be in protective custody and unable to return to work right now."

Patrice gasped. "For how long?"

"I have no idea. I wish I could give you a time frame, it's just . . ." Choked up, she didn't know how to finish that. "It could be days, weeks, even months," she confessed. "I hate to do this to you last minute."

"Finding a sub won't be easy, especially if it turns into a month or more." Patrice huffed out a breath. "But if we need to make accommodations, then that's what we'll do."

Kenna took that to mean they'd start calling substitute teachers, the few who lived in the area, to see who could take her classes. She really didn't want that. Her students could fall behind.

And in the back of her mind, she worried that she could be fired and permanently replaced. "I'm a good teacher," she reminded Patrice, feeling like she needed to defend herself. "My class test scores are twenty percent

higher than all the other teachers." Test scores were all
that administrators cared about sometimes.

"I know you are a dedicated teacher. To me, you're
irreplaceable."

That made her feel good.

"It's not just that your students test well. You em-
power them. You make them feel like they can achieve
anything. You go above and beyond, helping them apply for scholarships, getting them interested in STEM
programs that will help them succeed in life. I see that,
Kenna. The other teachers recognize it. Some of them
try to emulate it. Others are just jealous that your students love you so much, even though you're considered
the toughest teacher on staff, too." Patrice sighed. "I'm
sorry you're going through this. Hopefully the situation
will be resolved quickly."

If she could get her brother to turn himself in, maybe.
But that felt unlikely, given he'd gone into hiding. And
practically made her do the same.

"Ms. Arnett is subbing for you right now. Maybe she
can stay on another week or two. In the meantime, I'll
look for someone willing to take a long-term temporary
position."

Kenna sighed, grateful Patrice was trying to work
with her. "Thank you for understanding. I've emailed
lesson plans to you, along with assignments for the students. I've covered the next month, just in case, but I
hope to be back sooner than that."

And if not, she planned to throttle her brother for
mucking up her life like this.

She'd lost so much. Marcus. Her apartment. Her freedom in some ways. She didn't want to also lose the one thing she loved and had left. Her job.

"We'll take it a week at a time. Two of which coming up, the students will be off for winter break. So I'll have more time to find someone to take your classes in January if that's even necessary."

She hadn't thought about the upcoming holiday.

How would she buy her friends and family gifts?

Would she get to even see her parents?

There's no way she could intrude on the Wilde family's holiday and ruin it for Max.

Once she ran out of sick days, she wouldn't be getting paid. Her savings would quickly dry up.

Overwhelmed by the stress of it all, she closed her eyes and tried to take a steadying breath that didn't work at all.

"You'll keep me posted, right?" Patrice asked.

"I will. Of course." She hoped the feds would keep her apprised of their investigation and the time frame for how long this might drag out, but doubted it.

Patrice cleared her throat. "We're holding a memorial rally tomorrow before lunch. I think the kids would really like to see you. And since you were so close with Marcus, I thought maybe you could say a few words, even lead the ceremony."

"I'd love to do that, but it's too dangerous for me to come to school."

"I'm thinking we set up a video feed and you do it remotely. I know you can't tell the kids everything, but hearing from you, the person who was with him in the end, I think that would go a long way to helping them heal. Many of your students have expressed how worried they are about you."

That touched her deeply. She was close with a lot of her students, since she taught them multiple years in different math classes. "Yes, absolutely. Whatever I can do to help. I have an idea for something the students can do collectively to honor Marcus."

"The photography club put together a collage of images for the ceremony, along with video clips of Marcus speaking at other rallies and coaching the basketball and softball teams. I've seen portions of it. It's really touching."

"His family will appreciate it." She hadn't met his family officially as a girlfriend. Their relationship hadn't reached that level of commitment and introductions. But she knew them in passing, like you knew a lot of people in a small town.

"I was thinking you could get all the students pins and yellow ribbons to help the kids show their respect and remembrance of Marcus. It would be something they could hold on to in his honor as well."

"Brilliant idea. We've done ribbons for other events and to bring awareness to causes. I'll get right on that and enlist the basketball and softball teams to help, so they feel like they're doing something productive for him."

Kenna felt a little better herself, participating in this small way. "Great. I've got my laptop. I can connect with you tomorrow and you can put me up on the big screen in the gym, so I can make my remarks." They'd done this in the past to have guest lecturers from other states address the children.

"Sounds like a plan." Patrice sighed again. "He was such a good man. Someone I could count on. I don't know what I'll do without him, or how I'll replace him."

"He can't be replaced. If you choose someone who has the kids' best interests at heart, you might come close to someone like Marcus."

"I will definitely keep that in mind. I'll also be thinking about you. Take care. I'll see you tomorrow via video for the rally."

"Thank you again for being so understanding and letting me participate."

They said their goodbyes and Kenna ended the call. She found herself just sitting on her bed wondering what to do next.

The walls felt like they were closing in. She needed some air and walked out of her room.

Mike stood as she approached.

"Can I go outside?"

"Being out in the wide open isn't a good idea, but you could go down to the barn."

That made her feel like a toddler, but she didn't grouse at the poor man assigned to watch her do nothing.

Mike grabbed the rifle and slung it over his shoulder by the strap, then followed her downstairs and out the front door. She didn't go into the barn, just in case Max was working in there, and headed for the side of it and the covered outside stall where a couple of horses were penned.

Mike stood between her and the house. The cover and horses blocked her enough from anyone out past the pasture and tree line. It wasn't exactly relaxing to be out in the open after Mike pointed out it wasn't safe, but she liked the fresh air and space.

She simply couldn't stand the quiet and emptiness in the house one more second.

But she knew Mike would only allow this for a few minutes before he wanted her either in the barn or house, where it was safer and easier to protect her, so she used the time wisely and patted the horse who came over for some attention.

A dog ran out of the barn and headed toward her. A moment later, Chase walked out, too. She hadn't seen Max's brother in a long time and found a smile for him as she bent to greet the dog. "Hello there. Who are you?"

"Remmy," Chase supplied, closing the distance. "I heard you were here." Chase looked past her at her guard. "Given the circumstances, I won't ask how you are. I just wanted to say hi and let you know if you need anything, I'm here."

"Thank you. And congratulations on getting married. I've seen Shelby and Eliza around town. You're a lucky man."

"That doesn't even begin to cover it." Chase glanced over his shoulder. "Ah, Max is headed back with a sick calf."

"This time of year?" Winter in Wyoming was not the

time for calves. Way too cold. The potential for losing them too high for any rancher.

"Yeah. Fence got downed by a tree during a storm. Bull got out. We have a couple of babies."

"Sounds about right." It felt good to talk about things that didn't have anything to do with her brother and took her mind off Marcus.

Chase shrugged. "Anyway, he'll be here shortly."

"And I should disappear."

He shook his head. "I didn't say that at all. I thought you might like to see the calf."

That surprised her. She thought Chase would want to protect Max from being upset by her. "Oh. I would. But Max doesn't want to see me, so I guess I'll head back up to the house. I just wanted to—"

"Stop, Kenna. You're welcome here. You can go wherever you like on the property. Max let everyone know to keep an eye on you. He's worried about you. I bet it would ease his mind to see you outside."

"I don't know about that. Besides, Mike is not happy I'm out here in the open."

"I know it will make Max feel better to see you out of your room. He's looking a little worse for wear."

"Thank you for not saying I do as well."

"Believe me, I get it. You've been through a lot the last couple days. Give it time. You'll start to feel normal again."

"My life has been turned upside down. Now I've intruded on Max's life here."

"For what it's worth, I don't think he sees it that way."

"Every time he looks at me, I see that he's angry."

"Yet he hasn't said one word about you leaving."

Max came into view, cantering ever closer to the barn, the calf in his arms as he held the reins and guided the horse to a stop outside the barn.

Chase walked over to take the calf, so Max could dismount.

She hung back.

Max turned to her. "Hey, you busy?"

She shook her head.

"Do you want to cool down Ziggy while I tend to the calf? If you don't want to, I'll find someone else."

"No," she said quickly. "I'll do it." Mike would have a fit, but she desperately wanted to be helpful to Max, and she loved to ride and hardly ever got the chance anymore.

He nodded and rushed into the barn.

She didn't mind the abrupt dismissal, because she got to be with the horse. "Hello, Ziggy," she greeted him and took the reins, giving him a pat down his long face, noting his still heavy breathing from his ride. "Okay, big guy, let's walk until you cool down."

"Where do you think you're going?" Mike asked.

"Just into that pasture to walk him in circles. Mind giving me a leg up?"

Ziggy stood a good seventeen hands tall. Getting her foot in the stirrup wouldn't be easy on her own. She'd need to find something tall to stand on to mount. But an FBI agent would do the trick, too.

"This is not a good idea."

"Please. It's the least I can do, since I'm staying here."

Mike pressed his lips tight. "Only because the last report I received from our undercover agent indicates the threat is far away from here."

Good to know they had that much information. It eased her concerns about going out into the open pasture, too.

Mike cupped his hands.

She put her foot in them and up she went.

"In the pasture. Right there, where I can see you. That's all. I say *come back*, you ride like hell back to me."

She nodded, then gently kicked Ziggy to get him moving. He happily followed her lead and walked back to the pasture. She let her body move with the horse and felt the sun on her face and breathed in the fresh air.

For the first time in days, she breathed easy and relaxed into the saddle and the quiet moment.

Chapter Ten

MAX WATCHED Kenna from the barn. She looked calm and content for the first time since she got here, and it eased the tightness in his chest.

"I thought you said you were going to drop the calf with me, then go back and get the mama." Chase wrapped the calf in a blanket to keep it warm. Remmy, Chase's service dog, who helped Chase with his PTSD symptoms, lay next to the poor dehydrated calf.

"Jessie's on his way with the cow."

Chase stood and joined him. "You knew getting her up on that horse would make her feel better."

One look at her and he'd known she needed an escape. "She loves to ride. I thought it would cheer her up."

"Looks like you were right."

Because he knew her so well. At least he used to.

Chase leaned against the wall opposite him. "How does it feel to have her back here?"

"Worse than avoiding each other the last three years."

Chase raised a brow. "Why?"

"Because seeing her brings it all back. Everything

good we used to share. And how it all ended." The yearning was unbearable. "Now she's hurt and in trouble, grieving for and feeling guilty about a man she was seeing but had broken up with the very night he tried to save her life."

Chase gasped. "No shit."

Max sighed. "No one but me knows that, so keep it to yourself."

"Damn." Chase pressed his lips into a frown.

"Yeah. And she feels terrible about it."

Chase waited a beat, looked out at Kenna riding in a circle, back straight, head up, sun making her golden hair bright and shiny. "Maybe she's not over you, the way you're not over her."

"Doesn't matter how I feel, it is over. Has been for a long time."

"Is it, though?" Chase eyed him. "Look at the way you can't take your eyes off her."

Max loved seeing her up on a horse, the wind in her hair, a soft smile on her lips. She'd been so lost in her grief and reliving that night that he worried she was spiraling into a pit of despair. But one simple thing, a ride on his horse, had brightened her spirit. Maybe now, he could stop worrying about her every second of the day.

"Leave it alone, Chase. Hunt has meddled enough by setting her up here on the ranch." He held up a hand to stop Chase from defending, or agreeing, with Hunt's methods. "I don't mind." He didn't, even if it made it hard for Max to keep her in the past where she belonged. "I want her safe." He needed her to be okay, so he didn't have to worry or think about her. "But me and her . . . That's never going to happen again." He needed to keep reminding himself of that.

She'd moved on.

So did he. Even if his life hadn't turned out the way he hoped and it looked like that wasn't going to change anytime soon.

Chase took a step toward him. "Why?" he asked in a mild way that compelled the truth.

"Because when the one person you love more than anything and trust more than anyone thinks the worst of you and calls you a liar, there's no going back." Max turned away from Kenna to tend to the poor thing that actually wanted his help. "I'll get the bottle so we can feed the calf and get it well."

Max grabbed him by the arm. "If you care about her this much, don't you think it's worth talking to her about whatever happened between you? Maybe you can work it out."

Max pulled his arm free, his anger rising. "Don't you think I tried? It was too late the second she accused me, because she already didn't trust me anymore, even though I'd given her absolutely no reason to feel that way. So let it go." He stormed out of the stall and went to the office to cool off before he said or did something he'd regret. He and Chase were back on good terms after what happened with their mother, him leaving for the military and coming home a broken man. Chase was better, they'd mended fences, all was good. And Max wanted to keep it that way.

He just wished his two brothers would stay out of his personal life. Even if they had the best of intentions, they were making it damn hard to keep Kenna in the past and not popping up in the future he wanted for himself, one that looked as happy and fulfilling as his brothers' lives were turning out to be with the women they loved.

But that dream was never going to happen.

Chapter Eleven

⌒⌒⌒

KYLE PACED the dingy motel room, trying to decide what to do, even though he already knew what had to be done.

He never expected things to go down like this. But he should have known the government wouldn't back down until they got their top secret, we-have-good-reasons-for-using-this, program that would ruin people's lives. And the world, in his estimation.

People had a right to privacy.

They had a right to believe that when a business or some other entity said their private information and data was secure, that it actually was, or that that business or entity had done everything possible to make it so.

Kyle had been too caught up in creating a key that opened any lock to think beyond achieving it to the consequences of its use. Those intended. And those not.

The government said they wanted it to do one thing.

But Kyle created the key to everything.

No one should have that kind of power, or access.

Not a person, an agency, a country, the world.

It would cause utter and complete chaos.

Just because it could be done, didn't mean it should be done.

He'd kept that thought out of his head until it was too late.

And then he'd had to correct his mistake and someone got killed. His sister was a target. His parents, too.

He'd told Kenna to run, but he knew she wouldn't. She wanted him to trust the FBI.

He couldn't do that, but maybe he could use them.

His call was answered on the first ring.

"Agent Gunn."

He couldn't believe it had come to this. "Where are my sister and parents?"

"In protective custody. Your sister at the Wilde ranch. Your parents in a hotel somewhere safe." Agent Gunn hoped he would take the bait and go see her.

Not going to happen, no matter how badly he'd like to see Kenna again. It was too dangerous. He'd messed up her life already.

Or maybe not if she was with Max and finally told him the truth.

He'd leave that to her.

And maybe give her a nudge, if she didn't.

He couldn't see her, but he could contact her. It would be tricky to get past her guards, but not impossible. A risk he was only willing to take for one last goodbye.

But they hadn't reached that point yet.

Though it looked inevitable.

"You went back to your sister's apartment," the agent accused.

He couldn't leave the key to the vault there. Not that they'd find anything in it. He'd just wanted the feds to think the program was safe in something they thought was too secure to crack. After what he'd created, they should know better than to think anything was safe anywhere.

He'd already destroyed it.

Now he was the only one capable of re-creating it.

He was the asset everyone wanted.

He was the reason his family was in jeopardy.

"I've made some mistakes, trying to do the right thing." He'd thought he could hide the program, then go into hiding himself, and no one would get hurt. Naive. Stupid. A hope without a prayer of working. But he'd had to try, because the alternative sucked.

His heart broke for poor Marcus. He never meant for that to happen or for Kenna to get hurt.

"Hand over the program, go into protective custody like your parents and sister, and once we have the director and the man he hired in custody, your family won't be in danger anymore."

Kyle shook his head even though the agent couldn't see him. "That's a lie. You know it. I know it. And then what? You have the program and give it to the powers that be and they use it. That's never going to happen. I won't let it." He didn't have it anymore. But they'd have him.

Not going to happen.

"The government wants its property back. I'm authorized to use any means necessary to get it."

"Including holding my family hostage?"

"Protective custody."

"Semantics."

"You put me in this position. You did this to them. You're the only one who can fix it."

He rolled his eyes. "Turning myself in won't do that. That only makes me the hostage." Frustrated that his options were limited, he hoped he'd find a way to end this cleanly, but the only one that came to mind meant sacrificing himself.

He wasn't quite ready to accept that as the only alternative.

He'd done the right thing. He deserved to be rewarded for that, not to have his life taken away.

But it looked like he'd saved the world and ended his.

"Kyle, your family is a target. Anyone who wants to get to you will use them. Look what's already happened."

His heart thrashed in his chest. "A man died. I nearly lost my sister. I understand the situation and the consequences. I just . . . want to find another way, so I don't have to give up my family."

"You know your options."

Yeah. Jail. Protective custody.

"We could make you disappear. That way they won't know where you are. And if they don't know, then they can't be forced to tell."

And that one. Witness Protection. The only one that really protected everyone. Except he was still at the government's mercy.

But he had them by the balls. The government couldn't afford for him to fall into someone else's hands. They couldn't let someone force Kyle to re-create the program and use it against the U.S. and the world.

Kyle hit Enter on his computer and heard a ping on the agent's phone. "Can I get that in writing?"

The agent swore. "You already had a drop link ready?"

He smiled, though he didn't really feel it. "Just covering my bases."

"Then why not just ask for what you wanted?"

"Because I hoped you'd have a better idea," he snapped, the pressure and strain getting to him.

"If you haven't thought of one, there isn't one." The agent gave him credit for finally thinking things through.

Kyle wished it didn't have to be this way.

Agent Gunn sighed. "Tell me where you are. We'll pick you up."

"No. Not until I take care of a few things. And just so we're clear, the agreement you send is specifically for me to disappear without handing over the program. I know what you're going to say, you know I'm going to counter that you can't risk me giving it to someone else, so my only option is your only option. Follow through with my demands and send it to me in writing to the link I sent you."

"We need the director. If he blabs about the program, sends someone else for you, your family, someone who hears about the program comes after you all, too, it could make it that much harder to protect you. This needs to happen now."

"It happens when I say it happens. And it needs to be foolproof. I'm still thinking about how we do it."

"Stop stalling," Agent Gunn ordered.

"Maybe I can find another way." He hoped some brilliant idea would come to him.

"Kyle." Agent Gunn sounded exasperated. "There isn't one. Accept that, and let's get it done before someone else gets hurt."

"I'll let you know when I'm ready." He hung up, knowing the agent wouldn't be able to track the call back to him or call him back.

He stared at the box he'd packed on the bed. Once he sent it, it was the beginning of the end for him.

Unless he found another way.

Chapter Twelve

KENNA WAS brushing down Ziggy in his stall when the call came and brought her out of her peaceful bliss and took her right back to the night Marcus died.

"Hello."

"Is this Kenna?"

"Yes. Who's this?" She didn't recognize the female voice.

"This is Mrs. Perry."

Marcus's mom. Her heart dropped. "Mrs. Perry, I wanted to call you but I didn't have your number. I meant to ask the high school office staff if they had it, but I . . ." She'd been too busy trying to get through another day and find some joy with Ziggy before falling back into reality.

Mrs. Perry didn't care about any of that; she missed her son.

Kenna tried to think of the right words to express her sympathy and remorse. Nothing seemed enough, so she went with the banal. "I'm so sorry for your loss. I . . . I don't have the words to express how sad I am that he's gone." A fresh wave of tears hit her, even as she tried to hold it together.

Mrs. Perry sniffled back tears, too. "Just last week he mentioned seeing you. He said it was new, but going well. He talked about all you had in common, both of you getting out of long-term relationships and looking for someone new, who wanted to start a family and build a life. He seemed excited about the future."

Overwhelming guilt joined her grief. The two sent her stepping back into the wall and falling to her butt in the straw.

Ziggy went to his water trough and slurped up a gallon of water.

"And then this happens." Mrs. Perry's stern voice warned something was coming. "I spoke with Officer Wilde this morning. He told me this wasn't some random break-in, but that the man was after something your brother left with you."

"I didn't know that at the time." As defenses went, that one sucked.

"Yes, well, that doesn't change the facts."

No, it didn't. Nothing would now. "It all happened so fast. One second he was dropping me at my place, the next . . ." It all came back so clearly. Her breathing became erratic as the terror returned. "He w-was d-dead."

"He was murdered," she snapped. "Because he was seeing you."

Kenna understood Mrs. Perry's anger and kept her mouth shut to allow Mrs. Perry to have her say, to get it out, whatever it was she needed to do to help ease her grief, though nothing would diminish the aching loss of a child. Kenna could take it. She would, because that was the least she owed Marcus's family.

"I know it's not your fault." Mrs. Perry calmed.

"But it feels that way," Kenna acknowledged.

"I'm just . . . I'm angry."

"I completely understand. So am I. I can't change it. I can't fix it. I can't take it back, and I want to so badly." She couldn't even get her brother to do the right thing.

"I want to yell and scream at you. I want you to hurt the way I hurt."

Kenna's pain was all too real and all-encompassing. But she could take more. She would for Mrs. Perry's sake. "Go ahead. Do what you have to do. I deserve it."

Mrs. Perry let out a huge sigh. "No, you don't. I know that in my heart."

Kenna spoke from the heart. "I hurt for him. For you. For all the people who loved him. I want to make this right, but there's nothing I can do, so I'm left feeling as helpless as I'm sure you feel. I hope, in time, the sharp edge of your grief will dull, so it won't always feel so piercing. I don't know exactly who is responsible for all that happened, but I promise you, I will help in any way I can to bring them to justice for your son. For you and your family. And if there's anything more you need from me, please don't hesitate to ask."

"I know you'll be speaking tomorrow to the students about Marcus. I think that's good. The students need that. But . . ."

Kenna braced herself.

"Officer Wilde asked if you could attend the funeral with your . . . escorts."

She meant Kenna's FBI protection. She'd texted Hunt earlier asking if there was any way she could go.

"I wanted you to hear it from me. The answer is no. Not because of any malice, but because I want the focus to be on him, not your presence there. Tomorrow will be about his work, his friends, and his love for his students. The funeral I want to be about the family."

The punch of hurt to her heart pained her. She held back tears. "Of course. Whatever you want." She'd been prepared for the police and FBI to deny her anyway, but having Mrs. Perry do it herself cut deep.

"I'm sorry."

She was, too. "Don't be sorry for taking care of yourself and your family and asking for what you need. I don't want to be the cause of any more pain for you."

"I wish it didn't have to be this way, especially since he cared for you." Mrs. Perry's words held all her sorrow. As much as she didn't want Kenna at the funeral, she also regretted her decision to deny Kenna an invitation to attend.

"I understand. I will abide by your wishes and tell you now, you have my wholehearted condolences for your loss. I am truly sorry for what's happened. I will never forget your son. I will always think of him with warm feelings and good thoughts about the memories we shared."

Mrs. Perry sniffled. "You're a good person. I appreciate

that you suggested the kids all wear yellow ribbons in remembrance of Marcus tomorrow. That's very sweet of the children to do for him."

"I wish we were celebrating Marcus for a different reason."

"I know you do." Mrs. Perry gathered herself with a deep breath. "He loved being at the school and coaching. He loved helping young people."

"He will be missed by me and so many others," Kenna choked out past her tight throat. "Take care, Mrs. Perry."

"Stay safe," she said back and hung up.

Out of sheer frustration, she slammed her head back against the wall, then buried her face in her knees and wrapped her arms around them and let the tears fall. Her shoulders shook with every wracking sob.

Ziggy whinnied and stomped his hooves.

Someone put a hand on her shoulder, brushed at her hair, and pressed something to the stinging stitches. "You're bleeding," Max grumbled. "You tore two stitches. What were you thinking hitting your head like that?"

Ziggy bent his head low and nibbled her hair.

"Back off." Max pushed Ziggy's big head away. Max's body shifted and he slid his hands under her arms and pulled her up.

She went, because what else could she do, but she didn't look at him. Instead, she focused on the feel of his hands on her. The way he kept her steady. The warmth she felt being this close to him.

"You're upsetting my horse," he grumbled some more.

She tried to pull away, but he held on to her. "I'll leave." She needed to get away from him before she did something stupid and threw herself into his chest, held on to him for dear life, and hugged him until it didn't hurt anymore.

Max sighed. "You're bleeding. You're crying."

She didn't really care, but she sucked in a steadying breath, because it seemed those two things bothered him. She wiped at her tears and nearly fell over when the room took a spin.

"Whoa." Max scooped her up into his arms and carried her out of the stall.

"I'm fine." She did not feel fine.

"What's happened?" Mike asked.

"She tore her stitches and nearly passed out. Get the truck door. We're going back to the hospital."

"Max, I'm fine."

"No, you're fucking not. But maybe you can convince the doctor to say that after he checks you out and fixes your stitches." He set her on the seat in the truck.

Mike slid in beside her the second Max moved out of the way and pulled out his phone.

She tried not to move too much and set off another round of vertigo. "I don't know what's wrong with me."

Max started the truck and drove down the drive. "You've barely eaten in two days. You cry all the time. You don't sleep." He slammed his hand against the steering wheel. "It's my fault. I thought having you take care of Ziggy would distract you and make you hungry. I should have known you weren't up to it."

"It's not your fault—it's mine." She pressed her hands to her tired eyes and laid her head back.

Mike nudged her arm. "The other agent is following. We'll stay with you the whole time."

"Great." She'd disrupted Max's day and the agents protecting her.

"Who were you talking to on the phone?" Max asked, his voice soft.

"Mrs. Perry. Marcus's mom. I'm not invited to the funeral. She wants the focus on the family, not the woman who got her son killed."

"That's bullshit. It's not your fault. Your brother set this all in motion. He can end it. But where the fuck is he when you need him?" Max's anger didn't surprise her.

She'd put him out. He'd had to leave work to take care of her. "I'm sorry what's happening to me is interfering with your life."

"Don't apologize for things that aren't your fault."

"There are a lot of things that are my fault. The apology stands."

Max's hands tightened on the wheel. "I'm not doing this with you now." He was right.

They'd done this a long time ago. Probably best to let ancient history stay buried.

She didn't remember the drive. She'd never forget the feel of Max's hand on her face.

"Kenna, wake up. Open your eyes before I send for the emergency team."

She opened them, then squinted at the bright light. "What?"

"We're at the ER."

"Great. I'm like a toddler—you put me in the car and I fall asleep."

Max chuckled. "If you can't sleep tonight, I'll drive."

The offer made her tear up again.

"Don't do that. Please. Come on. Your guards are nervous enough about taking you from the ranch. If I make you cry on top of it, they'll probably shoot me." He was being nice and trying to make this less stressful.

"Thank you."

"I don't like this new super polite thing we do."

"Thank you anyway."

He frowned and backed away from the door, so she could slide out.

She wobbled a bit before she had her feet under her.

He took her gently by the arm to help support her, and they walked to the door and into the crowded waiting area.

Mike was on her other side, every eye in the room on the man with the gun. Luckily, he'd left the rifle—at the ranch, she hoped.

The other agent walked toward them. "Cubicle two. Doc will be there in a second."

She looked at all the waiting people. "But—"

Max leaned in. "Having you here puts everyone in danger. We need to be in and out as quick as possible."

"Then why did you bring me at all?"

"Because you need a doctor." Max tugged her toward the cubicle where Mike and the other agent waited. The second they were near the bed, Mike closed the curtain and left them alone. Kinda. The two guards were just feet away.

"Sit," Max ordered.

She did because she didn't feel steady. Maybe it was dehydration and lack of sleep. Maybe it was just being so close to Max she wanted to fall right into his arms.

She sighed.

"What's wrong?"

"Everything."

One side of his mouth drew back in a half frown of agreement.

The doctor came in carrying a tray. She recognized him from the other night. "I hear you popped a few stitches."

"Yeah. Sorry."

"It happens. Let's take a look."

"She's dizzy, has a headache that won't go away. She hasn't slept more than a couple hours the last couple days," Max supplied.

"How do you feel, Kenna?"

"Like someone I cared about died in front of my eyes and I got slammed into a wall by two hundred plus pounds of man who won't get out of my head."

"She hardly eats," Max added.

Mike pulled the curtain back for a nurse, who rolled in an IV stand.

The doctor pulled on gloves. "The IV will help. You

lost a lot of blood the other night with the head injury, which is probably making you feel tired, too. You need to eat, so your body can recover. I'd recommend some protein high in iron. A burger. A steak. Dark green veggies."

"I got that covered," Max assured the doc. He did raise cattle, so she'd bet he had some good beef in the freezer.

She didn't comment, just held her arm out so the nurse could put in the IV line, then she lay down with her back to the doctor so he could look at her head.

He hissed. "This looks nasty. It's dirty, too. What happened?"

"She bashed her head into a stall wall in the barn."

She looked up at Max. "Tattletale."

"We wouldn't be here if you'd take care of yourself."

"We're here because my brother took something that doesn't belong to him."

Max shrugged a shoulder. "It sounded like he had a good reason."

She sneered at him. "Now you're defending him."

"Just trying to keep things in perspective."

The doctor cut in. "Okay, Kenna, I've got the wound cleaned up."

While she'd completely ignored all the stinging pain because Max distracted her. She should probably thank him, but that would only make him cranky again about her being polite.

"I'm going to numb you up. It'll take a few minutes to kick in, then I'll do the stitches."

"Just sew me up without the numbing thing. We need to get out of here quickly."

Max leaned down close. "We can take the time."

She shook her head. "No. If something happens because I'm here . . . I can't." She turned to the doctor. "Just do it."

He held her gaze, his filled with sympathy. "The IV is going to take a while. We have the time to do this without causing you more pain."

"I have to go. I don't want anyone else to get hurt." She choked up.

Max planted his hands on the bed beside her and leaned down. "It's the middle of the day in a crowded hospital. The likelihood someone would come after you here is probably low. We're all just being overly cautious to keep you safe. Let the IV and the doc do their thing, then we'll go."

"You probably should have stayed at the ranch." She wanted to protect him, too.

"I'm good, right here with you."

"I'm ruining everything again."

Max ignored that and addressed the doctor. "Let's get this done."

The doctor finished the stitches in a matter of minutes once the numbing agent took effect. The IV finished in about half an hour. She used the restroom before the three men escorted her back out to the truck and Max drove them home and she went up to her room to rest again.

She must have fallen asleep, because the next thing

she knew, she thought she felt someone brush their hand over her hair. But then she opened her eyes and spotted Max and guessed she'd imagined it.

"Sorry to wake you, but it's dinnertime." Max held a plate with a thick steak, steamed spinach drenched in butter, and heaping pile of garlic mashed potatoes. "The doctor said to eat. So eat." He held up a fork and knife.

She sat up, wiped her tired eyes, then took the plate and utensils.

He headed for the door.

"Max."

He turned to her.

"Thank you for taking care of me, even if you don't want to."

His lips pressed tight and he looked annoyed again. "You're welcome." He turned back to the door, then back to her again. "Are you feeling better?"

She stared at the plate of food, then him, and thought about how she'd felt riding his horse today. The rest didn't matter. The fact that Max tried so hard to make her feel better did.

"Thanks to you, yes. I feel better."

He nodded, then left her room.

She spotted the bottle of water he'd left on the table by her bed. It warmed her heart that he'd gone to all this trouble. She needed to do what he wanted her to do and take care of herself so he didn't have to do it for her.

The meal was delicious. Her steak perfectly prepared the way she liked it. Medium rare. Salt. Pepper. Garlic butter. Spinach wasn't her favorite, but she ate it all. The mashed potatoes were divine. Also her favorite. Which Max knew and used to get her to eat.

She downed half the bottle of water, then grabbed her dirty dishes and headed downstairs. Mike was still there, sitting at the top of the stairs, probably listening to whatever game was on TV in the living room.

She rinsed her plate and utensils in the sink and put them in the dishwasher, then did the same with the other dishes left in the sink. She scrubbed the cast-iron pan with a little salt and water, rinsed and dried it, then left it on the stove. She washed the other two pots and left them in the strainer to dry.

Feeling better than she had in days, she walked out of the kitchen, Mike there keeping an eye on her and out the windows, and went to the living room.

Mr. Wilde sat in a leather recliner. Max was on the couch. They were watching a hockey game.

"Hi. Thank you both for dinner. It was delicious." She met Max's gaze. "I ate it all."

"Good." He turned back to the TV.

Mr. Wilde smiled at her. "You look better."

"I don't, but thank you for saying so. Mind if I watch, too?"

Mr. Wilde waved her into the room. "Not at all."

Max didn't say anything.

She took a seat on the other side of the couch, leaving a big gap between them. She wasn't a huge hockey fan, but found herself getting into the game. Mostly because

Max and his dad really enjoyed it and made a lot of comments and cheered when their team scored.

She tried not to think how nice it was to be here with them, or that if she'd been at her place, she'd be watching TV alone.

She spent a lot of time alone.

It made her sad and happy at the same time to be here. This is what her life might have been like had she and Max stayed together. This is what she'd lost.

She wiped away the tear that slipped down her cheek and sucked the rest back, not wanting to distract the men from their game with her inner turmoil.

Mostly, she shifted her focus and settled into enjoying the evening being with them, even if she was just taking up space and not really participating.

She'd spend the next however long she was here, doing this, being here, but not interfering in Max's life anymore.

The game ended with Max's team up two points. He looked so happy and excited.

Even Mike, who'd taken up a spot at the back of the room, looked pleased.

She stood and stretched her tense back. "That was a really good game. Thanks for letting me watch with you."

The muscle on the side of Max's face ticked. "Get some sleep."

"Good-night." She headed for the stairs, but caught Mr. Wilde's whispered remark.

"Ignoring her isn't going to fix things."

Max's reply was exactly what she expected. "Leave it alone."

It hurt her heart to know that, even though circumstances had brought them back together, he didn't want to change the status of their relationship from nonexistent to even friends.

She took the not-so-subtle hint, accepted that he'd been kind to nudge her into getting her act together, and now it was time for her to give him back the space he wanted.

She just wished it didn't have to be this way.

Chapter Thirteen

KENNA WAS in the stall with the mama cow and her calf. The little one was still too weak to nurse from his mother, so Kenna was giving him his lunch in the form of a huge bottle with a nipple. And the little guy was drinking it up. "Chase said you'll be back at your mother by tonight if you keep this up."

She hoped the little one didn't get attached to the bottle feeding.

The alarm on her phone went off. She needed to get into the office, where Mr. Wilde said the Wi-Fi was better for her video call with the school today. She was nervous about speaking. Patrice had emailed her the outline of what they had planned and a heartfelt message that the kids missed her, were worried about her, and couldn't wait to see her.

She intended to keep the focus on Marcus.

"Hey, what are you doing in here?" Max asked from behind the stall gate.

The calf finished off the bottle just in time. "Feeding the baby."

"He's looking much better today."

She gave the calf a rub behind the ear. "He's a strong one." She gave the mama a pat on the side, then walked out to the aisle where her agent for the day was waiting. She put the bottle on the table outside the stall. "I'll clean that after I call into the school. I hope you don't mind. I'm all set up in the office."

"Why didn't you do it up at the house?"

She eyed him. "Because the Wi-Fi is better down here."

Max frowned. "Who said that?"

"Your dad."

He sighed, looked up at the rafters, and said, "They're all getting in on the act."

She thought she understood what he was talking about, but said anyway, "What do you mean?"

"Nothing. Use the office. It's not like I didn't have a ton of paperwork to do." The annoyance was written all over his face and tinged every word.

"If you need to work in there, I'll do it up at the house." It would mean rushing and probably being late, but if it kept her from irritating him even more . . .

He waved his hand and sighed. "No. I'll just do what I need to do later."

"If you're just going to do paperwork, you can be in there while I do the video thing. Though I might distract you with the speech I'm giving."

His eyes went wide. "You're speaking?"

She nodded.

His voice softened. "Are you sure you're up to it?"

"I'd do anything for my kids. And right now, they

need to see that I'm okay. There are rumors about Marcus and me seeing each other. We'd only told a handful of people. So I want them to know I cared about him as much as they did. We all miss him. We all need to celebrate him."

Max nodded. "I'll stay out of your way."

She corrected him. "I'm the one in yours. But this won't take long, not like my staying here." She walked into the office and pulled her laptop around on the desk so it was facing the other way and Max could sit in his seat and work.

"You don't have to do that."

"It's fine." She logged into the chat and waited for Patrice to connect on her end.

Instead of the principal popping up on her screen, she got a view of the entire student body in the gym bleachers.

All the kids would be able to see her on the large screen.

It started slow, with a few of her students pointing at her and waving. Then everyone saw her and waved. Tears gathered in her eyes.

Max looked over at her, his eyes filled with concern, but he didn't say anything.

Patrice came into view. "We can see you. Can you hear us?"

"Yes. It's so good to see all of you. I miss you." She waved back at them.

She spotted the Perry family sitting in the front row.

Patrice turned and addressed the crowd. "Students,

faculty, the Perry family, thank you all for being here
to honor and remember Marcus Perry, beloved vice
principal, coach and friend. It's been a difficult few
days. We've all been trying to process this tragic event.
Counselors are still on hand to help anyone who needs
someone to talk to about processing their grief. Today
we gather to express our condolences to Mr. Perry's
family and to shine a light on the man who gave so
much to our school, and especially to all the students
whose lives he touched. I know you're all curious about
the details of what happened and why. I know you've
been worried about Miss Baker. As you can see, she is
well and here with us today. So I'm going to turn this
over to her."

Patrice turned and gave her a nod to go ahead.

A rising panic washed over her as she thought about
the night Marcus died and how she'd explain that to all
these kids.

Then Max leaned over, caught her eye, and whispered, "You've got this."

Her heart settled. Her mind cleared.

She let her heart lead. "Marcus Perry was not just
a colleague, he was my dear friend. Yes, it's true, we
were seeing each other. We'd gone to dinner that night.
When we returned to my apartment, Marcus walked
me to my door, like the true gentleman he was. I had
no idea at the time, he'd turn out to be a hero, too.
And just minutes later, he died trying to save my life.
Because that was Marcus. Someone who was always
there to help." She looked at the Perry family, hop-

ing they saw her grief and knew she wished it hadn't turned out this way.

She wiped away the fresh tears, gathered herself, and went on. "I'm sorry we lost him. I hate that someone took him from us. I wish with my whole heart it never happened. I wish he was here with us right now."

She paused to try to gather her thoughts. "The person who did this is still out there, but the police and FBI are working hard to bring him to justice. Marcus deserves that. And I will do whatever I can to make that happen. Unfortunately, that means I'm away from you for a while. I hope to return soon.

"But today, I get to celebrate Coach Marcus with all of you. He talked about core values. Dependability. Integrity. Trust. Respect. Being a good citizen, whether that was at school or in our community. Helping others. Raising them up. He did that for all of you. He lived it in his life. He showed me it in his last moments."

She wiped away a tear. "God, I miss him. I know all of you do, too. So let's honor him." She wiped away a few more tears. "Let's remember him and all he contributed to our lives."

She found a smile to go with a happy memory. "He loved to make us laugh. Remember last year on Valentine's Day, he dressed up as Cupid and went around at lunchtime dropping love bombs on everyone. He made sure every student got one, because he wanted everyone to know they were special." They were really heart-shaped papers in different shades of pinks and reds that he'd printed out with affirmative messages like: You're special. You're smart. You are enough. You are loved.

So many more she couldn't remember right now.

By the looks on the kids' faces, they remembered.

"He gave me one that simply said, You're amazing. He made me feel that way. He tried to make all of you feel that way because he believed it about all of us."

She touched her hand to her aching heart. "Who else has a story to tell about Coach Marcus?"

Drew, who taught biology and chemistry, came over and stood next to Patrice. Before he addressed the kids, he turned to the camera and looked at her, "I'm glad you're okay."

"Thank you."

Drew turned back to the kids and started what turned out to be a couple dozen stories about Marcus from him and everyone else who wanted to share a memory or story about Marcus.

Kenna tried not to look at Max. The compassion in his eyes touched her. He wasn't doing any work, but simply sitting behind the desk, his presence all the support she needed to get through this.

The last person finished speaking.

They watched the video montage. There wasn't a dry eye in the room.

Patrice nodded for Kenna to end the ceremony.

She sat up straighter. "I want to thank everyone who came up to share something about Marcus. He liked to end all our rallies with a falcon chant. Today, I want you all to join me in one for our beloved coach. It needs to be loud and proud and I want him to hear us." She started them off. "Coach, coach, coach." The voices and foot stomps in the stands grew to a deafening roar. One she was sure Marcus heard and felt, just like his family did in the gym.

She gave a last wave to the crowd, a nod to the principal, then closed her laptop even though the kids were still chanting.

Patrice would dismiss them to lunch with their spirits high.

Max reached across the desk, took her hand, and squeezed it. "You are amazing."

It made her smile that Marcus had thought the same thing and was maybe, through Max, reminding her again. "Thank you. I don't feel that way at the moment."

"Doesn't mean it isn't true."

"Except we both know I'm not."

Max's gaze narrowed. "Why would you say that?"

"Why would you call the woman who called you a liar and a cheat amazing?" All he did was remind her that her past self was a dumbass. And maybe her present self wasn't much better, because she still hadn't told him the truth.

"Kenna."

"Do you realize that's the first time you called me by my name?"

His gaze sharpened.

"Leave it alone. The last thing I want to do is make things worse between us."

Max opened his mouth to say something, but clamped it shut when her phone rang.

She looked at caller ID and frowned. "It's Mrs. Perry." She braced herself and answered. "Hello."

Mrs. Perry jumped right in. "What you did today, what you said about Marcus, he'd have appreciated it so much. That was an amazing speech. You reminded everyone who Marcus was and what he stood for. You reminded them and me how much he cared about everyone. I don't know how you're keeping it all together and are still able to show your heart to me, to them, to everyone."

"I cared about your son. I'm sorry he's gone and that being with me instigated his death."

Mrs. Perry squashed that notion. "You had no idea you were in jeopardy. Officer Wilde told me you even tried to stop that man."

"It wasn't enough."

"But like Marcus, you tried."

She didn't want Mrs. Perry trying to make her feel better. Not today. Not when this was about Marcus. "Thank you for the kind words. You will be in my thoughts tomorrow as you lay your son to rest. I'll be thinking of him, you, and your whole family. Take care, Mrs. Perry."

"You, too, dear. Stay safe."

They ended the call.

Kenna felt drained.

"I think we should talk," Max announced.

She put her elbows on her knees, her head in her

hands, sighed, then looked up at Max again. "I'll tell the agent on duty today that you want me to go. I'm sure they can have me out of here in no time."

Max stood, planted his hands on the desk, and leaned forward. "Damnit, Kenna, I'm talking about us."

She stood and matched his pose. "There is no us. Why? Because of me. I did this. I not only broke our relationship, I set fire to it on my way out, destroying any chance we might be even friends again. I know you hate me. I know you don't want me here. I know that every time you look at me, you want me gone. So excuse me, if after all that and what's happening now, I don't want to talk about it. I'll make this easier on both of us and go." She held back the tears until she cleared the office door and headed out of the barn.

Max yelled from behind her, "She's not leaving."

She guessed he was talking to the agent on her tail. Still, she threw up her hands and let them drop as the tears fell and she ran for the house.

Nothing in her life was easy anymore.

Her life had been upended, and she still felt like she was in a freefall and taking Max down with her.

Chapter Fourteen

MAX SLAMMED the office door, took the seat at the desk, and tried to wrap his head around what Kenna said. He expected her to put the blame for the breakup on him. Instead, she'd taken responsibility for it.

Why would she do that?

What the hell changed?

Did she regret the breakup, like he did?

He slammed his fist on the desktop. He couldn't believe how badly he handled things with her. She'd been a wreck after speaking to the students and getting that call from Marcus's mother, her eyes haunted, sad, and bloodshot from crying. She'd looked so fragile he'd wanted to take her in his arms and hold her.

But he couldn't do that because they weren't together anymore.

He'd done nothing but make things worse. For her. And between them.

He was starting to wonder if he'd put the whole blame on her all this time, but he was actually part of the problem, too.

He hoped to simmer his anger by doing the paperwork, but he ended up replaying the past and the present in his mind, wondering how two people who had been so in love let it all fall apart.

His emotions were too close to the surface. Too volatile.

Frustrated by the lack of any answer that made sense, he batted his hand at the cup of pens on the desk and sent them flying into the filing cabinet and across the floor.

It didn't solve anything, except to expend some of his pent-up energy.

"Feel better?" Chase walked into the office, concern in his eyes and written in the creases across his forehead.

"No." He didn't want to talk to or see anyone right now. "What are you still doing here? Isn't your wife and kid waiting for you?" Somehow he managed to make that sound like a bad thing, and it wasn't. Not at all. But Max saw Chase with his family, and it made him think of what he'd had a shot at and lost.

And he still didn't know how it all went to hell so fast, when he and Kenna had been together for so long.

But he guessed that was what happened when you lit a match to gasoline and it went up in flames.

Chase took the seat Kenna sat in earlier, pouring out her heart to her students. "What's wrong, Max?"

The simple question seemed all too easy to answer. "Everything. My whole fucking life is wrong."

"Why?"

He let the words fly without thinking. "Because this isn't what my life was supposed to be."

Chase tilted his head. "What was it supposed to be?"

"Like yours. Like Hunt's. A wife. Kids. The ranch. The person I want by my side. You got that. Hunt found it. Why the hell didn't it work out for me when it all seemed so perfect, and then it wasn't?"

"You tell me. You and Kenna did something most people can't. You sustained a long-distance relationship while she was in college. That alone would have broken up many couples. Then she comes home, starts working at the high school, and you two are planning a life. So you tell me what happened, because you've never really said, except that you had a fight and it was over."

Max's gut tightened with the memory. The last night they were together came back so clearly in his mind. "We went out for dinner and drinks at Cooper's with friends. Everything was great. We laughed and had fun, danced, and it was another great night out with my girl. But one of our friends had too much to drink and needed a ride home. I'd only had two beers the whole night, so I was good to drive. I dropped Kenna at her apartment because she wanted to take a shower and our friend's place was past hers. So I kissed her good-night, said I'd be back soon, and took the friend to her place."

Chase's eyebrow went up. "*Her* place."

Max narrowed his gaze. "Yes. And before you get any ideas about what happened, remember you just outlined my relationship with Kenna and that I loved her so much we made an eight-hour drive between us work for a long time because we were committed to each other."

Chase nodded. "Okay. So you took your friend home. Then what?"

"She was too drunk to walk, so I helped her to her door, opened it up for her, and helped her inside. I planned to leave right then, but she puked down my chest and collapsed to her knees on the floor."

Chase made a gross face. "Ugh. Not good."

"No. I couldn't just leave her like that, so I took off my seriously stinky shirt, picked her up, took her to the bathroom, cleaned her up, made her drink some water, and I tucked her into bed. By the time I finished all that, I figured Kenna was out of the shower and in bed asleep. I didn't want to wake her, so I didn't call or text her. I stayed with the friend—on her couch—until morning to be sure she was okay."

"The decent thing to do."

"I thought so. Until the next morning when I'm standing in the kitchen, drinking my first cup of coffee, when someone knocks on the door."

"Oh shit."

"Why would you think that? I didn't think anything of it, because I thought Kenna knew me and how much I loved her. Right up until Hillary wobbled out of the bedroom, opened the front door, and Kenna saw me shirtless in the kitchen and Hillary all rumpled and sleepy, saying, 'Yeah. So that happened last night.'"

Chase swore.

"I thought Hillary meant that she got drunk and I had to stay with her. Kenna thought she meant that we slept together."

"I'm sure you told her that wasn't the case."

"I did. And she called me a liar to my face."

"She was taken by surprise, angry in the moment." Chase offered the explanation like it made all the sense in the world.

"How would you feel if the woman you'd loved since sophomore year in high school accused you of sleeping with a friend when you'd never done anything, not one damn thing to ever make her think you'd look at another woman the way you looked at her?"

"I'd be mad. And heartbroken."

"You're damn right, because even when I told her the next day and days later that I never slept with Hillary, she wouldn't believe me."

"Why not?" Chase asked, his eyes narrowing and filling with suspicions. "If you and Hillary both denied it, why wouldn't she believe you both?"

Max went so still he felt like even a pinprick would shatter him. "Why wouldn't she believe us?" *Why would she take the blame now?* A cold shiver went through him.

"That's what I asked. Your relationship was solid. Hillary was friends with both of you. It should have been an easy matter to clear up."

Exactly. And because he couldn't do that with Kenna, he'd gotten even angrier. She should have believed him. But she didn't. Why?

"Hillary was more my friend than Kenna's." Time rewound in his head. The things he thought he knew took on a whole new dimension and truth. "Hillary had a crush on me. I always knew that, but I was with Kenna, so I ignored it."

"How did Hillary act after you and Kenna split?" Chase asked, only making things worse.

Max swore. "She pushed for us to get together. She showed up at the bar all the time, seemingly looking for me. But every time I saw her, I saw the end of Kenna and me, and I just couldn't go there." But he'd used a lot of other women to try to wipe away Kenna's memory and the mark she'd left on him.

It never worked.

She was tattooed on every bit of him.

He felt the reckoning that had been a long time coming building inside him.

"Before you walk out of here, you need to be clear what you want and what you can forgive, or you two won't have a chance at fixing this."

"I can forgive her for thinking I lied to her."

"Can you forgive yourself for letting her go and all you've done to try to forget her these last three years? Because we've all seen the way you've punished yourself."

If he could get Kenna to forgive him, maybe he could forgive himself.

"I need her to know that I see what happened now and it wasn't her fault. It was mine for not fighting for us."

"Good luck."

Max stood and walked out of the barn to face the woman he'd never stopped loving and to face a past he thought he understood but had not seen clearly, wondering if Kenna would ever forgive him for the way he'd turned his back on her. And them.

Chapter Fifteen

KENNA PULLED open the bedroom door wide enough for Max to see she was already done packing. He stood in the doorway, looking too damn good and still wearing that damn scowl on his face he always got when he saw her.

She brushed back the wisps of hair brushing her cheek. "I'll be gone in a few minutes."

"You're not going anywhere."

"Zander is making arrangements."

"No he's not. He's in the kitchen eating a slice of apple pie and drinking coffee, giving you and me a few minutes to talk alone."

"Just let me go."

He took a step closer. "I did that once. I can't do it again. Not with things the way they are between us now."

"Are you drunk?" That had to be the explanation for him saying something so crazy.

"I'm stone-cold sober. Though after an eye-opening talk with my brother, I think I may be the stupidest man on the planet."

That took her aback. "What?"

"Why did we break up?"

She tilted her head, totally confused that he'd even ask the question. "You know why?"

"I know I thought I knew why, but now I think I had it wrong."

"What?" Maybe she needed a couple drinks for this to make sense.

His shoulders sagged. "Just answer the question. From your point of view, why did we break up?"

Tears gathered in her eyes. Her throat clogged, her chest went tight, and her battered heart thrashed in her chest. "Because I hurt you."

He reached for her, but she stepped back. He sighed. "Kenna, talk to me."

"It's too late."

His eyes filled with hope and a plea. "Maybe it's not."

Yeah, right. That was too much to hope for. Either way, she finally confessed. "I accused you of lying to me. I didn't believe you. And then when I did, it was too late. I'd ruined it all and you'd moved on and never looked back."

A pained look came into his eyes. "That's not true."

She remembered every time she'd seen him around town after the breakup. "You couldn't stand the sight of me. You avoided me at all costs."

Max hung his head, then looked at her again. "I did. Because it hurt too much to see you and want you and know that you didn't believe in me."

"Exactly. It was my fault. And I'm sorry. I was so sorry, but it was too late to tell you that because I hurt you."

"Who hurt you, Kenna?"

She took a step back. "What? It's not about me."

"The hell it isn't." He closed the distance and stood so close she could smell the hay and horses and wind on him. "You lost me. I lost you. That happened to both of us. Now tell me exactly what happened."

"It doesn't matter now."

"It does to me!" He'd never raised his voice with her. Not once. Not ever. This really mattered to him. "Please, Kenna," he begged. "Start at the beginning and tell me what happened."

She gave in to the desperate need in his voice. "The amazing happened. You loved me, and I loved you, and it was perfect."

He rubbed his hand over his heart. "Yes."

"I didn't think anything would ever come between us."

"I didn't either." He looked so sad. "But Hillary did. Didn't she?" The anger came back. He knew. At least he thought he did.

"It was me. You said it then, you'll say it again now. I didn't believe in you."

He shook his head and started talking again. "You walked into her place and saw me shirtless and her just out of bed. I can see where your mind would go."

She sighed, feeling the inevitable about to happen. They'd relive this and still end up apart. He'd blame her again. Deservedly so. "You didn't call or text me that you weren't coming back to me. I woke up alone."

Pain filled Max's eyes. "I'm sorry."

"You don't have to be sorry. You didn't do anything

wrong." The shame and regret filled her up. "It was me. All of it was me."

"No. That's not true. I know that now."

She'd prove it to him. "I was worried about Hillary. She was in really bad shape. I thought I'd stop by her place and check on her. And there you two were together. At first, I didn't want to believe what I thought I saw, because you wouldn't do that. You wouldn't hurt me like that."

"Never," he swore, making it all worse, not better.

"And then she said—"

"'So that happened last night,'" he interrupted her, his memory as clear as hers.

"Yes. And everything inside me went haywire. It couldn't be true, but the look on her face . . . The triumph." The gut punch of pain hit her now just like it did then. "I thought she'd stolen you away from me."

Max looked thoughtful. "I was in the kitchen behind her. I couldn't see her face. I had no idea she made you think it was real, so that when I denied it, you didn't believe me."

"I . . ." She shook her head. "She denied it, too, but the way she said it, the look in her eyes . . . I didn't believe her either. I thought she was just covering for you. And after I left you two, she called me later."

"What?" Max's anger turned to fury.

"Over and over again, leaving messages that she was sorry, you two were drunk, things got out of hand. Neither of you meant for it to happen."

Max's eyes went wide with shock. "What the fuck."

He obviously didn't know, because Hillary had played her to get Max.

She shrugged and couldn't help the frown. "But I knew you weren't drunk. You'd never drive me home if you were intoxicated and put me in danger."

"Never," he confirmed.

"So I had to assume you wanted her and that's why you slept with her."

"The only woman I ever wanted was you."

"I thought so." Her frown deepened with memories of the last three years without him. "And then there were all the other women."

Max winced.

"And there was Hillary right there to tell me I wasn't special. You didn't love me. And oh yeah, she'd never slept with you, but she did manage to break up the perfect couple."

Max's eyes narrowed. "When did she tell you that?"

"On the one-year anniversary of our breakup," she choked out.

That shocked look came back to his face. "Are you fucking kidding me?"

"She followed me from school to the grocery store and confronted me in the parking lot, telling me how stupid I was to believe her over you and that I didn't deserve you because of it. I don't know what hurt more, the fact that I'd lost you, or that she was right. Definitely losing you and knowing that I let it happen."

"I never slept with her."

"I know. I think that's why she taunted me so much

and rubbed my nose in it that you had so many other women after me. I don't know what I did to make her hate me so much, aside from having what she wanted. I saw the way she flirted with you and always tried to get your attention. I never really worried about it, because I knew you were mine. And then she took advantage of a situation and I fell right into her trap. But you didn't. You never wanted her."

"Why would I want anyone else when I had you?"

She tried really hard not to let those words spark hope for something more with him than simply clearing the air. "She wanted that for herself. She wanted you to feel that way about her." Kenna shrugged. "I understand why." She swallowed a sob. "It felt really good to be loved like that."

He tried to reach for her again.

She stepped back. "Don't. I don't deserve your kindness after the way I hurt you. What I did . . . I'm so sorry. You were only ever kind and generous and loving to me. I had no reason to think you'd cheat. That's not you. I knew that and I—"

"You got hurt when you thought something that could never happen felt like it did, because Hillary manipulated you. And me."

"And now I've gotten to tell you I'm sorry. I've wanted to do that for so long, but you wouldn't . . . Well, it's done. Now we've cleared the air and it's all in the past."

"The hell it is."

"You've moved on. And that's okay."

"That's not true at all."

"The number of women you've dated over the past three years says otherwise." She held up her hand to stop him from talking so she could say the rest before she fell into a heap of tears again. "I don't expect you to forgive me for what I did to you."

"It wasn't your fault. Of course I forgive you."

She found a soft smile and felt her heart lighten. "Thank you. I needed to hear you say that. I don't like the way things have been between us these last few years. I hope now, we can see each other without all the pain making us want to avoid even a casual encounter."

"Kenna, you're not hearing me."

"I'm sorry, and you forgive me. That's all I want, Max."

"I want more."

She didn't hide her disbelief that he really meant it. "Everything is a mess."

"You're here. I'm here. We can fix this."

"I'm just happy you don't hate me anymore. I'll take that as a win after I've been filling up the loss column for a long time." She gave Max a reminder about her reality. "I've been alone since I left you, and I'm still not used to it. Being here, seeing you the last few days, God, it's been heaven and hell at the same time. My being here has put you and everyone here in danger. So maybe it's best that you continue to stay away from me, because I don't want to be the reason you get hurt again."

"I can't sleep for worrying that two feds and a cop sitting on the ranch and guarding you isn't enough. I hear you crying or screaming in your sleep and I want so badly to make it better for you. I want to wrap you up in my arms and protect you and love you the way I used to, but this damn thing has been standing in our way. And now it's gone and all I want to do is this." He didn't give her time to think, just closed the distance, cupped her face, and kissed her.

All his need for her poured into her. The kiss was passion and desperation. The years fell away and she was right back in it with him. All the love and desire she'd ever had and had dammed up inside her heart poured out. She clung to him. He wrapped her up close in his arms and slowed the kiss without losing any of the intensity. In this moment, everything else disappeared. She glowed from the inside out with a warmth and light like the sun, but it was his love and hers.

It was perfect.

It was right.

It was everything she ever wanted and more.

Max ended the kiss, but kept her close and pressed his forehead to hers. His gaze locked with hers, and in his she saw exactly what she used to see. He wanted her. He loved her. And the relief in his eyes matched her own.

"We can't get back the last three years, but we can let it go and be together again."

Someone pounded on the door. "Kenna, something arrived for you," the agent called out. "It could be from your brother."

She did the hardest thing she'd ever done and put her hands on Max's chest and gently pushed away from

him. "I'm sorry. This is not the time. Not when I'm putting your life in danger just by being here."

She sidestepped him and went to the door.

Max came up behind her. "I'm not giving up on us,
Kenna. Not now. Never again."

She really wanted to believe that they could start
again.

But here she was, hiding out on the ranch because
someone wanted her dead and her brother was a wanted
criminal, putting her life at risk.

She didn't know what the agent had for her, or what it
would mean for her future. She didn't know if the man
after her would show up here to try to kill her.

All she knew was that she'd never believe anyone
again who said something bad about Max Wilde. He
was the love of her life and the best man she knew, and
those two things would forever be true.

And she would do anything to keep him safe.

Chapter Sixteen

KENNA OPENED the door, her heart heavy and light at the same time.

Max forgave her. He didn't hate her anymore.

The kiss they shared had felt so much like the past, but also a promise of what they could have in the future.

If she didn't have a killer after her.

She stared up at the agent. Tom—she remembered his name. "What is it?"

He held up a plain brown cardboard box with a shipping label. "It just arrived."

"I'm surprised you didn't open it."

"Opening someone's mail is a federal offense. I don't have a warrant. And I figured since your life is in danger, you'd simply do the honors."

She liked Tom. Direct. To the point.

And since Max was right behind her, she figured he got the message, too. She was not someone he wanted to be involved with right now.

She took the box.

"What if it's a bomb or something?" Max asked.

"There's something hand drawn on the label. I'm guessing it's a message from Kyle to her." Tom pointed at the dog treat sketch. "What's it mean?"

"Ruh-roh."

Max chuckled. "It's a Scooby snack?"

"Apparently my brother has regressed to childhood fun and games. I'm also guessing the reference is to let me know he's in trouble."

"Like you didn't already know that," Tom said.

"I'm also guessing he's trying to solve a mystery. More than likely, how to get out of this."

"And he thinks you can help him do that?" Tom asked.

"I don't know. We'll have to open the box to solve the mystery." She took it from Tom just as his phone went off.

He answered the call and went on guard. "Got it." He hung up. "We have a suspicious vehicle on the main road that's gone past the entrance three times in the last twenty minutes."

Max took her arm and pushed her toward the door to his room across the hall. "I've got her. You go watch downstairs." Max opened the door and went to the bed.

He'd changed things after they broke up. All the rock band posters had been stripped from the white walls that looked like they'd gotten a fresh coat of paint. The room was neat, no dirty clothes strewn everywhere. The bed was perfectly made. He'd switched out the hunter green comforter for a dark gray one and added a large matching dark gray area rug under the bed. The hardwood floor looked clean and shiny. No dust bunnies in here.

The nightstands had two new lamps, one on each side, the left one had a stack of mystery and thriller books on it, too. The one on top, open and facedown.

Max's room reflected the grown-up version of him now.

He pulled a handgun out from under his pillow. "Go," he yelled at Tom. "I'll barricade us in here." Max went to the dresser next to the doorway and waited for Tom to close the door on them, so he could shove it in front of the door.

Tom frowned. "The agent canvassing the property is Rex. The cop on duty is Ward. Anyone else comes up here looking for her, shoot them."

"No one is getting to her," Max promised her with a look that he'd lay down his life for hers.

She didn't want that to happen. "You need to get out of here. Tom can protect me."

"I'm not going anywhere, ever, without you again."

While that made her heart soar, it also terrified her.

Tom slammed the door, taking the option out of her hands.

Max shoved the dresser in place, then turned to her. "Do you really not want to get back together?"

She couldn't lie. "I never said that."

"Then stop pushing me away when we both know this is what you want as much as I do. That kiss . . . it told the story. And that story was all of one word. Yes."

"There is literally someone out there right now who wants to kill me."

"We don't know if this is someone lost or the guy who killed Marcus. The cops are being cautious.

That's a good thing." He came to her and put his hands
on her shoulders. "I know you're scared. I am, too.
Because if something happens to you . . . I don't want
to live in a world where you're not in it. And if I've
learned anything the last three years apart, it's that
my life isn't the same without you with me. So will
you please do me a favor and sit in the corner by the
window and let me protect you, so that I can convince
you that maybe the timing sucks, but I'm not wasting
any more of it alone and wanting you."

"Max." His words touched her so deeply, she didn't
know what to say.

"As much as I'd like to kill your brother right now, I
should probably thank him first. Because if this hadn't
happened, and you weren't here right now, I don't know
if we'd have ever created the opportunity to clear the air
on our own. And I'm a little pissed you knew all this
for the past two years and never came to me. But that's
on me. I didn't make it easy for you. And I admit, I'm
ashamed of the way I used those other women to try to
get over you. It never worked, by the way."

She appreciated his candor, but now wasn't the time.
"Can we talk about this later?"

Max shrugged. "We've got all the time in the world now."

Except if she got killed. "I'm going to open this." She
took the box over to the corner and sat on the floor with
her back to the wall like he'd asked to make Max happy.

He went to the side table by his bed, set the lamp
on the floor, along with some other items, including the
change jar she'd returned to him, then picked up the

heavy wood piece and set it in front of her to block her from anyone coming in through the door. "Just in case." He sat on it, watching the door, pulled the gun from where he'd tucked it at the small of his back, and held it in his lap. "So, what did you get?" He glanced over his shoulder as she pulled the packing paper free.

She stared at the contents and shook her head. "An origami fortune teller and a lockbox."

Max raised a brow. "A what?"

She held up the folded paper on her fingers and moved the four corners showing him the different options of colors, numbers, and when unfolded, the fortunes told. In this case, her brother had written more numbers instead of cute little sayings like, "You'll be rich. You'll be famous." Whatever clever things grade-schoolers thought up for the silly but fun game.

Max grinned. "It's been a long time since I've seen one of those."

"I'm getting tired of the games."

"What is this game? The code to the lockbox?"

She held up the note and read it out loud. "Help Shaggy, Velma, Daphne, and Fred solve the mystery."

"I guess that makes you Scooby."

She was not as amused as Max about all this.

He notched his chin toward the paper game in her hand. "So, how do you play?"

"You pick a color and then a number."

"That's too random," Max pointed out.

"I'm guessing the message is a clue." She pulled out her phone and brought up a picture of the whole Mystery

Machine gang. "Since we have white, purple, green, and orange corners on the game, I'll assume that's based on the color of their clothes."

"Shaggy is named first, so we go with green for his shirt."

She put the fortune teller on her fingers and opened it up. "Green with it open this way has the number 5." She opened the flap to reveal the fortune. "Number 1."

"Velma is next, so orange."

"Orange has a 6 with a 4 as the fortune."

"Easy enough." Max looked like he was enjoying himself. "Now purple for Daphne's dress."

She caught his grin. "You had a thing for her."

His smile widened. "She had pretty hair, like yours." He brushed his hand over her head, avoiding the stitches at the back.

Kenna tried not to blush, but she did at the sweet compliment. She did the origami thing and came up with, "2 is a 'Nope.'"

Max chuckled. "I guess you need to move it the other way to get the right fortune."

She did and came up with, "3 gave us 9."

"And it's Fred for the win."

"The white 8 is a 'Nope' but the 1 gives us 7."

Max glanced at the lockbox. "So the four-digit combo is 1, 4, 9, 7."

She rolled the numbers to the right digits and popped the lock. "We solved the mystery!" She couldn't help getting caught up in the fun of it, because Max was into it with her.

"He could have just written down the lockbox code," Max pointed out. "Or skipped the lockbox altogether and just sent whatever is inside."

"What fun would that be? I'm guessing, wherever he is, he's bored out of his mind if he's doing this."

"He obviously knows you're here. Maybe he feels bad about what's happened to you and just wanted to make you smile again. I've wanted that since the second I saw you in the hospital."

She stared up at him. "I couldn't believe you were actually there."

"Hunt called and told me what happened. He knew I'd want to be there if you needed me."

"It helped and hurt seeing you."

"Same went for me every time I saw you around town. That's why I tried so hard to avoid you."

She popped the lock and stared at the slip of paper inside that read "Call Me" with a math equation written beneath it.

"Seriously?" Max grumbled. "I can't even read that, let alone solve it. Why are there so many letters? They're not even x and y. Isn't that usually how algebra works?"

"Exactly. Too many variables, not enough information to solve. So I'm guessing the equation itself is the answer."

"How so?"

"Like the first code I solved, this is all letters and numbers again. You think it's math, but maybe it's a word or just a number." She studied it again. "It's either 10 digits or 10 letters."

"A phone number," they said in unison.

She studied the nonequation. $3((ax0)) + 6d + i-(6d + 5f)$. She pulled out her phone and dialed as she changed the letters into the numbers they were in the alphabet. "I'm pretty sure it's 307 649 6456."

"Looks right to me. Go for it."

She hit the Call button and waited for Kyle to pick up.

"Put it on Speaker," Max coaxed.

She did, and her brother's voice rang out. "Scooby Dooby Doo."

She rolled her eyes. "Are you fucking kidding me right now? I'm locked in a room with Max, who has a gun by the way, because some whack job wants to kill me because of you!"

"There's no threat, sis. I just paid a guy to drive by a couple times to distract your babysitters so we could talk."

That made her angrier. "They're armed federal agents."

He ignored that. "So, you and Max, huh. Interesting that you ended up with him. I'm thinking Hunt had something to do with that." Amusement filled his voice.

Yeah, her brother and Max's had both helped bring them together. Not that she was counting her chickens on that just yet. "I swear to God, Kyle, this is not fun or funny."

"I know. But I'm happy something good came out of this mess."

"Max and I are . . ."

Max raised a brow, waiting like Kyle for her to finish that statement.

"Complicated," she explained.

Max shook his head. "It doesn't have to be."

"Listen to him, Kenna. You've wanted this a long time. Don't deny yourself a chance to be happy again because of what's going on. This will be over soon, and knowing you'll have him makes me feel a lot better."

Her heart dropped. "What do you mean?"

"Well, that's the trick. I can't give back what I took, and I can't come home because the people who want it will come after me. I've put a target on your back, along with Mom and Dad's."

"I've tried to call them, but I can't get ahold of them."

"The feds have them in custody, like you. Well, they're in a hotel somewhere. You're with the love of your life."

Max brushed his hand over her hair again and held her gaze. The moment seemed to stretch. God, the way he looked at her and made her feel so loved and cherished.

Her brother kept talking, not knowing anything about the interlude she shared with Max. "I think you got the better deal. Still, jail is jail, right?" Despite the light tone he tried to convey, she heard the strain in his voice.

"Maybe together we can figure out a way for you to come in safely and make this right."

"There is no making it right," he snapped. "I didn't take this thing because I could. I took it because it shouldn't exist. Ever."

Alarm bells went off just like the first time she heard about this mysterious thing. "Okay. It's that bad. So destroy it."

"I wish that solved the problem. The thing is, I know everything about it."

"Just because you looked at it, doesn't mean you can make it."

"I'm the only one of the three who created the project, who could finish it and make it work." Therefore, he was the one person who could re-create the whole thing. The person the feds and the company who hired him needed to get what they wanted.

"This is starting to sound like the plot to some doomsday movie where one guy saves the world by destroying the thing no one should have created."

"Is it so crazy?" He was dead serious.

"That it's some kid from some small town in Wyoming? Uh. Yeah."

"I'm not a kid. And this isn't some game or movie. It's as serious as it gets."

"I'm living the consequences of it," she grumbled.

Kyle sighed. She imagined him grabbing a fistful of his hair like he always did when he was frustrated. "I never meant for any of this to happen. You have to believe that. I've struggled with how to end this. It sucks, but there is only one way out of this for me. For all of us."

"Great. I'll go with you to turn yourself in. I'll contact Agent Gunn right now and set up a meeting."

Kyle sighed. "That's not what I mean. If I'm in custody, they'll find me."

"The feds can protect you."

"Maybe. Probably not. Because the only way I see this ending for everyone, is if I'm dead."

A cold shiver went up her spine. "Kyle, you're not thinking of doing anything—"

"No. Not that. Not exactly."

Her heart dropped.

"But that's the reality. I know it. The feds know it, because they don't want me helping anyone else either. So if something happens to me, just know that, even though I'm not with you anymore, I'm glad you're safe." Kyle choked up. "That's all I want now."

"Kyle, let's talk this out and find a way."

"I got myself into this. I have to accept what comes next and handle it myself. And I will, Kenna. I promise you that."

"What does that mean?" Her heart pounded. It sounded so final.

"Take this chance to build the life you always wanted with Max. Marry him. Have babies. Be happy again. It's a nice picture. A great life for you."

She couldn't look at Max. She needed to stay focused on the problem at hand. "Kyle. Please." She didn't know what she was begging him for, but in the back of her mind she knew she'd never see her brother again.

"I'm sorry what I did touched your life the way it did."

Tears filled her eyes. "You didn't mean for it to happen."

"I wanted to prove myself. I thought what I was doing was fun and cutting-edge and cool. I was riding so high on ego, arrogance, and success that I didn't stop to think about anything besides the victory and how it would open doors to bigger and better opportunities. And then it was too late. I'd gone too far. Now I can't turn back."

"There has to be a way."

"I told you, there's only one way. And I'm sorry for that, too, because I'd have really liked to see you marry Max and watch you bring new lives into this world. You're a really great sister. You're going to be an amazing mother."

Max leaned down and took her hand.

She immediately linked her fingers with his. "Stop, Kyle. Don't do this. Don't you say goodbye to me."

"Call Agent Gunn, tell him I finally accepted it has to be this way."

"Have you spoken to him already?" It sounded like they had talked.

"It doesn't matter now. Nothing matters but ending this."

"Kyle," she pleaded, tears streaming down her face.

"I love you."

"I love you," she rushed to say, knowing he was going to hang up.

Sure enough, the line went dead.

Chapter Seventeen

KENNA LEANED her head back against the wall, hit her stitches, winced, and righted herself again. She stared at nothing, replaying the call in her head. Any way she looked at it, the situation felt dire. And inevitable.

She wondered if she'd ever see her brother again.

Max moved the nightstand out of the way, held his hand out to her, and waited patiently for her to take it.

Reaching for him used to be so easy. Now . . . Oh, who was she kidding? He was the only thing she wanted right now. She took his hand, stood, and launched herself into his chest.

He caught her close and wrapped his arms around her. "It's going to be okay."

She appreciated the sentiment even if she didn't really believe it.

Someone pounded on the door. "It's Tom. Open up."

Max hugged her tighter for another few seconds, kissed her on the head, then slowly released her. "I've missed you."

"I missed you, too."

"I'm still waiting out here," Tom called out.

"Let him in." She gathered the box, origami fortune teller, and lockbox and set them on the bed, then shoved the nightstand back into place and replaced the lamp, coin jar, and other items Max left on the floor.

Max had the heavy dresser out of the way of the door in no time.

Tom opened the door, saw the box open on the bed with the items her brother sent inside, and eyed her. "What did you find?"

"A phone number. Probably to a burner phone. I need you to call Agent Gunn. I have a message for him from my brother."

Tom planted his fists on his hips. "You called him without waiting for me?"

She didn't care if she pissed him off. "Yes. Kyle paid the guy in the car to drive by and distract you so I could make the call."

"And you didn't think to call me from downstairs to come up and be a part of hearing what he had to say?"

"Agent Gunn will tell you how frustrating it is to try to track my brother. I wanted to give him a chance to open up to me. And it worked. So, if you'll call Agent Gunn, I'll tell him and you what he said. Max heard the whole call, so he can confirm I'm not lying."

"He's too wrapped up in you to remain impartial."

"That's bullshit," she snapped. "Max doesn't lie."

Max slipped his hand across her shoulders and pulled her close to his side. "Thank you for saying that."

"It's true." And believing that now didn't erase how badly she felt for what happened in their past.

Tom's eyes narrowed. "Is your brother turning himself in?"

"No." Her heart clenched so hard in her chest it ached.

Tom pulled out his phone and made the call. "It's Tom. Kenna opened the package and made a call to her brother during the distraction he created at the ranch." Tom took the phone from his ear and tapped the speaker. "You're on with me, Kenna, and Max."

"Is everything okay?" Agent Gunn asked.

"No. Everything is not fine. I spoke to Kyle. He said goodbye to me."

"I'm sorry to hear that. Anything else?" He sounded hopeful.

"Yes. A message for you. He said the only way for this to end is for him to die. He wants you to know that's the only way. And he's accepted it."

"I see." There seemed to be a volume of words left unspoken with that simple reply.

"That's it? That's all you have to say?"

"He's right."

Those words crushed her heart. "Can't you just arrest him and put him in prison?" That was better than dead.

"With the knowledge he has, he'd never be safe. Anywhere. We've promised him protection. We would do everything in our power to keep him safe and alive. But the person he stole from isn't the only one in this world who wants what he's got and what he knows."

"Kyle wouldn't kill himself."

"But apparently he'll sacrifice himself for the people he loves. For you, Kenna."

"I don't want that."

"Are you sure? The threat against you is still very real, even though we're monitoring it and believe we can keep you safe. For now. But if this goes on much longer, the people involved are going to get even more desperate. You are an easy target. The one thing that can be used to lure Kyle out into the open. Then there's your parents . . ." He left that hanging because she could fill in the blank. These people would use Kyle's family to get what they wanted.

Kenna sagged against Max. "We can't hide the rest of our lives."

"You could, but that means sacrificing the life you have and the people in it."

Meaning she'd have a new name, a new life. And no Max.

Agent Gunn went on. "Kyle understands what you'd have to do because of him. That's why he's come to the conclusion that this needs to end with him."

She sighed out her frustration that she couldn't come up with an alternative. "So what happens now?"

"Kyle will make the next move to end this."

"How?"

"Hopefully he'll bring all the players together. It'll be a volatile and dangerous situation. He knows that going in. In the end, it will be clear, to me, to you, to those after him that it's done, that he's no longer an asset for them to hold and you are not a pawn to force his cooperation."

"So this is going to happen soon."

"That depends on Kyle."

Frustrated, she snapped, "You're not very helpful."

"Neither is your brother. He could have ended this weeks ago, but he didn't, and Marcus died because of it."

She gasped and covered her mouth with her hand.

"I'm sorry, Kenna, that was blunt and—"

"True," she interrupted him. "I'm sorry, too. I want this resolved in a way that Kyle walks away from it clean. But it's too late for that, isn't it?"

"Yes."

"Will you at least let me know when this is all over?"

"The only thing I can say for sure is that you won't have agents watching you anymore once it's done. I hope having them there has given you some peace of mind."

"Not really. Not when you say you can't protect Kyle if he comes in."

"That's different."

"No. It's not."

"Fair enough. Stay safe, Kenna. This will all be over soon."

That didn't comfort her, because it meant she'd never see her brother again. She didn't want to think about how he'd sacrifice himself, how his life would end to save hers.

It didn't seem right.

She wanted to believe there had to be another way.

But even the FBI believed it had to be this way, or

she'd be in danger the rest of her life and Kyle would remain in hiding and on the run. Forever.

She truly wanted to wake up from this nightmare. But reality was more complicated than that. Her brother was in dire straits, her life in turmoil, yet she was happy and hopeful with Max.

How could everything have turned out this way?

How was it going to end?

With her brother lost while she was happy and in love with Max.

It didn't seem fair.

Max took her hand. "Come with me. I'll make you dinner. We'll turn on a movie. You don't have to do or say anything."

She appreciated so much that Max knew she needed to shut off her brain and not think or feel right now, because she was overwhelmed and in a loop of nothing but dire thoughts.

With him, being quiet didn't mean she was shutting him out. They'd never had to fill the silence. Being together had always been the point.

And she didn't want to be alone tonight.

But could they get back what they once had?

She couldn't go through losing him again.

She didn't want to put him through something like that if the man who killed Marcus came for her.

Chapter Eighteen

M<small>AX SAT</small> on the couch next to Kenna. He'd made her dinner and gotten her to eat most of it before he found one of her favorite movies and turned it on, hoping to distract her. If nothing else, it gave them time to be together and settle into this new and tenuous connection that felt just like before and would be again if only she'd stop holding back.

"Why can't protective custody be enough?" She put up her hands and let them fall onto her thighs. "Fuck. My parents, me, we'd have to give up our lives, everyone we know." The outburst came with a lot of anger and annoyance.

Max met her gaze. "You mean all of *us*."

A soft smile touched her lips, then disappeared. "I love that you said 'us.'"

He slipped his hand up the back of her neck underneath her silky hair. "It's you and me now. Always."

"I want that. I really do." She obviously needed to talk about the situation with Kyle, so she could come to terms with it.

Max knew, like Kenna, her parents wouldn't want to give up their lives and remain in protective custody. "Do you think your parents know what's really going on?"

"I doubt the feds have been as open and forthcoming as they've been with me. They wouldn't want my parents to know anything more than Kyle is in dire trouble and they need to cooperate. I can only imagine what they're thinking and feeling right now, not being able to talk to him or me, and know that we're all right. I wouldn't be able to lie to them and say that Kyle will be okay when this is all over. Not now. Intellectually, I understand Kyle's solution is the only thing that solves all of the problems he's facing. But my heart wants to find another way."

She looked at him again. "I feel like I'm counting down the seconds, waiting, and anticipating some sort of notification that Kyle is dead and this is over." She scrubbed her hands over her face, then let them drop. "Has it already happened? Will it be today? Tomorrow? Will I even know?" Her voice cracked and a stream of tears cascaded down her cheeks.

Max pulled her into his arms again. "I'm so sorry, sweetheart. I wish I knew what to do to fix this."

"Me, too."

The only thing he could do was hold her and let her cry herself out, knowing this wasn't the end of her grief, but just the beginning.

He felt for her and understood how hard it was to worry about someone you knew was in grave danger.

He worried about Hunt being on the job with the Willow Fork Police Department. At any time, he could be involved in something dangerous. He could be killed. It was always there in the back of Max's mind.

But Kenna knew it was coming. Soon. The stress and strain on her were tremendous. He wished Kyle hadn't told her his plans, as vague as they were. But maybe knowing, as hard as it seemed, would help Kenna process it. Maybe the final words they'd said to each other would be a comfort once the shock and grief receded and Kenna could think of them and all her good memories of the brother she'd loved and lost.

Max knew about that kind of loss. He missed his mom every day. And in the beginning, right after he'd lost her to cancer, he'd been angry. He'd wanted her to fight harder when all she'd wanted was an end to the pain. But that wasn't what really upset him. He'd simply wanted her back.

Kenna felt that way, too. She wanted her brother to be here with her, to share in her joy and her life.

Kyle was too young to die. She didn't want to live without him. But she would go on, always knowing he wanted to stay and wishing that he'd been here.

Max wanted to find another way for Kyle, but it seemed even the FBI didn't have a guarantee that wouldn't put Kyle at risk or on the run forever.

He appreciated that Kyle saw how hard it would be to ask his whole family to go into hiding with him. They'd all be separated. They'd lose the life and family they'd always known.

What was the point? Except they'd all be alive. But not together.

Kyle saw the bigger picture. He made the mess and wanted to take responsibility and fix it the only way he could without involving his family. It took guts and selflessness to make the sacrifice to do it.

Max appreciated that Kyle didn't want to put Kenna through that.

Selfishly, Max didn't want to leave his family either. They were finally back to being close after their mom's death had caused a lot of friction in the family, mostly because Chase had taken their mom away to die on her terms. It had been her request. One that wasn't easy for Chase to fulfill. They blamed him.

But they'd worked their way through the grief and anger and came back together as a family. They started new traditions, like Pancake Tuesday, and celebrated Chase's marriage and their birthdays and holidays as a family again.

They'd found love and expanded their family, too.

Shelby and Eliza. They were Wildes now. Cyn and Lana would be very soon.

And then, he hoped he and Kenna really put the pieces back together and someday soon she would be his wife. A Wilde. And they'd add a few new little Wildes, too. The ranch would be alive with little ones running wild, like he and his brothers used to do.

Kenna's tears dried up and she took a calming breath. He soothed her with soft strokes of his hand up and down her back, his other arm banded around her waist, holding her close. He hoped the comfort he offered did its job and made her feel better.

She looked up at him. "Thank you."

"For what? I barely did anything. Holding you is pure pleasure."

"Exactly. I'm all twisted up inside, but you unravel me. I find the calm in the storm when I'm with you."

He didn't have the words to tell her what that meant to him. "You do the same for me." He held Kenna through the rest of the movie, until the credits rolled.

"Max."

"Yeah?"

"I'm scared," she whispered. "I don't want to lose him."

He didn't know what to say. He hoped saying the words to her helped in some way. "He didn't mean for this to happen. He loves you. Hold on to that, because it doesn't go away, even if he does."

"I know. Still . . ."

He held her tighter and kissed the top of her head as she sat close with her head on his shoulder. He hated this for her. She'd always looked out for her brother. They'd always been close. If he could stop this from happening, he would. Because he wanted her to be happy. He wanted Kyle to live and be a part of their lives. He wanted Kenna to have everything she wanted and more.

But sometimes life dealt you a shit hand and there was nothing you could do but hope you could discard a few bad cards and pull a few goods ones in your favor.

Kenna had a lot of bad happening right now.

He touched his finger beneath her chin. She looked up at him. He kissed her softly. "I'm here for you. No matter what. Always."

"Maybe when this is all over, I'll believe that."

"You can believe it now. Everything we talked about in the past, we can have now, just like Kyle told you he wants for you on the call."

"Everything feels like it's happening, but also like it's unreal. Like me sitting here with you. Us talking like this. You not avoiding me, but saying all the things I've wanted to hear you say for so long."

"It is real, Kenna. Not all of it will end well, but you and me, that can be the good that comes from the bad."

"I want that. I really do." But she didn't sound convinced it would.

He wished he could stop what was happening with her brother. He'd spare her that loss and heartache if he could. But he hoped their being together and moving forward with their life would bring her the happiness they both deserved after they'd waited so long.

He wanted them to finally have the dream they shared and make everything official with a ring, a wedding, and a lifetime of shared memories.

It felt so close, yet still too far away.

Max refused to let it slip away again. He'd do everything possible to make it a reality, and make Kenna happy again.

Chapter Nineteen

Max sat at the table by the windows as the sun came up, drinking his coffee. He'd barely slept again last night and felt the fatigue in every muscle and bone in his body. He had a long day ahead of him. But just like last night, all he thought about was Kenna and the revelations about what happened so long ago.

How could he have not seen what Hillary did to him and Kenna?

His dad walked into the kitchen. "You and Kenna looked cozy on the couch last night." He'd gone up early to his room to watch TV, giving Max and Kenna some time alone together.

Well, as alone as they could get with an FBI agent in the house, checking all the doors and windows, making sure they were safe.

"She needed a quiet night of vegging on the sofa." He'd been more than willing to sit with her pressed up against his side, letting them both get used to being close again.

They'd gone up to bed just after ten. She'd been

yawning for an hour, but stuck it out to the end of the movie. He hoped because she wanted to spend more time snuggled up with him. He wanted to take her to his bed and hold her all night, but she'd gone to her door and offered a shy good-night, like she was unsure what he wanted or what she wanted to do.

"So I guess you two stopped fighting and avoiding each other."

"We started talking." It was a good place to start. But he wanted more.

His dad joined him at the table and sat in a chair facing the window. "That's good."

"I think so. There's a lot going on in her life right now. I feel like she's holding back. I thought that once we unraveled the past, everything would go back to the way it used to be."

"Nothing is that easy." His dad sipped his coffee. "What happened?"

"She got to say what she wanted to say for a long time, and I forgave her for believing a lie I didn't know someone else kept telling her even after we broke up." He sank deeper into his chair. "Who goes out of their way to taunt someone, to hurt them, to take something away from them, for no good reason?"

His dad's eyes narrowed with concern. "Did Kenna do that to you?"

"No. Someone did it to her. Someone I thought was our friend."

"Sounds like this someone wanted to hurt Kenna to make themselves feel superior in some way."

"Her name is Hillary." Just saying her name made him angry. "She wanted me, so she caused some trouble. Kenna and I ended, and I spent the last three years wishing I had what we shared back and thinking we couldn't get it back because Kenna thought I cheated on her when I didn't."

His dad blew out a breath. "So that's what happened. Damn, son. I had no idea."

"She blames herself for the whole thing, because she believed our so-called friend."

"This Hillary must have made it damn convincing."

That was the piece he'd missed. "She did. And still a part of me wishes Kenna had come to me and we'd have talked about it again until we figured it out."

"She never tried?"

He thought about the times he'd seen her around town, how she'd looked like she wanted to say something and he'd turned away.

"She did. And I didn't want to hear anything she had to say if she thought I'd do something like that to her. By the time she found out the truth, on the anniversary of our breakup no less, from Hillary herself, I'd cemented in her mind that I'd moved on."

"She knew you were seeing other women."

He put his elbows on the table and his face in his hands. "Yes. Damnit."

"Talk to her. Tell her they didn't mean anything. She'll understand."

"They meant she couldn't talk to me. They meant I didn't want her. That's what she thinks."

"Then prove her wrong. Show her that who you were with them is not who you are with her."

Actually, that was good advice.

His dad nudged him some more. "Show her that you don't blame her for what happened any more than she mistakenly blamed you. If you want her back, do something about it."

Max thought about the way she tried to keep things casual last night. While he'd reached out to her, putting his arm around her to offer comfort, to let her know he was there, and because he'd needed to touch her in some way, she'd somehow still remained restrained. "I think she's afraid to try again."

"If she missed you the way you've missed her, maybe she's afraid that if you try and fail and she loses you again, she just can't take it. Someone wants her dead. Her brother basically told her he's going to die to stop what's happening. I can see how that would mess with her head."

"She definitely isn't herself."

"After all the bad that's happened to her, I'm not surprised."

Kenna had a soft heart. Sweet. Kind. Loving. She couldn't stand that she'd hurt him. She didn't want to be responsible for anything happening to him again.

"She doesn't realize that living without her is killing me."

"Maybe you should tell her that."

"I will. But first I'm going to show her that she's still and will always be the only woman I want."

His dad put his hand on Max's shoulder and squeezed. "It'll be nice to see you happy again."

"I know I've been difficult the last few years."

"You were hurting. I knew that. I just didn't know how to help. Your mother was always better with the advice and knowing what you boys needed."

"You said all the things I needed to hear this morning."

"You already knew what you wanted to do."

"Yeah, but after what happened between me and Kenna, I guess I was scared to go after it, because what if she can't get past the way I spent our time apart using other women to try to get over her. That doesn't exactly speak well of me. I've been acting like a jerk. I probably owe a lot of women an apology."

"They knew what they were getting into with you. Kenna knows exactly what she can have with you, too. Don't complicate things. Simplify them. Tell her what you want and how you feel. Let the rest fall into place."

Max stood and smacked his dad on the shoulder. "Thanks, Dad. Next time I have a problem, I'll talk about it. Maybe if I'd said something to you or my brothers sooner, I'd have figured this out and Kenna and I wouldn't have missed so much time together."

"Time is precious. Don't waste it."

Max grinned. "You're just full of gems this morning."

"I've spent my fair share of time thinking about the mistakes I've made and how I'd like to change them. Problem is, I'm talking to your mom's ghost. You've got Kenna right here."

Max nodded and stepped away from the table to get another cup of coffee.

"It'd be nice to have a woman in the house again."

Max turned back to his dad. "Don't get ahead of yourself."

"I'm just saying, you're a grown man. You don't have to meet her down at the barn like you used to. She's welcome to stay as long as she likes, even once this business with her brother is over."

Max shook his head, not surprised his old man knew about his late-night rendezvous with Kenna back in the day. He'd never been able to keep his hands off her. "After seeing the way she reacted when we went to her place the other day, I don't think she wants to go back to her apartment ever again."

"Also," his dad said, to get his attention again. "You should start thinking about this house as yours. Your brothers are settled with their families now. Looks like you're stuck with me, but that doesn't mean you can't make this place the home you want to have with *your* family."

Max had actually thought a lot about fixing up the house on his evening rides. It gave him something to think about other than the lonely state of his life. But now he thought about the house in a whole new way. "Really? You wouldn't mind some updates?"

"No. Your mom always wanted to fix up this and that and I always put her off. Maybe if I spent more time doing things to make her happy, things could have been different for us at the end. Stubborn will only get you resentment from others."

"Dad, come on, Mom was happy with you. She loved being here."

"She loved her family, our life, but she wasn't always happy, because I was so set in my ways. So if you want to make some changes, I'm open to it. But if you're going to live here with Kenna, too, then you should probably ask her what she wants."

Max did something he hadn't done in a long time. He went to his dad and gave him a big bear hug, then stood back and smiled at him. "Who says you can't teach an old dog new tricks?"

"Just don't put this old dog out in the barn. This is still my home."

"Never, Dad. Who else is going to watch the grandbabies when I take Kenna out on date night?"

His dad grinned. "Now you're thinking right, son."

"Just remembering what my future is meant to be."

"Her. For you, it was always her."

No doubt about it. And this time he was going to get it right. And no one was going to get in their way or tear them apart again.

Chapter Twenty

KENNA NEEDED something to do. Staying in the house was safer. It made it easier for the feds to guard her. But she was going stir-crazy.

She thought about going down to the barn to feed the calf or just pet the horses, but then she might run into Max. She really didn't know what to say to him. Yes, they'd cleared the air; they'd even shared that amazing kiss. She wanted to believe they could just go back to the way things used to be, but she didn't want to push.

Deep down, she feared, despite what he'd said, he'd change his mind and decide they were better off to leave the past behind and move on to the future as friends.

She'd loved sitting on the couch with him last night, his big body so close to hers, his arm around her. It comforted her. And she'd needed that so much after talking to her brother. But as much as she liked it and wanted him to touch her more, he'd simply held her there, leaving her wholly aware of him and also wanting more.

It confused her.

And she didn't seem to be the only one. Max seemed

to want to say something last night, but then he didn't. When they parted ways, each of them going into their own rooms, it felt like the kiss they'd shared never happened.

Someone knocked on her bedroom door. "Kenna, it's me. Are you busy?"

She opened the door and found Max with his hands on the frame, leaning forward, at eye level with her. "No. Do you have something you want me to do? Please say yes."

He chuckled. "Bored?"

"Too much time to think, not enough to distract me."

"Then I'm your guy."

Oh, how she wished that was true. "What can I help you with?"

He stood tall and held out his hand. "Come with me."

She put her hand in his. He squeezed hers and drew her across the hall and into his room. She caught a brief glimpse of Mike and the knowing grin on his face before she was in Max's room and he closed the door.

She stared at the comforter laid out on the floor at the side of his bed and the picnic he'd set up.

"Mike said it's too risky to take you on a ride and a picnic on the property, so this is the best I could do under the circumstances."

Her heart melted at the sweet gesture. "You didn't have to do this at all. We could just eat in the kitchen like we always do."

"I want to spend time with you alone."

She raised a brow. "You do?"

"Yes."

Butterflies took flight in her stomach. "Why?"

"So we can clear the air."

Was he going to tell her now that it was nice they'd stopped avoiding each other but they could only be friends?

He held his hand out. "Sit. We'll eat. We'll talk. And hopefully by the end of lunch, we'll be on the same page again."

Her stomach dropped. She cocked a brow. "I haven't really slept in a few days, so I'm sorry, but I'm not following."

Max led her to the blanket, sat with his back to the bed, and tugged her hand to get her to do the same next to him. "Let's eat. You'll feel better."

She doubted it. She'd gone numb. Everything felt out of sorts and up in the air and strange. Nothing seemed to have an answer. Not Marcus's murder. Not her brother talking about dying to end all this. Not Max setting up a picnic in his room in the middle of the day.

"Aren't you supposed to be at work?"

"Hunt covered for me so I could be here with you."

"Isn't he getting married soon? Shouldn't he be helping Cyn with that?"

"It's in a couple of days. Nearly everything is in place. It's fine. And just an FYI, Cyn can't wait to meet you. Shelby, too."

She'd like to meet them, too, but it felt strange that Max sounded so casual about it, like it would happen soon. And because she was with him.

Is that what he meant?

Or did she have this completely wrong?

She needed answers.

"Why are we doing this?" she asked again, because it did not compute. And she liked things to add up.

Max pulled the large cutting board with their plates closer. He handed her a plate with a thick roast beef and cheddar sandwich on crusty bread stuffed with shredded lettuce and red onions. Her favorite. And so were the sour cream and cheddar potato chips, along with the cola. He set a small bowl of fruit salad in front of her, too.

She stared at all of it, touched he remembered so many details about her. "Did you make all this?"

"Yes. Well, I bought the fruit salad at the store. I made the sandwiches. I just wanted to do something with you, and for you, because you've been so upset since you got here."

"I'm fine." She didn't want to worry him, even though she had over the last few days.

"No, you're not. And that's okay, because something really bad happened. And after seeing you yesterday, how desperate you were to tell me everything that happened between us and because of Hillary, and how long you've carried that all alone . . ." Max raked his fingers through his hair. "I feel like the biggest asshole for what I did to you."

She didn't feel that way at all. "You didn't do anything to me."

"I tried to use a bunch of women to erase you from my life." That truth came with a dead serious look in his eyes as he held her gaze and let her see that he meant it and hated that he'd done it.

"Max . . ." She didn't know what to say.

"Please, eat. You didn't sleep again last night. You don't look well."

How could she sleep when her brain kept spinning thoughts of her brother and Max. So much to think about and consider and twist and unravel, but she could never really land on a clear solution or definite answer.

She didn't feel like eating. Breathing seemed to be a chore. But the pleading look in Max's blue eyes got her to take a bite of the sandwich. She rolled her eyes and groaned in appreciation. "It's really good," she mumbled, her mouth full.

Max's tense shoulders relaxed, and he settled back against the bed again.

Since he'd been so candid, she swallowed the bite and spoke her truth. "I was jealous as hell and miserable every time I heard about or saw you with someone else. And I hated myself, because I knew I made you do it."

Max's eyes went wide, then they filled with regret. "I'm sorry, Kenna. If I could take it back . . ."

"We can't take anything back, though, can we? It happened. It just is now. But we can remember the good. Like how you used to bring me lunch, just like this, when we were together." She took another bite of the sandwich, trying to focus on the fact that at one time they had been everything good for each other.

Max shifted toward her and leaned in close. "I want

you back. I want *us* again. If you can forgive me for . . . what I did."

She held his gaze and put her hand over his on his thigh. "Max, there is nothing to forgive. You and I broke up. You were free to see whoever you wanted to see. I knew that. I didn't like it, but I didn't blame you for moving on, even though I couldn't."

Max turned his hand and took hers in his. "That's just it. I never got over you. I couldn't stop thinking about you. I wanted you back, but I didn't know how we could get there if you, the one person who knew me best, thought I was the kind of person who'd cheat and lie and break your heart that way."

"You were angry, and I was caught up in a lie that made me think you were angry you got caught. I second-guessed myself and what I thought I knew was true about you. I didn't trust myself to know the truth when everything looked one way, but I knew you to be something else."

"Hillary planted the idea in your head, and then she reinforced it with her taunts. I'm surprised she ever came clean about the lie."

"I'm sure, like me, after a year it was clear to Hillary and everyone else you had no intention of ever speaking to me again."

Max's head fell back and he stared up at the ceiling. "Fuck."

She really couldn't blame him for the other women.

He was a good, kind, decent, and smokin' hot man. Women were always flirting with him and trying to catch his eye. She'd bet he didn't even have to try to get them into bed.

But when he'd been with her, she'd been his everything. And that's what made it so hard to believe she didn't see the lie. "I should have believed you. I'm sorry I didn't. Then you wouldn't feel the way you do right now. That's my fault. Not yours."

Max brought her hand up to his lips and softly kissed the back of it. The warm brush of his lips, the electricity that shot through her, made the longing deep inside her explode. He pressed his cheek to her hand, turned, and stared at her. "We both did things we regret. We both let the other go. So if we both still want to be together, why don't we fix this?" Max implored her with the earnest look in his eyes. "Please, Kenna, give us another chance. My heart has always been yours. Claim it again and come back to me."

Her heart overflowed with all the love she still had for him. Tears spilled down her cheeks. "I've wished for this to happen for so long."

"Then say yes, and it's you and me again. And this time we'll get it right."

She pulled Max close, pressed her forehead to his, looked him in the eye, and said, "Yes."

The kiss they shared was soft and sweet and filled with promise.

"This feels like the first time I kissed you. I was so excited and nervous and desperate for more."

She grinned and brushed her nose against his. "That was a long time ago."

"We were at school. At lunch."

She glanced at the spread he'd laid out for her. "You made me lunch that day." She remembered it so well now.

"I wanted you to know I wanted to be more than friends. Boyfriends do things for their girlfriends, like bring them lunch."

"You surprised me with it and when I said, 'Thank you,' you said, 'You're welcome,' and you kissed me."

"Right in the middle of the cafeteria, where everyone would see. They'd all know you were mine."

She put her hand on his face. "They already knew that because we did practically everything together already."

He leaned into her touch. "I'd like it to be that way again."

She sucked in a breath and held it for a second before she smiled. "Is this real?"

"One hundred percent." To prove it to her, he turned, slipped his hand over her shoulders and pulled her a little closer.

Her hands came up to rest on his chest.

The contact had them both going still.

"I've wanted this for so long," she admitted. "I thought you'd hate me forever."

"I could never hate you." He brushed the back of his knuckles across her cheek with his free hand. "You're not the only one who's happy about us clearing the air and getting back together. It's time we put all that aside and focus on us."

"I really want to do that."

"Me, too, which is why I think it's important you know that several months ago, I got sick and tired of myself and what I was doing with my life. So I stopped. I stopped going to the bar just to drink too much and be with someone who I didn't want to know anything about other than she wanted to be with me that night and that's all. I stopped being an asshole user and started asking myself what I really wanted."

He brushed his thumb across her cheek and stared into her eyes. "Chase was back in town and started working on the ranch again. The guys who work on the ranch are my buddies, but working with my brother . . . We found that connection again. I'd missed it. I'd missed him. I watched him struggle with his issues. No matter how hard things got, one thing was always clear to him. He loved Shelby. He had a single purpose. Love her and make them a family. Same thing happened to Hunt. He and Cyn . . . No two people were meant for each other the way those two are meant to be together."

"And you wanted that for yourself."

He cupped her face. "I had that and I lost it." He released her and took her hands in his. "I wanted to figure out how you could know me better than anyone and then call me a liar to my face. I needed to know what I'd done to make that happen before I tried to find someone new that I could have something close to what we shared, what I saw my brothers find with their partners. I didn't want to get it wrong again. I didn't want to think I had something, only to lose it again."

"That's the risk we take in all relationships."

"But ours shouldn't have fallen apart like that. You should have believed me."

Her gaze fell to his chest. "I didn't want to believe you cheated."

"I know. You were made to believe it. And not by me. Knowing what I know now, I wish I had tried harder to change your mind. Everything would be different now if I had at least tried."

"Max, you can't keep blaming yourself for what you did when we broke up. You can't blame yourself for not doing something in the moment when at the time you felt another way. I wish I'd been brave enough to come to you when I found out the truth."

"I made that impossible because of the way I treated you after the breakup. I acted like you didn't exist, like what we had never mattered, when it mattered more than anything to me."

Tears filled her eyes, but didn't spill over. "I knew you were hurt and angry."

"So were you. And that I can't forgive. Hillary orchestrated the whole thing because she wanted me."

She squeezed his hands. "The only thing that makes it any better is that she didn't get you."

Not that he'd been very picky after he lost Kenna about the women in his life. Any warm and willing body would do back then.

But something about the way Hillary tried to hold on to him those first few weeks after he lost Kenna didn't sit right. She never really understood how much it hurt him to lose Kenna. Even though he'd been upset and angry, he still didn't want to hear Hillary, or anyone else, bad-mouth the woman he'd still loved, even if they weren't together anymore.

"I know the rumor around town is that I started going to Blackrock Falls and my cousins' Dark Horse Dive Bar because I ran out of women in Willow Fork. The real reason is that I wanted to be around family and friends who wanted the best for me."

"You wanted to be with the people who know you best, who'd understand what you'd been doing wasn't you."

"They understood I was hurting and trying to heal in the wrong way and only making things worse. Being with them, just spending time by myself and thinking about the past and what I wanted for my future—it made things clear."

"You want a wife and family and someone by your side for the rest of your life, not just for a night."

"I want you. Not that it's a big revelation or secret. But I need you to hear it and believe it. I thought I'd have to find you in someone else, as impossible as that seems. So I stopped doing what I was doing and told myself to wait for it to happen, that someday soon a woman would walk into my life and I'd feel again. And then you were here with me and it was like an eruption. Everything I felt for you, it all came back, so vivid and intense and not enough because you tried to shut me out, and I tried to ignore it because I thought you thought the worst of me. But it ate me up inside because something terrible happened and you couldn't come to me because of how

I'd acted. You didn't believe that I'd listen to what you had to say about what happened to us. You didn't think I'd care about your situation or the past, when no matter what, I want there to always be the truth between us and for you to be safe and happy, even if it's not with me."

She leaned in and brushed her lips to his. "I have always been, I will always be yours until my dying day."

"Fuck, Kenna." He wrapped her in his arms, bent to her ear, and whispered his worst fear. "If something happened to you . . . I just couldn't take it. Losing you was hard enough. Without you in this world . . . I don't even want to think about it. I can't. Nope."

She put her hand on his chest. "You know what I'm going to do?"

"Stop doubting this is real and happening."

"Yes. Exactly that." She needed to stop trying to find roadblocks and saying things that made it seem like being with him wasn't exactly what she wanted. "Thank you for letting me stay here with you."

He slipped his hand beneath her long hair and against her neck. "I'm happy you're here." He kissed her on the forehead.

She melted at the sweet gesture because it was just another sign that Max was all in, their past mistakes behind them, and in this moment, all he felt for her was affection and understanding.

He'd let go of the animosity toward her and refocused it on Hillary, who'd caused all the problems between them.

And maybe that was the thing Kenna needed to let go of, her part in the breakdown of her relationship with Max.

She hugged him hard and held tight. "I don't want to lose you, or this chance we have to start over."

"Not over. To be together like we used to be. Like we are right now."

She leaned back and stared at him. "That's all I want. And a job."

He cocked a brow. "You have a job."

"That I'm not allowed to go to right now. So put me to work."

"You're serious?"

"Seriously bored and tired of my own company. And I desperately need a distraction from . . . everything."

"What do you want to do? Muck out stalls, vaccinate the cows—"

She smacked his shoulder with the back of her hand. "No. I'm good at math, not manual labor. I could do the paperwork. Maybe clean the house. Do laundry. Something like that."

"Paint the kitchen?"

"Sure." It seemed an odd request, but why not?

"Dad and I have been talking about making some improvements."

"You buy the paint and tape and stuff, I'll do the job." What else did she have to do but sit around waiting for a killer to come after her?

Dark, Kenna. Think happy thoughts.

Kissing Max again would make her very happy.

"Eat your lunch." Max picked up his sandwich.

She did the same. They ate in silence for a little while.

"This could work," he blurted out. "If you want to

catch me up on the paperwork in the office, that'd help a lot. I'll show you how to do it. You could count stock and reorder what we need. I have a list that shows what we should have on hand and how much. And yeah, you pick the paint color, and we'll redo the kitchen."

"You and your father should pick the color."

Max shook his head. "Nope. We'd probably end up with something equally as bad as what's in there now. I'm sure you can come up with something that's light and bright and makes it feel more inviting in there."

"If you're sure."

"I am. If it was your kitchen, what would you do?"

She hesitated because she didn't want to step on anyone's toes or insult Max and his family for the choices they made back in the day that did not age well. "I'd cover up the dark green with a very pale blue. It would be so much brighter in there."

"More cheerful, too," Max added. "The dark color makes it feel closed-in. My mom chose the color. Dad grumbled about it, but he put it up on the walls anyway because she wanted it. Once it was up, his grumbling continued. I don't think Mom liked it once it was on the walls either, but she didn't ask him to change it."

"She didn't want him to be right."

Max chuckled. "She didn't want to hear him grumbling more about having to do it again."

"Well, since I can't go with you to the store to pick it out, you'll have to either choose yourself or bring me some samples and I'll choose."

Max bumped his shoulder to hers. "I like the idea of us doing it together."

She stuffed the last chip on her plate in her mouth. "How did I eat all of that without realizing it?"

"I kept you distracted and thinking of other things."

"Thank you. It's nice to set everything aside for a little while."

"I'm glad I could help."

This all felt so sweet and perfect and like old times again.

"So, you said something about paperwork."

"You're the only person I know who'd get excited about spreadsheets."

She perked up. "You didn't tell me there'd be spreadsheets." She gathered her plate and his and her bottles of soda and stood up. "Let's go."

Max chuckled and stood but stayed right in front of her, smiling. "There she is."

She cocked her head and stared at him. "What?"

"The old Kenna. The one I think about all the time. Happy. Smiling. Joking." He cupped her cheek in one hand. "God, I missed you." His lips brushed hers in a soft sweep. "Come on."

She appreciated that he kept things light, even as he drew her into the relationship they were rebuilding.

This was a start of the next chapter for them. It felt familiar, yet exciting at the same time.

She'd come here reluctantly because she needed a safe place to hide. Now she didn't want to leave.

THAT NIGHT, AFTER she did the paperwork in the office and filed all of it, she made dinner to thank Max and his dad for letting her stay there. Then she and Max watched another movie on TV. After he saw her to her room and said good-night with only a whispered, "Sweet dreams," she found the beautiful bouquet of pink roses on her nightstand with a note from him.

> A new beginning.
>
> Love, Max

She thought she'd run out of tears over the last few days, but no. The sweet gesture and hopeful words brought them back. Her battered heart eased a little more. And she fell a little more in love with Max, if that was even possible.

She didn't know how he'd even gotten them for her. Then she remembered seeing Hunt's car pull out of the drive moments before she walked up to the house to start dinner. Max had probably asked his brother to pick them up in town and deliver them on his way home.

So sweet.

The flowers weren't the only surprise. He'd left the T-shirts she returned to him when they were at her place stacked neatly on the end of her bed.

And another note.

> These always looked better on you.
>
> Love, Max

She swiped another happy tear from her cheek, changed out of her clothes from today and slipped on one of Max's shirts. She settled into bed for the first time with happy thoughts in her head and a light heart. Finally she slept.

Chapter Twenty-One

M AX STARTED his day the way he wanted to start every one of them from now until he died. Kissing Kenna. He'd waited outside Kenna's room after she showered and dressed. The second she opened the door and saw him, she smiled and thanked him for the flowers and T-shirts, wearing one of his old Guns N' Roses tees.

He'd said, "You're welcome. Good morning," cupped her beautiful face, and kissed her until she melted into him. He loved that he could still make her smile the way she did when he ended the kiss, only because they had an audience. One of the feds was always close by. But the smile she gave Max, it was open and warm and bright and filled with joy to see him.

They'd walked downstairs together, and he'd left her in the kitchen with his dad and headed down to the barn to meet up with Chase and the crew.

He'd been busy with one thing after the next and hadn't seen her at all during the day. It amazed him that just knowing she was here, that they were trying again, made him so damn happy. It felt like his life was finally getting back on track.

And all roads led to her.

He found her in the barn brushing down one of the horses. Ray, her fed for the day, stood just outside the stall door.

He nodded to the guy, then slid the gate open and stepped in to be closer to her. "Hey, sweetheart, did you have a good day?"

Stormy shook his big head up and down.

Kenna laughed. "Yes. I finished all the filing, cleaned the office, because it looked like you hadn't swept the floor, wiped down the desk and cabinets, or tossed the trash in a while."

He shrugged, not the least bit cowed by her scolding that was more teasing than real. "I've been busy."

"Well, now you have a clean office." She looked proud of herself. "I also organized the supply cupboard and re-stocked the barn medical cabinet since the order came in. I'll leave the feed delivery to you and your men."

Most likely because it required a lot of heavy lifting. "Got it. And thank you."

"Sure."

"Any word on your brother?"

She stopped brushing the horse. "Nothing. Has Hunt said anything to you?"

"Nope. But he'll be here shortly to deliver the pizza I ordered for you, Dad, and your shadows."

She cocked one brow and glanced at him. "You did?"

"I thought you might like your favorite."

"Thank you. That's sweet. But it sounds like you're not eating with us."

"Can't tonight. I have a date."

That brow went even higher this time and she gave him a disgruntled look. "What? I thought . . ." She clamped her mouth shut.

He took a step closer, then another, until he was inches from her, her head tilted back to look up at him. "You thought I wanted you, and only you."

Her gaze fell to the floor. "I guess I misunderstood."

He touched his finger to her chin, made her look at him, and shook his head. "Not even a little bit. You're all I want."

That eyebrow shot up again.

"But I have a standing date with my niece Eliza that I can't cancel, or Chase and Shelby will kill me, because it's date night for them." He grinned, then kissed her softly.

"That's sweet." She relaxed.

"Eliza is amazing. She's going to love you. You have a lot in common."

Surprise shone in her eyes. "Oh, yeah, like what?"

"She loves numbers and flowers. She can count to thirty."

Kenna grinned with approval. "Impressive."

"I'm also her favorite person, just like I'm yours." His belly fluttered with hope that she still felt that way.

"A girl who knows a good thing when she sees it."

He let out his breath and let go of his reservations that maybe something had changed between them that he couldn't fix. Her feelings.

"I'm not one for sharing you, but if it's with your niece, I'll make an exception."

"Kenna."

"Yeah?"

He cupped her cheek. "I missed you so damn much."

She leaned into his palm. "I missed you, too. More than I can say. More than I ever want to feel again."

That made his day. "Same, sweetheart. It was killing me, living without you."

His dad was right about him telling her that. The amazed and stunned look on her face transformed into a look of pure appreciation and love.

"Max."

He couldn't help himself, he kissed her, holding her close, his tongue sweeping along hers, until the taste and feel of her was all he knew. "If I didn't have Eliza tonight, I'd be here with you."

"I understand. I'll just keep distracting myself by babying the horses until dinner."

"I'd really like to direct your attention my way, but I need to run up to the house and shower before I go." He regretted not being able to turn that kiss into much, much, more.

"Now there's an image."

He smirked. "You remember me naked, right?"

"Vaguely," she teased him. "I'll need a refresher."

God, he couldn't wait. "Anytime. Except right now, unfortunately."

She went quiet for a moment. "I wish all of this was over and that my brother was safe."

"Me, too. I'd take you with me tonight . . ."

She shook her head. "It's too dangerous. Bad enough I've put you and your dad and everyone here in jeopardy, I wouldn't want anything to happen to your little niece."

He cupped her face and brushed his thumbs across her soft cheeks. "I wish I could take you out on a real date."

"I'd like that. But I also like just being here with you."

He felt the same way. In fact, he didn't want her to leave. And that meant he needed to step up his game and make it so she wanted to stay.

KENNA WAS IN her room, in bed, reading a book when a text message dinged on her phone. She opened the text and smiled at the silly picture of Max and Eliza, who both had a bunch of colorful barrettes and hair ties all over their heads. They were making silly faces.

MAX: Eliza thinks Hunt's fiancé Cyn is better at doing hair than me
MAX: I think Eliza killed it on my hair
MAX: What do you think?
KENNA: You're gorgeous!!!
KENNA: And sweet
KENNA: What a lucky girl!

It pinched her heart just a little to see him having so much fun with Eliza, because it could be their little girl he was playing with. If they'd stayed together, they'd have been married by now and probably had their own bundle of joy. He'd be such a good dad, because he was a good man.

As if he read her mind, he texted . . .

> MAX: I want it all
> MAX: You
> MAX: The life we planned
> MAX: Everything! Now!

Her heart soared. She couldn't wait to settle into the reality of it all.

> KENNA: Me too!
> KENNA: Most of all I want you
> MAX: Done
> MAX: I'm yours

Kenna put her arm across her chest, her hand on her shoulder and stared at the picture Max sent. She saved it as her lock screen so she could see it all the time because it made her smile and think about him and how he'd do anything for the ones he loved, even if it made him look ridiculous. Or in this case, ridiculously cute.

> MAX: Time to put the little angel to bed
> MAX: Sweet dreams to you too
> KENNA: Like every night, I'll be dreaming about you.

She wanted him to know she'd never stopped loving him and thinking about him and wishing things hadn't ended the way they did.

She had regrets. So many of them. But being with him would never be one of them.

And now they had a second chance to get it right, to make it forever, to love each other the way they did.

MAX: I never stopped missing you

MAX: ♥

KENNA: ♥ x ∞

MAX: Math nerd

She smiled, thinking back to all the times he teased her with those words, and also how he loved that about her. He thought she was smart. More than anything else, that always made her feel like he saw and liked everything about her, because they were different in that way. She loved academics and teaching. She'd rather read a book, than go out most nights. Max loved being outdoors and working with the animals and on the land. Where she was quiet, Max loved a crowd and being with friends. She loved that he'd stay in with her for dinner and a movie, but also that he'd coax her to go out and be surrounded by people, dance, laugh, and have fun.

It didn't matter where they went or what they did. If she was with him, it was always a good time.

Tonight, even though he wasn't here, he still managed to connect with her. It was yet another way they were repairing the crack in their once solid foundation, building back the trust and intimacy they once shared.

She thought of him coming home later tonight and him standing outside her door, right across from his.

Would he knock and say good-night?

Would they share another heart-pounding kiss?

Would he be as desperate to see her as she was to see him?

How long before a kiss turned into the two of them tangled in the sheets?

Would this thing happening between them finally turn into a life together filled with happy memories?

The only way it wouldn't is if they got in their own way again.

Or a killer took her out.

With whatever Kyle had planned looming, that threat felt even more real and impending.

Chapter Twenty-Two

KYLE REGRETTED that he only had one way out of this mess. He'd sent the invitation to the director and gotten the response he expected. Now he needed to make the call.

"Agent Gunn."

He wondered if the agent would even bother trying to trace him this time. "The meet is set. Tomorrow night. The director and his man will be there. They think Kenna will be there, too. Just like we planned." On a previous call they'd had to confirm Kyle had his promise from the government that he got to disappear without handing over the program or creating it again for them.

Not that he trusted the government.

He'd probably end up in some black site.

He hoped to make sure that never happened. All he needed was a moment during the takedown to get free and do what really needed to be done.

Agent Gunn cleared his throat. "We'll have our teams in place. Kenna and your parents will be protected.

Once it's done, we'll get you out of there and handle
the notification with your family. They'll be safe. You'll
have a new life."

It sounded so good.

But it was an illusion, that life Agent Gunn offered.
Oh, the agent believed it. He had it all set up.

Kyle just wasn't that trusting and sure he'd get what
was promised, especially after all that had happened
and how desperate people were for what he'd created.

"I'll see you tomorrow night."

"Kyle, are you all right?"

"Just tying up loose ends before I go." He hung up,
picked up his Sharpie and continued working on his
final goodbye.

Chapter Twenty-Three

MAX REGRETTED spending another night away from Kenna. He loved that they'd settled into a kind of routine. He kissed her good morning, they had breakfast together, she worked in the barn or did chores in the house, they met for lunch and dinner, then settled on the couch to watch TV, and he kissed her good-night. It all felt good and right and moving forward.

But with each passing day and no news about Kyle, the threat of someone out there who wanted Kenna dead straining all their nerves, he wanted to remain close to her.

But tonight was about being with his brothers and dad and celebrating Hunt's upcoming wedding to Cyn. He was so happy about them becoming a family.

That thought led to what he wanted for his future. Kenna. For him, it had always been her. And what he wouldn't give to put his ring on her finger and for them to start a family.

He'd given up on that ever happening. But now it seemed not only possible but inevitable again.

They'd waited so long.

Now each day felt like a day closer to that dream becoming a reality.

He just wished this thing with her brother, the murderer, and the feds was over. More than that, he wished for a positive outcome for Kyle.

It seemed unlikely, given the circumstances and Kyle's own conclusion on what was going to happen. The weight of which hung heavy on Kenna's shoulders and darkened her usually bright and cheerful personality. She tried to hide it, but he saw the shadows in her eyes and the quiet way she retreated into herself.

Max walked out of his room, ready to meet his dad downstairs for Hunt's bachelor party. They were picking up Hunt and Chase and meeting Hunt's other friends at Cooper's. They'd reserved the back room for dinner, drinks, poker, and pool.

They'd have fun.

But he'd be thinking about Kenna, worried that something might happen to her while he was gone.

She wasn't in her room, so he headed downstairs.

Mike was on his phone in the dining room by the front windows.

"Everything okay?"

Mike nodded. "Everything's quiet. She's in the kitchen."

He found her at the counter reheating some pizza from the other night in the toaster oven. "Hey, beautiful."

She finally turned to him and seemed to come up short.

He looked down at himself to be sure he didn't have something on his shirt, then looked at her. "What?"

She eyed him up and down. "Wow. You look really good."

He loved that she thought so, even if all he'd done was shower and change into black jeans, a hunter-green, long-sleeve Henley, and his boots after he finished work. Nothing special. But, man, the way she looked at him. All he wanted to do was get his hands on her.

He walked right up to her and stared into her pretty hazel eyes. "You keep looking at me like that and the only place I'm going tonight is upstairs to bed with you." He'd been trying to give her time. It had been really hard not to knock on her door after he babysat Eliza the other night. Last night, the kiss they shared had all the fireworks to spark a long night of making love. He'd reluctantly let her go and abated his raging desire for her with his hand in the shower before going to bed alone.

They hadn't taken that next step yet. He didn't want to push or go too fast. They'd both needed time to reconcile the past and appreciate what they had now. A second chance.

But God, he wanted her. Desperately.

She grinned. "I think your brother would miss you being there for his big night."

"I wish you could meet Cyn and Shelby and be with them tonight for her bachelorette party. They really wanted you to be there."

Kenna gave him a sad look. "I would have loved to

be included. I can't wait to meet them, too. But . . ." She shrugged one shoulder and left it at that.

He closed the distance and put his hands on her hips, knowing, though she tried to hide it, that she was upset about having to stay here under guard and not being able to simply live her life and be with other people. He knew she specifically worried about him and his dad being in the house with her.

But he wondered if there was something more going on. "What I said about us just now . . . If you want to take things slow, I'm fine with that. Under the circumstances, it's not like I can date you and take you out, but we can definitely take advantage of being here together by continuing to talk and just being together."

She placed her hand on his chest. "It's not that. I want us to be like we used to be. No questions about what the other is thinking or feeling. No hesitation, because we know what we both want."

"It's been a while since we were that close and entrenched in each other's lives. We're getting there again. I feel it. I hope you do, too."

"The longer we're together, the more natural and right it feels. But this thing that's happening in my life, it complicates things. You're worried about me. I'm afraid something could happen to you because of me."

"It won't be because of you. And it's a risk I'm willing to take because I've lived without you for too long."

She stepped into him, her legs pressed tight to his.

He pulled her closer, because he needed to touch her and craved the connection.

"I want you desperately." Her honest words undid him.

Whatever reservations she harbored about him possibly getting hurt, that maybe they'd grown into different people during their separation and should take some time to get to know each other again—all of it—everything vanished from her hazel eyes and turned to need.

"I just want to let everything go." She kissed him softly. "All I want is to be with you."

He cupped her face and looked her in the eyes. "It's been too long and I want you so bad." He pressed his lips to hers and the same fire that used to burn in both of them exploded like a wildfire and consumed all the words he wanted to say, all the thoughts in his head, until all he knew was her pressed to him and the glorious taste of her.

She clung to him, her nails biting into his back, her mouth as greedy as his, their hearts pressed together and finally beating as one again.

He slipped his hands beneath the soft T-shirt she was wearing and found her warm, smooth skin. She immediately arched and rubbed her belly against his thick erection. Her groan was music to his ears. He wanted to hear a whole damn symphony from her tonight.

And then a thought broke through his lust-hazed mind and he broke the kiss and pushed her away with his hands still gripped on her hips because he really wanted to pull her back. "I nearly forgot."

"I can't remember anything right now but that kiss."

He chuckled. "I'm right there with you, but any second

now my dad is going to come downstairs, ready to go to Hunt's bachelor party."

Her eyes dipped to below his belt, so to speak, then came back up with a question in them. Like, *Are you crazy? You want to leave now?*

He swore under his breath and cursed Hunt for getting married, even though he didn't really mean it. "I'm sorry. My timing sucks."

She inhaled a calming breath and brushed her hand over his heart. "It's okay. That's been building for a while now."

"I don't know how much longer I can wait," he confessed.

She rubbed both hands up and down his chest. "I'll be here when you get home."

He slipped his hand up under her hair and pulled her in for a soft, lingering kiss. "I hope this good luck holds through tonight and I take the others for all their worth at poker before I come home to you."

Her earnest gaze met his. "I look forward to seeing you later tonight."

Now that was an invitation he'd never turn down.

Chapter Twenty-Four

MAX HAD a great night at Hunt's bachelor party. He ate a great meal, toasted his brother and wished him a long and happy life with his soon-to-be wife, left the poker table a hundred and twenty bucks richer, and arrived home mostly sober and thinking about the woman who was never off his mind.

"It was a good night," his dad said, cutting the engine and opening his door.

"Hunt's happy." Max exited his side and met his dad at the front of the truck.

"I haven't seen you this happy in a long time. I hope when this business is over, I see just as much of her then as I do now."

Max grinned as they approached the front door, where Tom was standing guard. "You like having her here."

"I like seeing you with her."

"Thanks, Dad."

"Good-night." His dad slapped him on the back and headed inside.

Max stopped to talk to Tom in the foyer. "Everything okay?"

"All good. She's in her room. Light's still on." Tom remained professional, but Max caught the gleam of amusement in his eyes.

Everyone on the ranch knew they'd gotten back together.

Max preferred it that way and hoped Kenna was waiting up for him. "Any news on Kyle or Marcus's murderer?"

"I can't be specific but I think this will be over soon."

"Good to hear." He hated that it meant more heartache for Kenna. But the sooner Kenna had her freedom back, the better. She missed teaching, her kids, and seeing her friends and family. She hadn't been able to speak to her parents since this happened.

Max headed up the stairs, anticipation riding him hard, his heart speeding up the closer he got to Kenna's door. He tapped lightly, just in case she'd fallen asleep.

Nope. There she was, opening the door wearing just a T-shirt with a chicken on it that said, My Hen Can Count Her Own Eggs. She's a Mathemachicken.

He chuckled. "Cute shirt."

"If you like this, you should see what's under it."

Max dropped his voice, so Tom didn't overhear him. "Are you ready to show me?"

She stepped right up to him, went up on tiptoe, and kissed him softly. "So ready."

He brushed a kiss to her lips. "You sure?"

"That I want you and can't wait to be with you again? Yeah. I'm sure."

Max took her hand, slapped the light switch off in her room, then led her across the hall and into his. He wanted her in his arms and in his bed tonight. Every night.

He closed the door, shrugged off his jacket, tossed it on the dresser, and turned to her. With the drapes open, the moonlit night gave them enough light to see each other.

But all he wanted to do was feel. His hands on her body. His lips on her skin. His body moving against and inside hers.

"Max."

"Yeah," he answered, slipping his hands onto her hips.

"You don't have to go slow."

"What if I want to?" He said the words against her neck, kissing a trail up to her face and taking her mouth in a deep kiss, his tongue sliding slowly along hers.

She showed him what she wanted and gripped the hem of his shirt and brought it up to his chest and right off over his head as he raised his arms and broke the kiss long enough for her to get his head free. He kissed her again. She tossed the shirt and put her hands on his pecs. "You feel so good. I want more." She slid her hands around his sides and up his back.

He fell to his knees in front of her and trailed his fingertips up her legs and under the shirt. His fingers found nothing but soft skin. His hands slid over her ass as he pulled her close and kissed her belly over the shirt, then looked up at her. "God, I've missed you."

She brushed her fingers through his hair. "I'm so tired of wanting you and not being with you."

His hand moved to the inside of her thigh and up

until his finger slid along the seam of her damp folds. She wanted him just as desperately as he wanted her. "Neither of us has to feel like that anymore." He slid his finger deep inside her. "I want you just as much as I can feel you want me." He pulled that finger out slowly, then pushed it back in like he had all night to drive her crazy with need.

He put his other hand on her belly and nudged her back toward the end of the bed as he crawled forward with her. She went because her legs were about to give out and did when he thrust two fingers inside her. Her rump hit the mattress. Max pulled his fingers free and had her legs draped over his shoulders and his face between her thighs before she even settled back on the bed. He licked her all the way up to her clit and she nearly shattered right then and there, but he stopped for a moment and slid both his hands up her body to her breasts and squeezed them to distract her and make the pleasure last.

She moaned and rolled her pelvis right up to his mouth. He licked her with his flat tongue and she shivered with need. "Oh God, Max."

His heart soared at how responsive she was to all he was doing. "I remember everything you like." He kissed the inside of her thigh. "I've dreamed about doing this and everything else to you night after night."

She slid her hands down his arms as he squeezed her tight nipples between his fingers and his tongue and mouth moved over her sensitive flesh, turning that shiver into a ripple until it erupted and quaked through her whole body and echoed through his.

Max gave her a moment to come back to herself and laid a trail of soft, open-mouthed kisses from her knee up to her hip, on one leg and then the other. He rose at the end of the bed and kissed his way up her belly. "I love this shirt, sweetheart, but it has to go because I want these next." He kissed the swell of one breast and then the other as he slipped one hand beneath her back and pulled her up to sitting. With the shirt already rucked up at her waist, it took him no time or skill at all to pull it right up and over her head.

He took a second to admire her bare breasts and groaned with approval before he dove in, taking one nipple into his mouth and sucking at her as she fell back onto the bed again, sliding her fingers into his hair and holding him to her. He licked and laved and growled a little, then moved to her other breast. She tried to pull him on top of her, but he held himself up on his hands, bent over her.

"Max. Please."

He kissed his way back down to her belly, then stood at the end of the bed. He pulled his wallet out of his back pocket, opened it, and tossed a condom on the bed next to her.

"I appreciate that, and I also have my IUD," she reminded him.

Good to know they had backup, even though a baby would make him overjoyed.

But tonight was about them and reconnecting on a deeper, baser level.

He pulled off his boots, undid his black jeans, and

shucked them and his boxer briefs, along with his socks, like they were on fire, then crawled up the bed and over her, hungry for her in a way that put an appreciative gleam in her eyes.

This hadn't changed. And it comforted him to see the unabashed desire in her eyes. For him. The way he wanted her.

He settled his body over hers. They both sighed at the contact. He dove in for a kiss. She grabbed ahold of him and held him close, not one millimeter separating them.

They moved together, against each other, kissing and touching until they were desperate for more.

Max found the condom by her ribs and tore it open. He sat back, sheathed himself, then leaned over her again, rubbing the round head against her wet entrance, sinking in, watching as he pushed in deeper. The sensation of him once again filling her sent a wave of euphoria through him. Finally, they were together again.

And then Max moved, pulling out and filling her up again. She rocked away and into him, taking him deep. She gripped his hips and pulled him into her again and again. They lost themselves in the sensation and joy of being back together like this, until they were both panting and writhing and desperate for the release that overtook them and had them clinging to each other as the shock waves rocked them both.

Max collapsed on top of her, crushing her into the bed. She held on tight, apparently not minding his weight, his love, everything surrounding them and filling them up.

Their breaths sawed in and out at each other's necks.

She held Max close, her arms around his back, her fingers brushing against his overheated skin.

The quiet held them in its intimate embrace, giving them time to settle into each other once again as a couple. The afterglow of what they'd shared washing away any doubts or hesitations they may have held on to until this moment when everything real about what they felt for each other solidified into absolute knowing.

They were good together.

They belonged together.

Max rose up on his forearms, stared down at her, and brushed a lock of hair from her cheek. "This is where I belong. Right here. With you."

"You read my mind."

"Stay."

"I'm right where I want to be."

He left her only long enough to deal with the condom cleanup, then sank into bed beside her. She immediately rolled into his side and settled her head on his shoulder. He lay content with her in his arms, skin to skin, hoping this was the first night of the rest of his life that she was right here beside him.

He'd spend the rest of his life doing everything possible to make her happy.

Seconds before he fell asleep, happier than he'd been since the last time they were together like this, footsteps pounded up the stairs and his bedroom door flew open.

Chapter Twenty-Five

~━⊷━~

MAX SAT up in bed, gun in hand pointed at the man standing in the open door.

"Don't shoot," Tom called out.

Max sighed and dropped his hand, his heart pounding with fear.

Kenna held the sheet to her chest. "What's happening?"

Tom tossed a bunch of clothes at her. "Get dressed. Now. We have to go. Now, now, now." Tom moved just enough away from the door that he couldn't see them getting dressed as he covered the stairs, gun drawn.

Max grabbed his clothes off the floor.

Kenna threw her legs over her side of the bed and started pulling things on. "I need shoes."

Tom rushed into the room across the hall and came back and tossed her a pair of sneakers.

Max was already dressed and pulling on his boots.

"Ready?" Tom's voice rang out, sharp with impatience.

"Ready," Kenna called out, taking Max's hand and heading to the door with him.

They headed down the stairs to the front door, where Tom stopped and caught Max's gaze. "You and your dad get into your truck and take off. Do not follow us. I need to get her as far from here as possible."

"I'm going with her." Max refused to leave her or let them just take her without telling him where they were going or when she'd be back.

Tom shook his head. "I don't have time to argue. We've got an undercover agent who says she's in immediate danger. She is my priority. You're a distraction."

Kenna turned to Max. "He's right. You need to get your dad and get as far away from me as possible so you aren't a target."

He slid his fingers into her hair and gripped it softly. "I'm not leaving you."

She kissed him quick. "I need you to. I couldn't live with myself if something happened to you or your dad. Please, Max. Do this for me."

He couldn't do it. "No. Where you go, I go, and that includes into whatever danger is coming our way." He saw his dad coming down the stairs and tossed him his keys. "Take the truck. Go to Hunt's place. I'm going with Kenna."

Tom took Kenna by the arm. "Let's move. We're running out of time to get out of here safely."

Max stayed on Kenna's tail as Tom opened the door, and the other agent, who covered the outside, flanked Kenna. Tom took the lead. They got to the fed's sedan, and he and Kenna got in back.

Max watched to be sure his father got in the truck

and headed across the property, the opposite way of them, toward Hunt's place.

The agent started the car and floored it, kicking up dirt and gravel as they headed for the main entrance to the ranch. Max kept his gun in hand and on his knee, ready to take out anyone who tried to get to Kenna.

Tom turned in the front passenger seat and held up his phone. "This is the guy who killed Marcus. Get a good look at him. He is the only person you shoot at if he's threatening you. Do not draw on or shoot anyone else, even if they are with this guy."

Max remembered they had an undercover agent on the killer. "Got it."

Tom eyed him intensely. "You better."

Just before they reached the ranch gate, he noticed it was open. Before he could warn the agents something wasn't right, a truck barreled out of the trees and rammed the side of the vehicle hard enough to push them off the edge of the narrow road and partially into a ditch.

Stunned by the surprise of it and the impact of the hit slamming him into the side of the car as the momentum threw Kenna's body into his, Max tried to keep his wits and focus on the truck.

The sedan's doors on the driver's side of the vehicle were caved in. Blood marred the windows front and back where Kenna and the agent up front hit their heads.

The driver sat with his head hanging forward, the seat belt holding him up, but he wasn't conscious.

Kenna moaned beside him and grabbed her head, too.

He shifted and cupped her face, turning it so he could see the gash on her left temple, the blood pouring out of it, down the side of her face and into her ear.

Tom opened the front passenger door, climbed out, then pulled open Max's door. "Get out! Run!"

Two men climbed out of the truck. The driver took a shot at Tom, who ducked for cover.

Max undid his seat belt and Kenna's, then pulled her out of the car with him. He put his hand on her head and shoved her down low by the rear tire. "We need to run for the trees."

Kenna looked stunned and out of it.

He'd need to push her along to keep her safe.

"I'll cover you. Go!" Tom fired at the driver of the truck, who returned fire.

Max helped Kenna stand in a crouch, then they ran the few yards to the trees, more shots ringing out. She suddenly screamed, stumbled, and fell, hitting her chest hard on the dry leaves and grass. Something dark and wet started to spread just to the right of the middle of her back. "No!" he screamed, realizing she'd been shot.

A terrifying rage came over him, and he turned and fired at the driver, who fired at Tom again.

One of Max's bullets hit the guy high in the chest more toward his shoulder, but another bullet hit him in the side of the head, taking him down.

Max caught a glimpse of the guy on the other side of the truck, right before he climbed in through the passenger side, slid behind the wheel, backed the truck up, and sped away without Tom firing a single shot to stop him.

Max dropped beside Kenna and pressed both hands to her back to try to stop the blood. "We need an ambulance!"

"They're on the way," Tom shouted back.

Max glanced over at him. He was checking on the agent in the front seat, who appeared to still be passed out.

Kenna groaned in pain. "Max." She barely got his name out.

"I'm here. You're okay. You're going to be okay. Help is coming."

Oddly enough, sirens rose in the distance, which didn't make sense, given how far out of town they were. He hoped it was an ambulance and not just more police.

Tom knelt beside him and handed him gauze pads from a medic kit. "We had emergency vehicles headed this way just in case. Use these to apply pressure."

Max took one after another, pushing on Kenna's wound, trying to get the blood to stop, but it just seemed to keep seeping out of her. He hated to leave her lying in the dirt and leaves, but he didn't want to move her and make things worse.

"Kenna, baby, you stay with me."

A car skidded to a stop on the nearby road. A minute later, Hunt dropped to his knees beside Max. "Ambulance is here. How bad?"

"I don't fucking know. She's shot. That's how bad."

Hunt's hand gripped his shoulder. "She'll be okay."

Max looked at Hunt, whose image blurred with the tears filling Max's eyes. "We . . . Everything was perfect tonight. How did this happen?"

"I got a text earlier from Agent Gunn. Kyle set the meet for tonight with all the players."

"And?"

"Things went south all the way around. Kyle is dead."

Max didn't have time or the patience to even ask about it, but his heart sank for Kenna. She'd be devastated to lose her brother. Max considered Kyle a friend, even if they hadn't seen each other in years.

The only thing he could do for Kyle now was take care of his beloved sister.

The paramedics nudged their way in to get to Kenna.

Hunt moved out of the way to give them room.

Max released the pressure on Kenna's wound to allow the paramedic to replace the soggy, bloody gauze with a clean one. Max took Kenna's hand and squeezed it.

She squeezed him back.

"Hey, sweetheart. There you are. I'm right here. They're going to move you now. To the ambulance. We're going to the hospital. The doctors will take care of you. I won't leave you. I promise."

Her hand went limp again. He could only hope she'd heard him.

"Sir, you need to let us take care of her now."

Max hated to let her go, but he stood and moved back so the two men could do their jobs and save Kenna's life. Because things were looking really dire at the moment.

One of the guys checked out the gash on her temple, winced, then pressed a thick gauze pad to the wound and taped it in place.

The two worked together to roll Kenna to her side, despite her protesting groans of agony.

"I've got an exit wound." They kept Kenna on her side and pressed a new pad to the front of her.

Didn't matter what they did to her at this point, she'd passed out completely and didn't move or respond. Not even when they put a backboard beside her and gently laid her out on it. They put a neck brace on her just in case, strapped her down, lifted her onto the gurney, and put her in the back of the ambulance, where they could get her warm and work on her. An IV line went in, her vitals taken again. Monitors were put on her chest and finger.

Both guys frowned. Apparently they didn't like anything they saw.

He kept vigil right outside the ambulance, his hand on Kenna's foot, a thick blanket tucked around her legs.

He didn't even feel the cold.

This wasn't how the night was supposed to end.

They were supposed to spend the night in each other's arms. He was supposed to wake up with her beside him in the morning. He'd have made love to her again as the sun rose. He'd have told her with his body and the words just how much he loved her.

"What's the word?" Hunt asked, stepping up close to Max. "Is she stable?"

"No," the blond one said bluntly. "We need to go. Now."

Hunt put his hand on Max's shoulder. "This is my brother, Max. Kenna's boyfriend. He stays with her."

The paramedics both nodded, the dark-haired one jumping out the back, so he could take the driver's seat.

Max jumped into the ambulance. "Can you get in touch with her parents?"

"Agent Gunn is on it." Hunt closed the door.

They were off in a flash, the paramedic beside him monitoring Kenna and relaying information to the hospital. They'd be ready when Kenna arrived.

It felt like an interminably long drive, even though they raced down the road with lights and sirens, speeding through every red light once they hit town. By the time they pulled up in front of the emergency room doors, the medical staff was waiting right inside for Kenna.

He barely got out, "I love you," and a squeeze of her hand before they took her away and he found himself in the waiting room not knowing if he was going home with Kenna, or alone.

Did she hear him?

Did she know how much he loved her?

Would he get a chance to tell her again?

Chapter Twenty-Six

MAX PACED the waiting room. He sat. He stood. He paced some more. Time didn't matter, except that it was taking too damn long for the doctor to come and tell him what was happening. He'd tried to call the Bakers, but only got voice mail. He'd had to leave them a message that their daughter was critical and in the hospital. He couldn't imagine what they were going through, losing a son. Now they had to wait and see if their daughter lived.

"Max." Shelby ran into the room and threw her arms around him.

He gave her a quick hug, happy to see her and Chase. Surprisingly Cyn walked in looking a little worse for wear, since she'd also had her bachelorette party tonight.

Max couldn't believe they'd gone from celebrating the upcoming nuptials to this. But he appreciated his family so much for being here.

Cyn came to him on not so steady legs. "Hunt will be here soon. I'm still a little drunk, but I couldn't not come. Is she okay?"

"I don't know. The bullet went right through her—apparently that's better than it still being inside her."

Chase was the last to hug him. He held his brother a little longer than he had his sisters-in-law. "Tell us what happened."

He stepped back from Chase and the others and tried to make sense of things. "It happened so fast. Kenna and I had just fallen asleep when one of the guards rushed in and said we had to go. I sent Dad to Hunt's and stayed with Kenna and the two feds. We were just about at the ranch gate. I noticed it was open, but by the time I realized what that meant, a truck T-boned our car."

He didn't have any idea how badly the agent driving had been hurt. He'd gotten a glimpse of Tom talking to Hunt before Max left with Kenna in the ambulance.

"Damn," Chase said by way of taking all that in.

"The guy driving the truck started shooting. The fed covered Kenna and me so we could run for the trees, but Kenna got hit."

"I hope they got the bastard," Cyn said.

"Me and, oddly enough, the guy who came with the killer in the truck shot him. He's dead."

"Then he's no longer a threat." Chase nodded.

"Well, Kenna is tough. Now that you two can finally be together again, she'll fight to get back to you." Shelby's positivity bolstered him.

"The head wound from the car accident didn't look that bad, but for all I know she's got another concussion to go with the gunshot wound. I just wish they'd tell me what's happening."

"Max," Mrs. Baker called out from the waiting room door.

He rushed to her because she didn't look too steady either, but from grief and fear more than anything. "I'm so sorry to call you down here like this."

"Is she . . ." Mrs. Baker's already bloodshot eyes filled with tears.

"They stabilized her and took her into surgery, but it's serious."

"What happened?"

He took her by the arm, led her to a chair, and helped her sit. "Where is Mr. Baker?"

"He's . . . He's with Agent Gunn. With Kyle's b-body."

Max wanted to ask what happened to Kyle, but didn't want to put Mrs. Baker through telling him the story. So he stuck with what happened to Kenna for now and gave her a bare-bones outline of what happened.

Mrs. Baker paled. "It feels like it was all so coordinated to kill my children."

"That asshole got what he deserved for hurting Kenna," Cyn snarled, apparently the alcohol helping to keep her anger amped up.

Max made a quick introduction of everyone to Mrs. Baker, who already knew his brother Chase, but hadn't met Shelby and Cyn.

"It's been so hard to be separated from her. When we heard she was staying with you . . . Well, it eased our minds to know she was with someone she loved." Mrs. Baker waved her hand and frowned. "I know you two broke up a long time ago, but she never stopped caring about you."

"I feel the same way," he admitted, filling her in on how they'd reconciled their past, how Hillary had been the instrument of their relationship's destruction, and how they'd gotten back together.

Mrs. Baker teared up again. "I am so happy for you both."

Max's heart soared at that news. He didn't want her parents to still harbor resentments about him, or be apprehensive about them getting back together.

She clasped her hands tight. "I just want Kenna to be happy and have the life she wants. This can't be the end."

"It's not." Max couldn't even entertain the notion that Kenna wouldn't make it.

The doctor stepped into the room. "I'm Dr. Conway." He looked to Mrs. Baker. "Are you Kenna's mom?"

Mrs. Baker shot up to her feet, anxious as Max for information. "Yes. How is she?"

The doctor gave them all a sweeping glance. "May I speak about her medical information in front of everyone?"

Mrs. Baker nodded. "Just tell us. Is she going to be okay?"

Of course, the doctor didn't answer that directly. "Kenna is stable and in recovery at the moment."

That only frustrated and scared Max more. He wanted details.

"She has a slight concussion and stitches on the side

of her head. We removed the ones in the back of her head. As for the gunshot wound, there was no major internal damage, though she lost a lot of blood. She has two cracked ribs. It could have been a lot worse. I expect her to make a full recovery, though the ribs will take the longest to heal."

Mrs. Baker let out a heavy sigh. "Thank God."

Max felt his world right itself.

The doctor tried to look reassuring. "You can see her as soon as she's out of recovery and in a room. Because of the blood loss, we gave her a transfusion, but she'll be fatigued for days to come because of it."

"Is she awake?" Max desperately wanted a yes.

"She is, though she's tired. With the head injury, we'll be monitoring her closely as well as giving her antibiotics to stave off any sort of infection. Give us another twenty minutes or so to get her settled, then I can let you see her. Just one or two of you at a time for now. She needs to rest."

Max understood the doctor wanted to give Kenna the best care possible, but that didn't make it any easier for him to wait. "Doc, she's my . . . everything. How long before I can take her home?"

"I'd like to keep her here for a couple of days. What's your name?"

"Max Wilde."

"I'll tell her when I go in to see her that you're here and waiting for her."

It wasn't the visit he wanted, but he'd take it. "Thank you."

"You're welcome. Now I better get back and check on her."

Chase left to get them all coffee right after the doctor stepped out. Shelby and Cyn talked about the bachelorette party with Mrs. Baker, trying to distract her. Mr. Baker showed up half an hour after Chase passed out coffee and Max left his untouched on a small table.

Hunt joined them, assuring them the threat against Kenna was over and so was her protective detail. Cyn passed out with her head on Hunt's shoulder.

Max couldn't sit down. He couldn't be still. He paced and waited and thought of nothing but Kenna, their lives together, what happened between them over the years, what he wanted for their future. Every thought about her.

When he finally walked into her room an hour later and took her hand, he looked into her happy, teary eyes and knew he didn't want to spend another day without her knowing how much he cared.

"Max." She said his name with utter relief and a need so desperate he leaned in close to comfort her.

"Yeah, sweetheart."

"I love you. I've always loved you. I've only ever loved you."

He leaned down and pressed his forehead to hers and looked deep into her eyes. "I know, sweetheart. I feel the same way." He kissed her softly. Reverently. Longingly. Then he gave her the words back. "I love you, too. Forever."

She held his gaze. "That's all I want. You and me for the rest of our lives."

"Done." He sealed that promise with another of those slow, deep kisses that went on and on, until they were lost in each other and nothing else mattered but them in this moment.

Chapter Twenty-Seven

KENNA SPENT most of yesterday in a fog—lethargic, sore, and heartbroken to hear that her brother died, though she still didn't know the details. Every time she opened her eyes, there was Max, right beside her, holding her hand, reassuring her everything was going to be all right. She was safe now.

This time when she opened her eyes, she found Max and Chase seated beside her, their heads together as they whisper-argued.

Chase frowned. "The wedding is in two hours. We need to go. You have to be there."

"I'm not leaving her. Hunt will understand."

Chase fell back in his seat. "We all need to be there. It's family. We're brothers. We all stand up for each other."

"*She* needs me here."

"She can hear you." Kenna's groggy voice drew their attention.

Max jumped up and came to her, resting his hip on the bed and taking her hand, careful of the IV line in the back of it. "You're awake."

She smiled at him, tears coming to her eyes because he was a sight to behold and she was so grateful he was here and so was she.

His eyes filled with concern. "Are you in pain?"

It hurt to breathe because of her sore ribs, but it didn't matter. She was alive. "A little, but mostly I'm just happy to see you."

"You say that every time you wake up."

"I mean it."

Max leaned down and kissed her softly. "How are you really feeling?"

"Guilty," she admitted. "Chase is right. You need to be at your brother's wedding."

Chase stood and put his hand on her shoulder. "You look better today. I'll give you two a little time alone." He squeezed her shoulder, then patted Max on the back and left.

Max sighed. "Sweetheart, I'm not leaving you here alone."

"I'm sure my mom and dad will be back soon." They hadn't left her for more than an hour or two at a time.

"They're busy for the next few hours." Max looked away from her.

"What aren't you telling me? Are they okay?"

He still didn't look at her. He didn't respond.

"Max?" Her mind was finally clear enough after a day and a half in the hospital to put more than one thought together. "This is about Kyle."

"Now is not the time to talk about him. You need to stay calm and keep your blood pressure down."

"You need to tell me what happened."

Max planted a hand next to her head and leaned over her. "Please calm down." He eyed the heart monitor, then looked at her again. "The nurse is going to bust in here any moment and make me leave."

"Good. Then you can attend Hunt's wedding."

Max hung his head and sighed. He looked so tired with the scruff darkening his jaw and the circles under his bloodshot eyes.

He was still wearing the same clothes he wore to Hunt's bachelor party and pulled on as they were rushed from the house.

"Have you slept at all?"

"I'll sleep when you're home with me in our bed." Tears gathered in his eyes. He'd had a rough couple of days.

"Max." She reached up and softly brushed her fingertips over his cheek. "I love that you want to protect me and be with me and love me."

"I love you more than anything."

"I know that. I feel it. And I'm going to be fine."

"You had major surgery. You still have a concussion to go with the nine new stitches in your head," he growled out.

"All of which is keeping me here. But none of it means I won't be here when you get back after the wedding. Please, Max, go. Come back with pictures and a smile on your face because you're happy for your brother and you have a new sister-in-law and niece and it's all official and beautiful. Bring me a piece of wedding cake and I'll feel like I got to experience a small part of it. I wish I could be there with you. But I'll feel even worse if you don't go."

Max hung his head again.

She brushed her fingers through his hair, simply needing to touch and soothe him. She'd give him everything she had, even if she wasn't at her best right now, to make him feel better.

She knew the moment he decided.

He pressed his forehead to hers and looked into her eyes. "I won't be gone long."

"Stay for the ceremony, the dinner, the cake, the toasts, all of it."

"It's brunch." He looked at the closed blinds. "It's coming up on nine in the morning. The wedding is at eleven."

She frowned. Maybe her head was still foggy from the pain meds. "Don't miss a moment. Take it in. Be happy with them. You don't have to worry about me. I'll be right here, safe, watched over by the nurses. You've got to be tired of watching me sleep by now."

"Never." He kissed her on the nose. "I'll come back as soon as I can."

"Or you could get some sleep and see me in the morning."

He shook his head all through that. "I'll be back tonight. With cake," he added.

"Stubborn."

"Look who's talking." Max settled beside her again and stared down at her hand in his. "We'll talk about your brother tomorrow. Your parents are making all the arrangements for him today. Your aunt and uncle came into town this morning to help them out."

A wave of sadness and anxiety washed over her, though she couldn't reason out why the second overwhelmed her. Probably just the trauma of what happened the other night.

She'd never been more scared in her life.

Chase poked his head into the room. "It's getting late," he warned Max.

"He's ready to go," she answered, hoping Max didn't back out now because she couldn't hide the aftershock of fear that came over her.

The nurse called out from behind Chase, "Excuse me, but Kenna is due for another brain scan."

"See," she said brightly, "I have places to go, people to see, too."

Max grumbled under his breath. "Maybe I should stay until the results come in."

Kenna shook her head once, but stopped immediately because it sent the room spinning.

She tried not to show it, but Max put his hand to the side of her face. "Be still. Be quiet. Be calm."

"I will. While you're gone. And the nurse will call you and tell you my results." She glanced at the nurse without moving her head.

The nurse nodded confirmation. "I'll call as soon as they come in, though the doctor expects to see improvement, just like the last scan."

"See. All is well."

Max didn't look convinced, but leaned down and kissed her softly. "I love you."

"I love you."

"I'll be back soon."

"I'll be a little bit better then. And a little better tomorrow. And so on. But I'll always be happiest when I'm with you."

Max kissed her, his lips soft and sweet against hers. The nurse sighed.

Chase waited patiently.

Max stood and gently set her hand on her thigh. He gave her one last longing-filled look, then left with Chase.

The nurse checked the monitors and took her blood pressure. "You're really lucky. He loves you a lot. He's barely been out of this room or away from your side. All the nurses have been sighing over him and how he takes care of you. Oh, the way he washed your face last night and brushed your hair. He makes sure you're warm enough and holds your hand. It's so sweet."

"Max is the best man I know."

"I'm sorry to hear about your brother. My condolences to you and your family. So much tragedy in one night. Your parents . . . They've been through a lot."

"Thank you." She appreciated the sympathy. She tried not to let her grief overwhelm her, but the tears came in a flood.

Soon she'd find out how Kyle died and what else she didn't know that everyone was keeping from her.

Chapter Twenty-Eight

Max was in his tux and just about to escort his cousin Lyric down the aisle to stand up as Cyn's bridesmaid. He was about to stand beside his brother Chase as co-best man when his phone finally rang. He didn't even hesitate to answer it, needing to hear good news about Kenna, or he'd race back to the hospital to be with her.

The nurse confirmed what the doctor had anticipated. The swelling in her brain had decreased. No signs of infection after surgery. She was slowly getting better. Which meant he'd get to bring her home soon.

He couldn't wait.

Even though she still faced some tough times ahead in her recovery and burying her brother.

He tried to do as she asked throughout the late morning and stay focused on Hunt and Cyn as they exchanged vows. The happy couple stood under a trellis he'd helped Chase and Hunt build for the outdoor ceremony. They'd strung tiny white lights all through it and the florist had made it beautiful with bouquets of white and purple flowers.

He felt so full of joy for them when they finished their vows, exchanged rings, and kissed for the first time as man and wife. He wished so badly that Kenna had been here to see it and be by his side.

Even more special, Hunt and Cyn signed the adoption papers. They were officially Lana's mom and dad. The ceremony was as profound and special as the wedding.

And now Cyn and Lana were officially Wildes.

Though the wedding was small, the cheers were huge. The love abundant.

He couldn't wait for it to be him and Kenna.

But first, she needed to heal. He needed to propose.

They needed to set a date and make it happen.

Soon.

Because he didn't want to wait.

He wanted her to be the next Mrs. Wilde. The one and only for him.

Since it was early December, they moved into the house for brunch, champagne, and the rest of the celebrating. Hunt and Cyn had rearranged the furniture in the house to accommodate the dining tables. The florist had decorated the mantel and tables with the same purple and white flowers they'd done outside. The fireplace blazed, keeping the house warm and inviting.

Max sat through it all, happy for his brother, but anxious to get back to Kenna. He sent pictures to her phone. But since the doctor told her no screen time, she didn't see them. He'd shut off her phone and tucked it into the bag Shelby had been kind enough to pack for her and

stash in the little closet in her hospital room so she'd
have something to wear home.

She could look at the pictures later.

Lyric tapped his shoulder. "It's your turn to give a toast."

Right. Max stood and held up his glass. He'd listened
to Chase's heartfelt speech. Now he needed to come
through for his brother. He'd thought he'd have time
to prepare before the wedding, but he'd forgotten everything he needed to do while sitting next to Kenna's
hospital bed replaying the events of that night over and
over, thanking his lucky stars Kenna survived. A few
inches to the left and that bullet would have killed her.

He saw himself shoot the bastard who tried to kill
her. It played out like an action movie, him as a de-
tached spectator. He was glad the guy died and couldn't
harm Kenna again. But still he knew at some point the
reality of what he did would hit him.

He'd been justified. But still, he helped take a life.

He looked at Hunt and Cyn sitting next to each other,
Hunt's arm around her shoulders, her hand on his thigh.
Their smiles said it all. They were so happy and in love.

Max didn't want to dwell on the past, but focus on the
here and now and what mattered most.

He met Hunt's joyful eyes. "I spent my whole life
watching you and Chase, wanting to be like you. I
sometimes laughed and mostly sympathized when you
two screwed up. I cheered when things went right. I saw
how hard you both worked to build a life for yourselves.
How you strived to be the best at what you do. How
selfless you both were in wanting to help others. How

hard you fell when the right woman walked into your lives."

Chase looked at Shelby and smiled.

Hunt couldn't contain the smile he laid on Cyn.

"I see the happiness and love that's enriched your lives and given you both a sense of peace and belonging. It wasn't easy for you. You had to protect that love, build on it, fight to hold on to it." He looked between Hunt and Cyn. "You had to put your lives on the line for each other. For Lana. And now, after all that, you get to be what was always meant to be." He thought of him and Kenna. "A family." He couldn't wait for him and Kenna to be officially one, too. "I wish you both nothing but happiness from here on out. You've earned it. You deserve it." He held his glass out toward little Lana sitting in the car seat on a high chair beside Cyn. "Welcome to the family, baby girl." He held his glass out to Cyn. "Mrs. Wilde. I love you, Hunt." He swept his glass across them. "This is perfect. This is everything. Cheers."

"Cheers," the crowd said in unison and drank to the happy couple.

Max took his seat.

Lyric put her arm over his shoulders and hugged him to her side. "That was really sweet. I know you're desperate to get back to Kenna, but it's good to have you here with the family."

"How come you didn't bring a date?"

She eyed him. "Who would I bring?"

"That guy at the bar who is always watching out for you that Jax is always grumbling about."

"This is a family thing and he's . . ." Her gaze went to the wide windows.

He didn't like the forlorn look that came over her whole face. "What?"

She looked at him again, confusion in her eyes. "Complicated."

"Why? Because he's some kind of outlaw biker?" Max didn't know if that description actually described the guy or simply what he looked like.

She scrunched her lips and shook her head. "I'm not so sure he's what he seems to be."

Max wasn't either, because the guy who shot the killer who was after Kenna the other night was the same man they were talking about right now.

He bumped his shoulder to hers and gave his cousin a bit of encouragement. "Maybe you should find out exactly who he is and uncomplicate things."

"Why?"

"Because I've seen the way he looks at you." He leaned in and pinned her in his gaze. "And the way you look at him."

She scrunched her lips into a pout. "Everyone keeps warning me away from him."

"Take it from me—sometimes you think you know something, but you're wrong and just don't know it."

"I guess. I mean, he looks a certain way. He belongs to that biker club. He goes by that ridiculous name. But everything he does is . . . kind."

"People will show you who they really are by their actions."

Lyric hugged him again. "Thank you."

"For what?"

"Confirming for me that my instincts about him aren't wrong."

"Then you should ask yourself, is there something there worth going after, or are you two so different that it would never work?"

"I don't know. I haven't really given it a chance." She frowned. "Truthfully, I think I've really frustrated him by staying neutral."

"Are you okay with that, or are you frustrated, too?"

Her face went all disgruntled. "I am. He's always there, but he never comes out and says much of anything to me. He's always saying things under his breath. I think he's trying to tell me something, but I keep missing it. And it's infuriating." She glared at nothing.

"Then start paying attention. Catch him. You might discover exactly how he feels but can't seem to say."

One side of her mouth quirked back. "He's hiding something."

"Maybe he's just waiting for you to be ready to know it."

She frowned at him again. "When did you stop putting bugs in my hair and grow up?"

He chuckled. "It used to be fun to watch you squeal in disgust. Now I just want to see you happy." He really meant that. He wanted everyone in his family to feel loved and accepted and joyful about their lives. Like he felt with Kenna.

She leaned her head on his shoulder. "I want that for you and Kenna, too. It's sad what happened to her brother."

"They were really close." He looked around the long table and the room at all of his family, Cyn's, and their closest friends. "He won't be at our wedding. It will be a hole in her life, a yearning she can never fill because he's gone. I hate that for her."

"Me, too."

His phone vibrated in his pocket. He pulled it out and answered, even as he stood from the table and walked back to Hunt's bedroom. "Hello."

"Mr. Wilde. This is Kenna's nurse, Tina."

"Is she okay?"

"Yes. Everything is all right. She asked that I call and give you an update. Her concussion symptoms have improved. I changed her dressings and everything looks good with her incisions. She's resting comfortably."

"Thank you for calling. If she needs me, please call. I'll come right away." They still had to clear brunch and cut the cake. He didn't know what else Hunt and Cyn had planned.

"I spoke with her parents. They'll be here shortly."

"Okay. Good. I should be there in a couple hours as well. Thank you again."

"You're welcome." The nurse hung up.

He turned and found Hunt just inside the room. "Sorry. I didn't want to disturb anyone taking the call."

Hunt waved that off. "Is everything all right with Kenna?"

Max nodded and sighed out his relief. "Everything is looking good. She's asleep right now. The doctor was right about the blood loss sapping all her energy."

Hunt rubbed his hand over the back of his neck. "That's great. Good."

"Congrats on the wedding. I know you and Cyn are going to be very happy together."

"You're next up. When's it going to happen?"

He pulled the black velvet box out of his pocket. He didn't know why he had it with him, but before leaving the house for the wedding, he'd picked it up, opened it just to look at the diamond again, and stuffed it in his pocket to have something that would be Kenna's with him today.

He opened the box now and turned the ring to Hunt. "Do you think she'll like it?"

Hunt whistled at the big diamond. "She'll love it." Hunt slapped his hand on Max's shoulder and squeezed. "When did you have time to pick that up?"

"Right between picking up our tuxes and your bachelor party."

"The day Kenna got attacked."

"I almost lost her before I could even give this to her." Just like last time he bought her a ring.

Hunt hugged him to his side. "The important thing is that she's okay and you will put that ring on her finger. You will marry her. You will make a life with her." Hunt squeezed his shoulder.

"Come on. Back to the party. Your bride is probably wondering what happened to you."

"Cyn sent me in here to make sure you're okay. She's worried about you, just as much as I am."

"I'm fine. Kenna is the one in the hospital."

"Believe me, I know the toll it takes on you to sit and wait for news and watch over the woman you love while she recovers. Been there, done that with Cyn too many times."

"But that's all over now."

"But the nightmare is still in your head. If you need to talk about the shooting, I'm here. Chase is here. There's counseling available."

He knew all that. Maybe he'd take them up on it. But right now . . . "I just want Kenna home with me."

"I get that. But what you've been through . . . It's traumatic."

"I just keep telling myself I had to stop him from hurting Kenna again."

"You did. She's safe. That's what matters most." Hunt squeezed his shoulder. "Come on. We're going to cut the cake. Then I'm going to kick everyone out so I can be alone with my wife. Chase and Shelby plan on going with you to see Kenna. Dad's going to watch the kids. We'll pack up some cake for Kenna."

"Thanks, man."

"What are brothers for?" They were for being by your side offering comfort and support, knowing what you needed without you having to say it. And so much more. Max was lucky to have brothers like Chase and Hunt.

He gave Hunt a bear hug before they rejoined the party.

Chapter Twenty-Nine

KENNA STARED at her parents' haggard faces. They appeared to be barely functioning. She'd assured them she was fine and ordered them to go home and try to get some rest.

Max showed up with Chase and Shelby. Kenna ate her cake while Shelby showed her pictures of the wedding and filled in all the details.

Chase and Shelby only stayed an hour. Max stayed the night. Again.

He'd been quiet, but content to hold her hand and watch reruns of *The Big Bang Theory*.

He ran home this morning to get cleaned up and changed.

Her parents arrived a few minutes ago, looking like they hadn't gotten any rest at all. They gave her a hug, took a seat, then both of them had remained silent, waiting for something.

"Mom. Dad. Are you okay?"

"Fine," her mother automatically said.

"Nothing to worry about, dear," her dad assured her.

They did not bluff well.

"Did the doctor tell you something about my condition that I should know?" She felt better today, less tired, more alert. They'd lowered her pain meds. Her wounds ached, but didn't scream with pain anymore. Everything seemed like it was going in the right direction.

But maybe she was wrong about that.

Her mom put her hand over Kenna's. "Everything is fine. The doctor said you're making wonderful progress in your recovery."

She sighed out her relief. "Then why are you both so on edge?"

Her mom's eyes narrowed with anger. "We just want some answers. No one will tell us what exactly happened to Kyle."

"I'd like to know that, too." None of them would give her any of the details they did know.

"I can answer that." Agent Gunn walked in, Max right behind him.

She liked Max in the fancy suit he wore to the wedding yesterday, but he looked damn good in black jeans, a gray thermal, and a black-and-white plaid shirt over it.

Max came right to her, leaned down, and kissed her in front of everyone. He stared into her eyes, checking to see that they were clear and focused on him.

She gave him a smile. "I feel a lot better today."

Relief filled his eyes. Max turned to her parents. "I'd ask again how you both are, but I can see the strain. If there's anything I can do to help, just name it."

Her dad stood and shook Max's hand. "You're doing it by taking care of Kenna."

"Well, that's my pleasure." Max took her hand and held it, then looked to Agent Gunn. "You called this meeting. What can you tell us about Kyle?"

Agent Gunn stood at the end of her bed. "First, I want to say that I'm sorry about what happened to you, Kenna."

"How the hell did that guy get to her before your men got her away? You said you had someone watching the guy who killed Marcus." Max's anger rang in every word.

Agent Gunn took it in stride. "It's complicated, but I'll try to lay it all out so it makes sense. Kyle set up a meeting with the person he took the program from and offered to sell it back."

"But that was a trap you set," Kenna filled in, because it had seemed on her last call with Kyle that the two had spoken about what needed to happen to end all this. "Kyle was working with you."

"Yes. The FBI would be there to apprehend the director who stole government property, plus the guy he hired to get it back from Kyle, but who ultimately ended up killing Marcus. All the players would be there and we'd sweep them up all at once."

"But something went wrong," Max guessed.

"In setting up the meeting, Kyle promised that Kenna would retrieve the hard drives and bring them to him at the meet. It was their condition that she be there."

"But I don't know where they are, or how to get them. Kyle took back what he left at my place."

"I know that. They didn't. I had my undercover guy hint that maybe the reason you were in protective custody had more to do with you having the thing they wanted, than you being able to identify Marcus's murderer. So the businessman, not having dealt in a lot of shady deals, assumed you'd be the one to bring Kyle the hard drives at the meeting. The businessman would get them back, his guy would kill Kyle and you, eliminating anyone who tied him to the theft and murder."

"Because once the businessman had back the thing he wanted, he didn't need Kyle. He wouldn't want Kyle to be able to tell anyone about it, how to defeat it, or make another one," she guessed. "The only way it ends is with Kyle's death. If he lived, people would use him if they had him, or they'd continue to try to find him."

"Exactly. And he was willing to make the sacrifice. We hoped to stop it and save him."

"But you didn't," her father snapped.

Agent Gunn hung his head, then met their gazes again. "Things didn't go to plan. The agent following the killer backed off once the killer was at the meeting to protect his cover. There were other agents surrounding the scene, so we thought we had the killer contained."

Agent Gunn continued. "Kyle arrived first, then the businessman and the hired gunman. Kyle and the businessman faced off. Just when we were about to move in and make the arrest, everything went sideways. The killer accused the businessman of not paying him and lying about you being there, so he could eliminate you. He threatened to kill Kyle unless he got paid. They argued about it, and the killer shot Kyle in the chest."

Her mother gasped. "Why?"

"Because if he didn't get paid, the businessman didn't get his asset. Kyle."

"But you said he died in a car crash."

"Kyle took advantage when the agents I had on scene swooped in to make the arrests and somehow managed to drive away. I went after him. But he didn't get far before he veered off the road and hit a tree. He wasn't wearing a seat belt and died on impact." Agent Gunn sighed out his regret. "I'm so sorry for your loss."

"How could he just drive away?" her mom asked.

"The killer didn't want to go down without a fight. Bullets started flying. Kyle ran. Adrenaline gave him the strength and speed to do so, but ultimately it wears off and you're left in a lot of pain." It sounded like Agent Gunn knew that firsthand.

"Did Kyle hit the tree by accident?" Kenna wasn't so sure based on her conversations with Kyle.

Agent Gunn shrugged as his only answer, leaving Kenna to wonder if it was an accident, or intentional.

"Of course it was an accident," her dad snapped. "So you captured the businessman, but not the killer?" her dad asked.

Agent Gunn took her father's anger in stride. "Unfortunately, he ran into the trees and got away. We had people out looking for him. Then my undercover agent texted me that the killer asked for his help in taking down the agents at the ranch, so he could get to you. I warned my team at the ranch that they were close and to get you out immediately. And you know how that turned out."

"Your undercover man took him out," Max said.

"You helped," Agent Gunn replied.

Kenna gasped. "Wait. You shot the killer?"

Max sighed. "He shot you. I had to stop him before he killed you. I thought . . ."

Tears filled Kenna's eyes. "You thought I was dead."

"I wasn't sure you'd make it," he clarified, his eyes watery.

Agent Gunn sighed. "I'm sorry you were put in that position, Max. Tom praised you in his report for keeping Kenna safe and saving his life."

"Your man did that."

Agent Gunn didn't let Max downplay his role. "You helped save lives."

"How is the agent who got hurt driving the car?"

"Like Kenna, he suffered a mild concussion. He was released from the hospital yesterday."

Max nodded. "Good. That's a relief."

Agent Gunn finished the story. "The only thing missing is what Kyle stole, but he was adamant he destroyed it." Agent Gunn looked at her, like she could confirm it was destroyed.

She couldn't, except to say, "Kyle knew how dangerous it was, and he really didn't want it out in the world. If he said he destroyed it, I believe him."

"Are you ever going to tell us what the thing is he stole and what it does?" her dad asked, agitated by all the secrecy.

"No." Agent Gunn didn't look apologetic at all for not revealing the answer. "But the world is a better place without it. Everyone's private business should remain private." He looked her in the eye. "You and your family are safe now."

She turned to her parents. "Did you see Kyle when you made arrangements for him?"

"Briefly," her father said, then dropped his head and wiped at his eyes.

"So he's really dead?" She couldn't believe it for some reason. Something niggled at the back of her mind.

"The service is the day after tomorrow." Her mom squeezed her hand. "We hope you'll be released from the hospital by then."

"The doctor said I could go home later today."

Max looked at her, surprised. "When did he say that?"

"Right after you left this morning."

"Best news I've heard in a long time." Max kissed her on the head.

Agent Gunn looked at all of them. "If you have further questions, please contact me. I'll try to answer, if I can." He gave them an apologetic look to convey his sympathy. "I'm really sorry for your loss. Take care, Kenna, though I think you're in good hands."

She glanced up at Max, who looked down adoringly at her. "I'm in the best hands."

"Goodbye to all of you. Sorry we met under these circumstances." Agent Gunn left them alone.

Her mom and dad shared a sad look.

"Are you guys okay?" she asked them.

Her mom closed her eyes briefly, then turned to her. "It's just so senseless and wrong. This wasn't how it was supposed to be. We were supposed to go first. Not him. He had such a bright future. He'd barely had time to live."

She sympathized with her parents. Losing a child couldn't be easy. Especially in this way. Her heart broke for them. For Kyle.

But something deep inside her told her this wasn't the tragedy it should be. She couldn't explain it. But it felt like this was as inevitable as Kyle had said it would be, but also not as it seemed.

Maybe like many others, he'd predicted his own death with a sense of dread but also hope that somehow he'd cheat it.

But Kyle hadn't.

And maybe she was simply numb, because she didn't feel his loss the way she thought she would.

Max slipped his hand beneath her hair and rubbed at the back of her neck. "You look tired."

It wasn't even lunchtime. "I am." It seemed her energy came in spurts, then left her drained.

Mom leaned in and kissed her cheek. "I bet, like us, you're looking forward to being free of protective custody."

Kenna grinned. "I want my life back."

Her mom glanced up at Max. "Looks like you got something else you've wanted back for a long time."

She leaned into him. "My something good in all the bad."

Her dad gave Max a nod of approval. "It's good to see her happy again."

"It feels good to be this happy again." Max kissed the back of her hand.

Her mom brushed a tear from her cheek. "Well, I know you don't want to return to your apartment, so you'll come stay with us until you find a new place."

"She has one," Max blurted out.

All of them stared at Max.

Her parents looked to her to explain, but she couldn't, because she couldn't believe Max was saying what she thought he was saying.

"Stay with me. I'll take care of you while you recover. We'll build on what we've restarted. Maybe you think we're going too fast and jumping ahead. I think it's more like we're just getting to where we should have already ended up. Having you there these last many days, it's been a glimpse of what I always wanted, for it to be the place you want to be. The place that feels like home to you now. Or at least when we make it ours. I don't want to miss you anymore. And I will every second you're not with me. I don't want to wait for what we both want. Say yes," he implored.

Her parents looked expectant and excited that she'd do it.

So she said, "Yes. I'd love to stay with you."

Max's grin and joy eclipsed all the worry in his eyes and written in the lines on his face. He looked over at her parents. "I'll take really good care of her. I'll make her happy."

Her mom reached across the bed and held his arm. "You already do, Max."

Her dad nodded his agreement.

She wanted to be alone with Max to talk about this next step. "Mom, Dad, you two need to take some time for yourselves. Go home. Max will get me settled at the ranch. He'll let you know I'm there and that everything is okay."

Her parents needed the reassurance after losing Kyle and her nearly dying the same night, too.

Max confirmed this with a nod. "I've already spoken to the principal at school. Kenna will continue to have a substitute in her class for the next two weeks and be on paid medical leave."

She frowned. "You did? I am?"

Max gave her another soft smile. "Yes. You need time to recover. Doctor's orders."

"Okay." She looked at her parents. "See. Max has it all covered. Um . . ." She didn't know how to broach this subject. "Will you call me later with all the details about the service for Kyle?"

"Of course," her mother assured her. "All you have to do is attend. If you're up to it," her mom said, like it was okay to miss her brother's funeral.

"I'll be there no matter what."

Her father hugged her. "You need to take care of yourself."

"I will," she assured him, hugging him back.

He stood and held her by the shoulders. "I love you."

Tears filled her eyes. "I love you, too, Dad."

Her mom hugged her goodbye and softly brushed her hand down the ends of Kenna's hair because she still had a big bandage on her head. "See you soon. If you need anything, you call us."

"I'll be fine," she assured her mom and dad again.

They reluctantly left, even though they obviously needed a break and some time at home to just be together and be quiet and take the time they needed to let everything settle.

She needed the same thing at home with Max.

Her parents left and Max propped his hip on the bed, but didn't meet her gaze.

"What's wrong?"

"Are you sure you're okay?"

"I'm feeling better. Why?"

"You seem to understand that Kyle's dead, but you're not sad. Not like you miss him. Your parents are wrecked. But you're not. Not like you were about Marcus." He studied her face, looking for something he didn't see.

It hit her that he was right. "I don't know what it is. When I think about Kyle, I logically understand what happened. But it doesn't feel real. It feels wrong. I can't explain it. I miss him. I want to see him. I want him back. But . . ." Tears slipped down her face.

Max brushed them away with his thumbs. "I know. I'm sorry. People grieve in their own way. You've had a lot happen in the last couple days. You're dealing with a lot. I guess I'm just worried that at some point the grief is going to hit you and make you worse."

"Maybe it will. And that's okay. It's supposed to be that way. I'll get through it, because I have you to hold me when I'm sad and love me through it, just like you've done while I've been here in the hospital."

He cupped her cheek. "I just want you to be okay."

She tried to reassure him. "I am for the most part. The rest will come in time."

He gave her another sweet kiss, and a huge smile spread across his handsome face. "I'm taking you home."

She took a minute to think about what moving in with him really meant. "Is your father okay with this?"

"He wants me to be happy. He said it's been nice having a woman in the house again."

"That's not the same as me moving in."

"It's going to be fine," he assured her. "We'll figure it out as we go. We'll clean out your apartment when you're feeling up to it. It'll be a long drive for you to get to work, though."

"Then we'll both be up early."

A serious look came over him. "Do you mind living there with my dad?"

"It's a big house, Max. We'll have our privacy on your side of the house. He has his on the other. I think we can make it work just fine."

"Whatever you need to feel comfortable there, we'll make it happen."

"I know you will. I'm looking forward to coming home to you and not an empty apartment anymore."

"I feel the same way."

"Promise me something."

"Anything," he readily replied.

"That whenever something happens between us, we'll always take the time to talk about it, no matter how hard it may seem to say something or how long it takes for us to solve it." She didn't want to ever repeat past mistakes.

"I promise."

"I promise, too." She smiled at him. "One more thing."

"What?"

"Can we stop for pizza on the way home? I'm starving."

He leaned in and kissed her. "Anything you want."

"You. Always you."

"That's good. Because you're stuck with me." He kissed her again, this time holding the sweet touch as he stared into her eyes.

"You and pizza. I could live on that forever."

Max smiled again and laughed. "We've got so much more ahead for us."

She didn't doubt it. But first, they had a few things to do to finish off this chapter so they could start a new one.

A happier one that included them making their dreams a reality.

Chapter Thirty

MAX WASN'T a morning person by nature, but after all these years working the ranch, he enjoyed the quiet, a cup of coffee, and the sunrise. Though today he'd have rather stayed in bed with Kenna.

They'd gotten home a bit late last night. After she'd been discharged from the hospital, he'd taken her out for pizza as promised. Their first date now that she wasn't being guarded by the feds. He thought they'd pick it up to go, but she'd wanted to eat at the restaurant and just be out in the world.

By the time they got home, she was tired again, so they called it a night early. He didn't think he'd sleep, but apparently the second he had her in his arms, all the fatigue he'd carried since the night she was shot caught up to him and he fell into a deep sleep, missing a chance to talk to his dad, who'd been over at Chase's place playing with his granddaughters.

His dad came down the stairs and raised a brow. "I thought I heard the shower upstairs."

"You did," he said, pouring his dad a mug and holding it out to him.

His dad gave him a grin. "I assume it's not one of your brothers upstairs. They're too happy living with their women to end up here for a night."

Max returned his dad's grin. "It's Kenna."

The smile widened. "I knew that."

"Her place is still a mess. With what happened there, she doesn't want to go back."

"And you want her here."

"Yes. In fact, I asked her to stay." He blurted it out, like a confession. Maybe he should have asked first, but . . . He was a grown man who wanted the woman he loved under the same roof as him.

"I knew once she was here, you weren't going to let her go again. I want you to be happy. You're happiest when you're with her. And, for what it's worth, I've always liked her. She'll fit in here just fine."

"Thanks, Dad. We'll sort out any details later." Max turned to the dining room entrance when Hunt and Cyn walked in with Lana. "What are you guys doing here? I thought you were leaving on your honeymoon today."

Hunt hooked his arm over Cyn's shoulders. "We are, this afternoon. But first, we wanted to stop by to check on Kenna."

Max glanced at Cyn. "And you're dying to meet her." And she finally could because Kenna was free to do as she pleased.

Cyn beamed. "She's family, right?"

He grinned. "Yes. She is. But we just got back together, and while things are falling right back into place, they're also moving quickly, so maybe you all could give us both a little breathing room to settle into it."

Cyn nodded. "Of course. Shelby and I just want her to know we're here for her, too."

He hoped Chase, Shelby, and Eliza didn't show up next. Kenna didn't need this kind of overwhelming welcome when she was still recovering.

Lana started fussing in Cyn's arms.

Max loved his nieces dearly and plucked the little one right out of her new mom's arms. Lana's mom's death was still all too fresh for all of them, especially Cyn, who had been very close to her sister. Lana was lucky to have Hunt and Cyn jump right in to love and raise her as their own. And now they were an official family.

Not that they needed a wedding license and adoption papers when love made it as real as it gets.

Lana settled in against his chest and went back to sleep. He couldn't blame the little girl, it was early, even for her.

Hunt took a seat at the breakfast table. "How is Kenna?"

"Sore. Tired. We crashed early last night. She had a nightmare, but went right back to sleep." He rubbed Lana's back, taking in her sweetness and the comfort of holding her.

Cyn frowned. "She lost two men in her life. She nearly got killed. That's a lot to keep her up at night."

Max nodded. "Wait. How did you know she was here?"

Hunt gave him an amused look. "It runs in the family."

"What?"

"You find the one you want and hold on with everything you are," Cyn said, kissing Hunt on the head.

Hunt hooked his arm around Cyn's waist and pulled her close. "Damn right. I'm never letting you go."

Kenna walked into the kitchen, stopped short, and gasped. "Um. Hello *everyone*." She took them all in, but her gaze came right back to Max.

"Hey, sweetheart, I poured you some coffee." He held the mug out to her.

She hesitated for a moment, then came further into the room and took the mug, her eyes locked on Lana in his arms. Her gaze met his again. "You and she make a very sweet picture."

"Anytime you want to do this, I'm in," he said, not caring that all eyes were on him now.

Kenna rolled with it. "I'll let you know." She ducked her head to hide her blush, then glanced at everyone in the room. She turned to the one person she didn't know. "You're Hunt's Cyn."

"I am." Cyn beamed with happiness.

"Shelby showed me wedding photos. You two looked so happy."

"We are." Cyn kissed Hunt's head, then turned back to Kenna. "I would love to get my hands on your hair."

Kenna grabbed a chunk of the long blond locks. "Really? Why?"

"I'm a hairdresser, and you've got amazing hair. The color. It's like golden wheat. I have clients who would kill for that color."

Kenna laughed. "It could use some attention. I haven't had it cut since . . ." Her head slowly turned to Max.

He knew exactly what she was thinking. "Before we broke up." He loved her long hair. He'd always told her to just leave it alone, let it grow. He used to slide his fingers through it all the time. He couldn't wait to do it again.

"Yeah." Kenna ran her hand through the long strands. "I never really thought about it."

"It's beautiful, sweetheart. Short, long, somewhere in between, I don't care as long as you're happy."

Cyn shrugged. "Whenever you feel like it, just come to my shop and I'll take good care of you."

"Mostly she wants to get all the details about us," Max supplied. "I'm kind of surprised Chase and Shelby aren't here, too, though they saw you at the hospital."

"They're on their way." Hunt smirked.

Max chuckled under his breath. "Of course they are."

And right on cue, the front door opened and closed. A moment later, Chase and Shelby walked in with Eliza.

"Unc!" Eliza yelled holding her hands out to him.

Chase set her on the floor and she ran to him and wrapped her arms around his legs.

Max put his free hand on her back. "Morning, sweet girl. Want to meet my friend Kenna?"

Eliza looked up at him and nodded, then turned to Kenna. "Hi."

Kenna squatted to Eliza's level and held out her hand. "Hello."

Eliza took Kenna's hand and shook. "You pretty."

"Not as pretty as you."

"It's a tie." Max brushed his hand over Eliza's hair and smiled at Kenna.

Remmy, Chase's service dog, walked over to Kenna and brushed up against her side.

"Hello, there." Kenna had seen Chase's service dog a lot down at the barn.

Kenna looked up at Chase. "You've got a beautiful family."

Chase hugged Shelby close to his side. "Thank you. It's good to see him"—Chase notched his chin up toward Max—"happy again. How are you feeling today?"

Kenna gave Remmy one last pet, then planted her free hand on her knee and stood with a groan.

Shelby rushed forward, took Kenna's arm, and helped her stand without spilling her coffee.

"Thank you," Kenna said. "It's nice to see you again."

"You, too. That's a nasty head wound."

Kenna brushed her fingers over the line of stitches on her temple. "Everything is sore today. But at least I'm alive."

Shelby put her hand on Kenna's back. "We are all happy about that."

Kenna bit her bottom lip. "It's a little overwhelming to be welcomed like this, but I'm so happy to be here with all of you. Especially you," she said to Max. "Like for real. We had a really close call."

"Too close." Max brushed his fingers along the cut on her head. "Drink your coffee. Want something to eat?"

"One of those peanut butter granola bars you picked up for me."

"I want," Eliza said. "Peanut butter my favorite."

Kenna smiled down at his niece, then pulled the box from the cupboard. "Then it's your lucky day, sweetheart, because I have two." She pulled the treat out of the box and handed it to Eliza.

Shelby rolled her eyes. "You already ate breakfast."

"I want it." Eliza held it to her chest.

Shelby looked at Kenna. "Do you really have another one?"

Kenna pulled out the second granola bar. "I do. No worries. I'm like a squirrel, I always have snacks. Some of my students don't always get enough food at home. It's well known that I keep a stash of things in my classroom."

"That's really nice and thoughtful," his dad said, addressing Kenna for the first time.

"I wish it wasn't so necessary."

His dad acknowledged that with a nod. "You need help restocking, we're happy to help."

Cyn touched Kenna's arm. "I could put a collection box in my shop. Lots of moms and grandmas come in. I'm sure they'd love to drop off food for the kids."

Kenna's eyes shined with joy and unshed tears. "That would be amazing."

Cyn held her hands out. "Then consider it done. I'll drop the food off here with you once a week."

"Thank you. It's been my dream to set up a food pantry in my class, where kids can grab what they need without feeling like they're being judged."

"I can talk to my work about doing the same thing," Shelby added. "I'll even ask the juice place next door about donating fresh fruit. They seem to throw away a lot of stuff. Maybe some of it can go to the school."

Kenna nodded, obviously touched. "The more the better. If it's too much, I can distribute some to the elementary and middle school."

Cyn nodded. "Great idea. So we're talking snacks, fresh fruit . . . Anything else?"

"Cereal. I pick up an extra box every week for one of my kids. Sometimes she doesn't get breakfast or dinner. Lunch is provided free to her at school. This way I know she's got something to eat at home for several days. It's not ideal, but it's something."

Cyn sighed. "I'll start spreading the word right away. I'm opening a shop in Blackrock Falls, too. I can do the same there and talk to the principal of their school about a food pantry, too."

"That's above and beyond." Kenna choked up. "Thank you. I keep thinking about how I lost my brother, but this morning I have a whole family willing to help with something that means so much to me. I'm so appreciative and humbled by you all showing up this morning."

"Get used to it." Max handed Lana off to Cyn, then kissed Kenna like he might never kiss her again.

The room went quiet.

He didn't care that all eyes were on them. He ended the kiss and pressed his forehead to hers. "I love you." He wanted her to hear it, for his family to know it.

"I love you, too."

Max surveyed his family. They were all smiling at him, barely containing their joy. "So I love her. She loves me. What of it?" He didn't know why he suddenly felt embarrassed.

"We're just happy for you," his dad said for all of them.

"Okay, well, great. I need to get to work." But first, he took Cyn's and Shelby's hands. "Thank you both for accepting her with open arms and helping her with her kids. They mean everything to her."

"No child should go hungry," Cyn said.

"Not when we can buy a few extra groceries and ask those around us for help." Shelby kissed his cheek. "I'm off to work, too."

Shelby, Hunt, and Cyn said goodbye, then Hunt and Cyn helped Shelby take the kids out to her car so Shelby could drop them at day care while she worked. She'd pick them up at the end of her workday and take care of Lana for Cyn and Hunt while they were on their honeymoon.

Chase, Remmy, his dad, Kenna, and him remained in the kitchen.

Max looked to his dad, who sat at the table, an amused and content look on his face. "You good, old man? Want some more coffee?"

He held up his mug. "I'm good. This is perfect," he said, meaning having them all here this morning. "I just wish your mom was here to see how this family has grown and how happy her sons are now."

"She knows," Chase said. "But she always liked Kenna and thought she'd be the first to join us. Now that it's happening, I think she's smiling down on Max, happy to see he finally got her back."

"No one is happier than me about that," Kenna said, smiling at all of them as she refilled her mug.

Max grabbed his jacket off the hook by the back door. "Let's get to it," he said to Chase. Their dad would join them when he was good and ready, because he and Chase had taken over the bulk of the work on the ranch and managing the crew who worked here.

He couldn't wait to get through this day and be back with her.

Halfway across the yard to the barn, Chase stopped and turned to him. "She's going to be okay. The women in our lives are tough. Look what Shelby and Cyn went through and survived. Kenna is a lot like them."

"I nearly lost her twice. I know she's okay, but now every second I'm away from her, I worry."

Chase squeezed his shoulder. "I know exactly how you feel. It gets better. That hyperaware thing you've got going will dissipate as you two settle in here together and start living some ordinary days."

"I'm looking forward to that." No matter what, he knew that whatever came at him and Kenna next, they could handle it, beat it, and live the life they wanted together.

Chapter Thirty-One

Max woke Kenna with a soft kiss on her cheek. He loved seeing her in his bed. He spent every free moment with her, soaking up the feeling that he was living the life he wanted with the woman he loved.

He wanted to say the difficult times were behind them, but he knew better. Now, though, they'd face them together, head-on, by each other's sides.

They spent last evening together on the couch binge-watching a comedy series, though Kenna had to hold back some of the laughter due to her injury and cracked ribs. Still, it lightened her mood and brought them closer together.

They went for a walk down to the stables in the mornings. Kenna loved to be with the horses, and was disappointed she couldn't ride until the doctor cleared her for such activities.

They'd sat together and eaten all their meals, talking about nothing and a little about the future. She spoke with her parents on the phone for about half an hour after dinner last night, reassuring them she was okay.

Though her sadness over Kyle's death lingered, he saw the joy and pleasure she took in being with him on the ranch.

"Kenna, baby, it's time to wake up."

Last night, he'd joined her in the shower, pampering her with soft strokes as he scrubbed her clean from head to foot. He'd dried her off and slipped one of his T-shirts on her, so she'd be comfortable. Then he'd tucked her into bed with him and held her all night.

She woke up screaming and trying to ward off an attack in the early morning hours. When he asked her what she remembered, she said *nothing* and fell back onto the bed, still shaking and sweaty. He kissed her softly and brushed his hand up and down her arm, holding her until she fell back into a peaceful sleep.

And now she didn't want to wake up.

He kissed her soundly on the lips and hers tilted up into a grin against his. "Good morning," he said, stealing another kiss as her eyes finally opened.

"I smell bacon."

"I brought you breakfast in bed." He notched his chin out toward the plate he set on the nightstand beside her, along with a cup of coffee.

"That looks yummy, but I have a problem."

"What's that?" he asked, wondering about the mischief in her eyes.

"I think I've forgotten what you look like naked."

He had propped himself over her on his hands, giving her a perfect view of his bare chest, all the way down to his flannel pajama pants he only wore to walk around the house in the morning. "Is your eyesight not work-ing?" He tried to hide a grin as her gaze traveled over his face, down past his shoulders and chest.

"I think I need to get a bit closer, so I can get a really good look at you." She rose, using her hands to push her up so she didn't have to strain her midsection muscles and pull at her injury. She kissed his neck, then trailed kisses down and across his shoulder, then down his pecs until she licked his nipple.

He groaned. "Baby. I love you. I love this. But your food is getting cold."

She sat up, making him sit up to give her room. The sheet dropped, revealing her bare breasts. She slipped her arms around his neck and kissed him softly, press-ing her hard nipples to his chest. "You can heat it up again later." She kissed him again, this time slipping her tongue right past his lips and along his.

She tasted like mint.

He leaned back. "You're not wearing the T-shirt I put on you last night. And you brushed your teeth."

She dove in for another kiss. "You're so smart." She kissed him again. "And sexy." Another kiss. "And warm." A soft peck. "And overdressed. And not in this bed with me." She kissed him soundly this time.

Who was he to argue with any of that?

The doctor said she needed to take it easy. But she seemed fine this morning. He didn't want to deny her what she so obviously wanted.

He'd go slow. "We don't have much time," he re-minded her.

"We have time for this." She kissed him again. Then she looked him in the eyes. "We should always make time for us."

She was so right. They'd wasted so much time, nearly lost their chance to be together like this more than once. Nothing should ever be more important than their relationship and making each other a priority.

He stood and dropped his pajama bottoms and kicked them off his feet.

She took one long sweeping glance at his naked body and grinned. "Just as I remember. Sexy as hell."

He chuckled and slid on top of her just after she kicked all the blankets down the bed and out of their way. She was naked and warm and welcoming in every way.

He took his time kissing her, touching her, rubbing his body against hers, though he tried to keep most of his weight off her midsection and ribs. The feel of her skin against his heightened his need for her. Every kiss was an invitation for more. He loved her fingers trailing over his back and shoulders, the way her body rolled beneath his bringing her hips into contact with his, her breasts pressing to his chest.

He slid down and took one hard pink nipple into his mouth, swirling his tongue around it and sucking until she moaned. She planted her hand on his head, spread her legs wide, and gave him a gentle push in the direction she wanted him to go. With pleasure, he trailed kisses down her belly and gave her what she wanted, his mouth on her soft folds, the very essence of her on his tongue as he licked and laved and sucked on her clit until she was rocking against his mouth and crashing over the edge.

"Mmm, baby." She hummed out the words. "I like it when you do that."

"I like doing that to you." He kissed his way back up her belly, over one round breast, up her neck to her lips, until he was staring down into her beautiful, bright eyes and seeing all the love he had for her reflected back at him. She held up a condom. He took it and rolled it on, then settled between her thighs again. He nudged the head of his aching cock at her entrance. She grabbed his ass and pulled him home. It felt so good, he moaned and lost himself in her wet warmth, the feel of her body holding his, the connection they shared shutting everything else out and pulling them closer to each other.

The pleasure took hold once again. He tried to hold out, make it last, a chance for them to savor this precious time together. But eventually the physical demands of his body and his desire to make Kenna feel as amazing as she made him feel won out and they came together, ending with a deep kiss that lasted all through the cascading aftershocks.

Mindful of her condition, he held most of his weight off her and whispered in her ear, "I can't believe you're mine."

She kissed his cheek and hugged him close. "I feel so lucky to still be here with you."

He held himself up above her on one hand and brushed his fingertips lightly along the side of her beautiful face. He kissed her forehead. "I never want to feel the way

I did when I saw you lying in the dirt and thought you were dead."

She brushed her thumb across his bottom lip. "I wish you didn't have to go through that."

"Seeing you all bloody like that and not moving . . . God, the relief I felt when I knew you were still breathing. I meant it when I said I can't lose you again. I love you so much. My whole world is you." He wanted to propose. The moment felt right. But he didn't want her to be reminded of her brother's funeral every time she remembered his proposal. So he'd have to wait to make it perfect.

Because she deserved that.

They both did.

"And now it's our time to have our life together." She hooked her hand at the back of his neck and pulled him down for a sweet kiss. "This is how we should start every morning."

He grinned. "With me bringing you breakfast in bed, making love to you, and you eating cold food."

"I wouldn't mind, because I'd be feeling as good as I do right now."

He brushed his nose to hers, then rolled off her and the bed. He did the condom cleanup, pulled on his pajama bottoms, and picked up her plate. "I'll go heat this up for you, then take a shower while you eat." He glanced at the clock. "We don't have much time."

"I know." She didn't look eager to go. "Everything is going to be okay now. I'll miss Kyle every day, but I've come to terms with his decision. He gave me my life back, and soon the sense of security I lost will return. We'll live our lives, knowing he played a small part in making it happen."

Max stared at her, getting that same odd sense that she refused to grieve for her brother. Maybe it was too painful to do right now and the grief would come later. But something seemed off. "Sweetheart, are you still feeling like maybe it's not real?"

She slowly sat up and turned to him. "If I tell you something, will you promise, like a real promise, you won't repeat it to anyone? Ever. Because if I'm right, and the wrong person heard it, it could be very bad for Kyle."

"He's dead. Nothing can hurt him now."

She tilted her head, waiting for him to promise.

"I swear. Whatever you say, I won't tell anyone. I'll never mention it again." He even crossed his heart and leaned down and kissed her to seal the bargain. "Okay?"

She grinned. "Yes."

"So, what is it?"

"I don't think Kyle is dead."

He worried she was in denial. "He was shot and hit a tree while driving, sweetheart. Your father saw his body."

"I know all that. But I think Agent Gunn and Kyle made it look that way. Because the only way for Kyle to be free and for his family to be safe, was for him to die. What better way than to make everyone think he did, then put him in witness protection."

"But he's not a witness to anything. There are no bad guys to testify against."

"What if his knowledge was enough to get him in the program? They have to hide him, so no one can get to him and what he knows."

Max sat on the bed beside her and cupped her cheek. "I would really like to believe that's true."

"I think it is." She leaned into his touch, her gaze steady and filled with a strong belief that she was right.

"But isn't it more logical that what Agent Gunn told us happened, really did happen?"

"Maybe. But the last time I spoke to Kyle, I got the impression that he was trying to tell me something when he told me to tell Agent Gunn that he'd finally accepted it had to be this way."

"I remember him saying that." Max started to believe that maybe the words held more meaning.

"Why would Agent Gunn need to know he'd accepted it?" She didn't wait for Max to give an answer. "I think it's because he'd already spoken to Agent Gunn, who offered him the only way out that protected everyone. Including Kyle. Kyle said, *'That's the trick.'* Why use that term? It doesn't make sense. Unless he was trying to tell me his dying is a trick."

Max rubbed his hand over the back of his neck. "I'd like to think you're right, but we'll never know. Kyle won't be able to reach out. Agent Gunn will never confirm it."

"I know. And so we'll hold a funeral for my brother today, never knowing if he's dead or alive. At least, I won't."

"Well, now I'm not so sure either."

She looked relieved to hear him say that. "Maybe it's

wishful thinking. Maybe it's my way of denying reality, so that I can cope."

So what if it was. "You know your brother. You'd know if he was trying to get you to hear what he couldn't say. Maybe you're right."

She leaned over and hugged Max. "Thank you for not dismissing it. Thank you for having even a little doubt on my behalf. And thanks for not calling me crazy."

"What I think is that you're crazy smart and maybe your brother was counting on that to help you cope with his loss. Because even if he is alive, he can't ever come back. You'll never see him again."

"I know. And maybe I spend the rest of my life pretending that he's out there, living a whole new life. But you know what? I'm okay with that. Because I hope it's true. And I will miss him like he's dead. But I'll keep him alive and a part of our lives in my own way, even if it is far-fetched."

"It would be nice to know for sure, though."

"I'll have to settle for believing it even if I can't confirm it."

"Some things, like love, are like that."

"Oh, I don't know. I think you confirmed how much you love me. Especially this morning."

Max grinned. "Happy to do it again anytime you want. But right now, we need to get ready to go."

"Right. But maybe you could do something for me first."

"Anything."

She wrapped her arms around his neck and kissed

him. "Help me shower. You know, in case I get dizzy. You wouldn't want me to fall."

Max put the plate back on the nightstand, slipped his arm under her legs and scooped her up against his chest, then stood, and carried her to the bathroom. "I'll be sure to *wash* every bit of you."

Max actually *loved* every bit of her under the warm spray before he helped her soap and rinse and dry off. They hadn't rushed in the shower, but they did to leave the house.

And they made it to the funeral on time.

Chapter Thirty-Two

THE PAIN hit Kenna the second she arrived at the funeral home and saw the urn amongst the many bouquets of flowers and the picture of Kyle behind it all. There he was, smiling back at her, but not here.

Whether dead or somehow alive somewhere, it finally sank in that he wasn't coming back.

As she sat in the pew with her parents, Max's family—minus Hunt and Cyn, who were on their honeymoon—she realized that from this day forward, he wouldn't be a part of the family. He'd miss birthdays and holidays, her wedding, the birth of her children, the family dinners and milestones to come.

The tears didn't come in a torrent of sobs like her mother. They streamed down her face in a cascade of lost days turning into weeks and months and years without Kyle.

She grieved not just the loss of him but all the things they'd never share. The things she'd never know, if he really was alive. She'd never know if he fell in love, married, had kids of his own. She'd never know where his life took him, what career he'd have, successes or losses or ordinary things about his new life.

And so, sitting there with Max's arm around her, his comfort easing her pain, she silently thanked her brother for the sacrifice, for doing the hard thing. For giving up his life for hers, even though that meant they would forever be apart.

She prayed that somehow, someway she'd see him again.

And it gave her comfort to know that her brother was smart enough, canny enough to make that happen if he was still alive.

He'd know where to find her. At home on Split Tree Ranch with Max and their family. The only place she wanted to be with the man she couldn't wait to marry and make that life of home and family a reality.

The service was lovely. Her mom and dad accepted all the condolences and love their family and friends showered on them. Everyone gathered shared stories, laughed, and cried. And said goodbye.

Max stayed by her side the whole time. Most of all, he held her hand, offering his comfort and support. And he told great stories about Kyle. Because as long as he'd known her, he'd known her brother, too. And the two of them had some good times together with and without her.

It was nice to know that from now on, she could share stories with Max, and he could remind her of the things her brother did and said.

Max would keep her secret, whether it was true or not, and help her keep Kyle in their lives, even if it was just to share a memory now and again.

Max took her home after the funeral and their visit to her parents' home where everyone gathered after the service. He took her into the kitchen for a cup of tea, then disappeared for a minute before he came back in carrying a brown delivery box.

He set it in front of her on the table and pointed to the words written next to the ranch's address.

Max,
    Give this to her after the funeral.
    Thanks to you, I know she'll have a great life.

                                                    Kyle

She looked up at Max. "When did this get here?"

"The day after Kyle died. I was at the hospital with you, but my dad brought it in and showed it to me when I came home."

"And you didn't say anything about it to me?"

He brushed his hand over her hair. "I wanted to honor his last request."

Tears gathered in her eyes. "I don't want to open it."

"You don't have to until you're ready."

"If I open it, then it's over. If I don't, there's still possibility."

"For what, Kenna? He's gone. Nothing will change that. Opening this box will at least tell you what's inside,

and hopefully bring you closure. He'd want that for you."
Max took the knife from his pocket, opened it and held it
out to her.

She took it, slit the tape, then opened the flaps and
stared at the white sheet of paper on top of dozens and
dozens of Reese's Peanut Butter Cups all with black
marker that said, "I'm Sorry" across them.

Max put his hand on her shoulder and squeezed.

She read the note:

> What is 1 + 1?

"You and me," she answered out loud for Max. She
looked up at him. "When I was little, it's the first math
problem I ever taught him. I wanted him to know no
matter what, it was always going to be him and me.
Whenever we were in trouble or something happened in
our lives and we needed each other, we'd ask the question and give the other the answer."

"Finish reading," he coaxed.

> Now it means you and Max.
> I don't think these are enough apologies for everything I'll
> miss in your life. It kills me that I won't be there to see your
> dreams become reality. But I know you're going to make
> them all come true.
> I'll be watching over you.
>
> Love, Kyle

Tears cascaded down her cheeks.

"It's sweet that he sent you one final goodbye," Max said.

And he'd given her one more reason to believe that maybe he wasn't as dead as everyone thought, because Kyle used to hack into her computer, delete all her cookies and trackers and leave her little messages about how he'd saved her from getting her identity stolen or whatever. When she complained and told him he'd violated her privacy, he'd always say, "I'm just watching over you."

She didn't say anything to Max about her suspicions. She'd laid enough crazy on him already.

So she opened one of the candy packages and took a bite of the first peanut butter cup. Then she looked up at Max. "He's right. This is not enough chocolate."

Max sat next to her. "I'll buy you more."

Kyle was right.

From now on, it would be her and Max.

Chapter Thirty-Three

❧

Max pulled into the diner parking lot and found a spot right next to Chase's truck. Hunt's patrol SUV was a few spots over. He and Cyn were back from their honeymoon. His dad slipped out of the truck to head inside. After attending Kyle's funeral a few days ago, Max had something to say about the importance of today and turned to Kenna.

Just before she slid across the seat to hop out, too, he touched her arm to halt her.

She turned to him with a smile. "Everything okay?"

"Over the last however many months it's been since Chase came home, I've watched my brothers fall in love. Pancake Tuesday began with us starting a tradition with Shelby and Eliza to show them they're our family, too."

"That's really sweet."

"Well, the tradition was Shelby and Eliza's. Dad, Hunt, and me, we insinuated ourselves into it as a way to get the family back together after it fractured when Mom died."

"Still sweet."

"And then Hunt brought Cyn. I think he had a thing for her longer than she had one for him, but it was so clear they belonged together no matter how different they seemed from each other. She fit right in with all of us."

Kenna tilted her head and her eyes grew wary. "Are you afraid I won't?"

He shook his head. "You're what was missing every Pancake Tuesday when I sat at the table with all of them."

Her eyes softened with love. "Oh, Max, that's so sweet of you to say."

"I mean it. I tried so hard not to think it or wish for it, because I didn't think we could ever get back what we had, and I missed so much."

She took his hand. "I missed us, too. All the time."

"And now you're going to walk in there with me, sit at that table with my family, and it's all I ever wanted. So I want you to know, this means a lot to me."

She scooted closer to him. "It means a lot to me that you'd bring me today and include me not only in the tradition but in your family. I know this is still new between us."

He kissed that thought right off her lips. "Not new. We're continuing what we started."

"I feel that way, too."

They planned to go to her place after breakfast to clean it up and pack the rest of her things. Another step closer to forever.

He kissed her. "Let's go stuff ourselves with pancakes with my family, who are all happy for us."

"Your dad has been really warm and welcoming. Every time he walks in on us together in the kitchen or living room, he gets this smile on his face."

"He misses my mom. He's happy that all his sons are with someone they love."

"I still can't believe this is real."

He kissed her softly. "You and me, we're an algebra problem. You're an x and I'm a y. We started with attraction and lust that turned into love. A variable we didn't expect tore us apart, but now we've subtracted the bad stuff, found more of the good, multiplied our happiness and the love we share, and now we know for sure that $x+y=$forever. Right?"

She grinned and chuckled. "That's the perfect equation for us."

"I'm glad you agree, because soon it will come with a ring and babies, I hope."

"I look forward to our love multiplying and there's a sweet little Max running around the ranch. Though I'm not sure how your nieces will feel about that."

He chuckled. "They'll love him. Or her. And it will be amazing to see them all riding horses one day and squealing over the calves like me and my brothers used to do."

"It's a sweet picture of a happy, simple life," she agreed, making his heart soar because they'd talked about this a lot in the past.

He'd thought they'd have it by now.

And he still couldn't wait for it to be a reality.

"Let's head in before they send a search party for us." Max slid out of the truck and held his hand out to Kenna so she could slide over and exit. He held her hand all the way to the diner and smiled at his family, sitting across the dining room at their usual table.

"So it's official. You two are back together." Hillary came out of nowhere and got in Kenna's face.

"Back off," Max ordered.

Hillary kept her gaze locked on Kenna. "You think you're so smart and put together and have everything you ever wanted."

"I do." Kenna stood her ground. "My life may not be perfect, no one's is, but I finally got a second chance to be with Max and I'm taking it. After what you did, I'd think you'd stay away from us. I don't know why you care about what Max and I do."

"He was supposed to be mine. But you got in the way."

"No. I was right where he wanted me. With him. You saw how much we loved each other and you wanted that for yourself. I get it. It's an amazing feeling to know someone cares about you that much. But you can't take it. You can't trick your way into it."

Hillary glanced at him. "Why her?"

That was easy to answer. "She's the best person I know. Better than anyone I've ever met. A true friend. She wants only the best for me. She loves with her whole heart. You betrayed me, her, yourself, and look what happened. You ended up with nothing."

Max put his arm over Kenna's shoulders and dismissed Hillary by giving her his back. He led Kenna to their table, every eye in the restaurant on them, including his family's.

Hillary stormed out of the diner, the bell over the door clanging wildly with her exit.

Kenna leaned into Max. "I think I've earned some chocolate chip pancakes after all that."

"Definitely." Max held a chair out for her at the table.

"Are you all right?" Shelby asked, all of Max's family looked concerned.

"I'm fine. She's just . . ." Kenna waved it away. "Not worth even talking about." She sucked in a breath. "I'm going to let it go. Thank you for inviting me to your special Pancake Tuesday."

"We're happy you came," Cyn chimed in.

Shelby tapped her shoulder. "Cyn and I get together every Wednesday for lunch, since we work close to each other. You know, a girls' thing. But you can't leave campus and join us, so we thought we'd start girl's night out every Thursday. We don't always have to go out, we can get together at one of our houses. We'll kick the guys out, of course."

Chase grumbled out a "Hey."

Kenna laughed. "Sounds fun."

Hunt looked at his brothers. "We'll get together, drink a beer, and watch a game or something."

"You'll have the kids," Cyn reminded him.

"They like beer, too," Hunt teased, and got an elbow to the gut from Cyn.

The waitress arrived and took everyone's order. Max kept his hand on her thigh beneath the table and kept glancing at her, sharing a smile and his happiness that she was here with him, even as he, his brothers, and their dad talked about the ranch and their hopes for their hockey team.

Max ended up with Eliza and Lana in his lap multiple times. The little girls adored him. He didn't mind being wrapped around their little fingers. Or that Eliza ate all his bacon.

Kenna kissed his cheek. "You're a really good uncle."

"I love being with them." He leaned over and whispered in her ear. "I love that you're here with me. This is how it's supposed to be."

She pressed her forehead to his and didn't have to say a thing because he saw reflected in her eyes everything in his heart.

"What are your plans?" Chase asked Max.

"Marriage and babies," he responded, still looking at her. He turned to his brother and the whole family. "Just like you guys."

Chase grinned. "Good to know. I'm sure I speak for everyone when I say it's been a long time coming and we're all happy for you."

Max nodded. "Thanks. We're not wasting any more time."

"You shouldn't," Chase agreed. "But I was asking about your plans for today." Chase's grin and everyone else's made Max chuckle.

"Oh. Yeah. We won't be back to the ranch until later. Kenna's place is still kind of a mess after the break-in. Plus she's moving in with me, so we're going there to box up her stuff and turn in her keys to the landlord."

"Are you excited about moving to the ranch?" Shelby asked.

Kenna didn't hesitate when she answered, "Yes. I've always loved it out there."

"And you're okay with the commute to work?" Cyn asked. "You start much earlier than I do at my shop, so the extra-long drive means you'll be up early."

"Max is up early anyway, so it won't be so bad. Plus I won't be going home to an empty apartment. My place was only supposed to be temporary because Max and I had planned to get married. I've been wanting to move into something bigger for a long time—I just never did."

"I'm so happy everything is finally working out for you two." Shelby said the words, but everyone around the table nodded and smiled their agreement.

It was so nice to know that everyone wanted her and Max to be happy.

Well, Hillary didn't want them to be happy. But Kenna wasn't going to think about her anymore.

Unhappy people sucked the life and joy out of others and Kenna wasn't going to fall into that trap. She had better things to think about, like moving in with Max and waking up in his arms every morning.

Kenna settled into the cozy diner atmosphere, the family chitchat, and her chocolate chip pancakes and let everything else go. It took at least five minutes to say their goodbyes. Mostly due to Eliza smooching Max's whole face a dozen times because she wanted to and it made her uncle laugh, so she kept on doing it.

By the time Kenna and Max made it to her apartment, she was filled with a sense of peace she hadn't felt in a long time.

"Looks like you lost some of your worry," Max pointed out as they parked outside her apartment.

"I wasn't sure this morning if I'd ever let it go, but being with you and your family, them accepting me the way they did—it makes me feel one step closer to the future we planned."

Max leaned over and gave her a long soft kiss. "Good. Next step, we take care of your apartment. Are you sure you're ready to go back in there again? If not, I'll do it myself and you can wait out here."

She shook her head. "I need to face this to close the chapter on the past. I can do it. I feel like I need to literally clean up the mess so I can move forward."

"I get that. But if at any time you feel overwhelmed or like you simply can't finish, take a break, walk out, and I'll do the rest."

Max was always so supportive and caring about her feelings. "I'm fine. Let's just get it done."

He slipped out of the truck on his side and grabbed the flattened boxes they'd brought out of the truck bed.

She met Max in front of the truck. Their hands went to each other's just like they always used to and their fingers linked. She squeezed to let him know how much she liked being connected to him. He smiled at her and gave her a little tug to go ahead of him at the door so she could unlock it.

She hesitated for a moment.

"What's wrong?"

"I just got a creepy feeling that I'll find something bad inside again."

Max frowned. "Another thing I can hang on your brother. You shouldn't be afraid to walk into your place."

"It used to just make me feel lonely."

Max slipped his hand up under her hair to her neck. He stared deep into her eyes. "I know how you feel." He sighed and his gaze dropped away, then came back to meet hers. "I tried to fight that feeling in all the wrong ways. I drank too much. I spent time chasing a feeling that, in the moment, chased away the lonely, but it always came back. Faster and faster, until it never went away, because I hadn't found what I needed."

"What was that?" she asked on a whisper.

"What I lost. A real connection. Trust. Love." Max dropped the boxes and pulled her into a hug. "You." Max pressed his cheek to her hair. "I missed you, even when I didn't want to think about you. I loved you, because love like that doesn't go away. I hated that we ended the way we did, and I wanted you so damn bad anyway."

She tilted her head back. "Do you trust me again?"

"Yes. Because I know we won't walk away again without fighting for us."

"I felt so stupid for believing her lies. Every time I see her, *I* want to hit *her*."

"She's her own worst enemy. She sabotages herself while she's going after other people. One of these days, she's going to do something that really gets her into trouble. And when that happens, we'll still be together and happy and she'll still be alone and stuck in the same self-destructive behavior."

"I know. It's just . . ."

"She makes you mad."

"Furious."

Max softly brushed his thumb over her cheek. "Me, too."

She turned and kissed the pad of his thumb, then opened her apartment door and went completely still. She saw the attack happen all over again.

"Kenna, breathe."

She sucked in a breath.

Max bent and put his face right in front of hers. "You are safe. No one is going to hurt you."

She knew that in her head, but the echo of that night still rang through her body and mind with a wave of fear and the need to flee.

She fought it, because she didn't want it to control her. "I'm okay."

"We're here to get your stuff." The reminder helped her brain focus on the task, not the past. Max nodded. "It won't take us long to clean up."

They'd done a lot of the work the day after it happened, when she came back to look for whatever Kyle had left with Agent Gunn and Hunt.

He'd tried to keep his distance, but that hadn't worked.

The last few days, just hanging out on the ranch with him, had been peaceful and wonderful. A glimpse into their future life together.

But to fully be there with Max and live that life, she needed to finish this, even though it brought up all the bad memories.

She walked into the apartment, but stopped short.

"Kenna? What's wrong?"

She picked up the little cat figurine from the dining room table. "Kyle left this. It's the cat he brought the night he left and Marcus died. He'd put it on the shelf with the others."

"The one we came here looking for the next day?"

"Yes." The one she couldn't find, but now sat, prominent as could be, in the middle of the table.

"He came back and left it for you. When? Before or after he 'died'?"

She appreciated that he still entertained her notion that Kyle could still be alive. "I guess we'll never know." Even if in her heart she wanted to believe this proved he was still out there somewhere.

If nothing else, it was a message that he'd been thinking about her and loved her even when things looked so bleak.

Max hugged her.

She held on to him, letting his strength and love seep into her and dull the grief again.

Max cupped her face and made her look up at him. "He will always be with you."

"And so will you." She believed that with her whole heart again.

"You and me, sweetheart. Always. Forever." He kissed her softly. "I'll start in the living room. You take the kitchen." He looked down into the bedroom at her bed. "I don't think your bedding survived."

The pretty white bedspread with embroidered leaves in several shades of green hadn't just been torn from the bed and dumped on the floor, but a lamp had been smashed on it, then the person walked over the shards, which had torn the fabric.

"That was my favorite thing in the room."

"Maybe it can be repaired." Max didn't sound convincing in the least.

"Not without it being completely noticeable." She sighed over the destruction of her things. "And every time I look at it, it will remind me of this. I don't want that."

"Me either. I'll go get the rest of the boxes out of the truck. We'll pack up what you want to bring to the ranch. Anything that's trash, we'll throw out here in one of those big bins in the parking lot. Anything you want to donate, we can drop at the thrift store later."

She loved that Max knew how to get her back on track by laying out a plan. "Sounds good. I'll work on folding all the clothes that got dumped in the bedroom and packing those up. Most of my kitchen stuff can probably be donated."

"You can bring it to the ranch if you want to keep it. We'll make room."

"Most of it will probably be duplicates of what you already have there."

"But these are yours, and if you want them, keep them."

"Max, I appreciate that you're being sweet, but we also need to be practical."

"I just want you to be happy there and not feel like you're a guest in someone else's house."

"I don't feel that way," she said quickly to reassure him.

"Are you sure? Because you asked if it was okay last night if you took a soda from the fridge, then you asked if you could use the washer, even though it was empty."

"I was being polite."

Max shrugged. "If it was just you and me, I don't think you would have asked. Which makes me think you're being polite because you feel like the house is my father's and we're just living there."

"It does feel that way," she admitted, even though she was now sleeping in Max's room. The rest of the house felt like someone else's. She felt weird about using things without asking, or even just plopping down on the sofa and watching something on TV. As soon as Mr. Wilde walked in, she always felt like she should hand him the remote.

Max put his hands on his hips. "It is your place now, too. I want you to feel that way, and so does my dad. In fact, we talked about the house yesterday morning when you slept in. He thinks you and I should make some updates and changes, since it's going to be our house one day."

"What about Chase and Hunt? It's their place, too."

"The ranch is split between all of us, but they already have their own places, so everyone agrees the big house will go to me."

"Okay." That relieved her concerns that there'd be some sort of dispute down the road.

"I have some ideas for the house. But I'd like your help to make the place ours."

She looked up at his earnest face. "I've been saving up to buy my own place. I don't have much, but I'd like to contribute to whatever changes we make."

"Okay, but the ranch is doing better than ever. I've got money to do it if you want to save yours for something else. Or just as an emergency fund."

"I may have to use some of it to pay for repairs here." She'd already received an email about the repairs to the front door. There was a small hole in the wall where she'd been slammed into it and broken the picture frame. The floors were scuffed and scarred from the broken glass and figurines. Who knew what else she'd find as she cleaned up the rest of her place today.

"Focus on the future. Name the one thing you wish you could change at the house to make it feel more like yours."

She scrunched her lips. "Don't you think your father will be upset if we change what your mom loved? He sees her in that place. I don't want to take that away from him. He'll resent me if I do."

Max closed the distance between them. "And you'd live with all the stuff that's hers and makes you feel like you're a guest to spare his feelings?"

"Yes." Because she wouldn't want someone coming in and erasing the things that reminded her of Max if she lost him.

"My mom lives inside all of us. We don't need the paint on the walls to remember her or all the good times we had in that house. It's not the things, sweetheart, it's the feelings and memories we have of her that matter." He kissed her softly. "And Dad wants to update the house."

"Really?"

"Yes." Max tapped her chin with his finger. "Come on, sweetheart, there's got to be something you hate about the house."

She gave in and spilled the beans on what she didn't like. "It's not just the paint color in the kitchen. The whole thing needs a remodel. I think we should paint the upper cabinets white and redo the dark wood stain on the lowers with something lighter. New countertops. Something that looks like marble, but is more durable."

Max grinned. "Sounds good to me. What about the floor?"

"What do you think?" She wanted to give him a chance to voice his opinion and choices.

"The linoleum has to go. Maybe hardwood. Or a tile that will set off the wood cabinets."

She squished her lips. "I guess it will depend on our budget."

"We don't want to skimp on the kitchen. There are hardwood floors everywhere else, so maybe we'll pick tile. But I want large tiles. Less grout lines."

She smiled. "Okay."

He smiled back. "Okay."

"Should we run this all past your dad?"

"We will, but I'm telling you, he'll love it, because he wants us to make that place ours."

She let that settle. "Then we better get me packed up and moved in."

Max squeezed her hand. "Feel better?"

"Yes."

"Good. Because I have some plans for the upstairs rooms. It involves us picking a crib."

A burst of excitement shot through her. "Will we need it right away? Or is it for later?" She'd wanted to be a mother for a long time. She loved kids. That's why she went into teaching.

"Soon. Ish. We still have a few things to do before we put a baby in the crib, but I don't want to wait too long. If you're on board with that."

"I am. I just need to have my IUD removed, and maybe give my body a couple months to get back on cycle."

"I'll leave that to you to decide when you're ready."

"Now," she said without question. "You're a great uncle. You'll be an amazing father. We planned on starting early and it feels like we're behind."

"Okay. If that's what you want, I'm in."

She put her hand on his forearm. "But I want us settled first."

He slipped his hand up her neck to the back of her head underneath her hair. "Absolutely. We'll get us and the house in order." He kissed her again, making her think of the bed just steps away, even if the mattress was off-kilter on the frame, the sheets and blankets a tangled and torn mess.

When Max leaned back, ready to get to work, she

distracted him with another long, deep kiss. They lost themselves in each other's arms for a moment that seemed to stretch with every kiss and caress. She leaned into Max, rocking her hips against the thick erection pressed to her belly.

But it was Max who pulled back and took a steadying breath. "We need to get this work done so we can go home."

"Are you sure?" She rubbed her front against his, tempting him.

His eyes heated with desire. He kissed his way down her neck. "Bed's a wreck." He kissed the swell of her breast in the V of her shirt. "There's glass everywhere."

"You'll have to pick another spot."

He nipped at her hard nipple over her shirt and bra. "I like this spot." He slipped his hand down her belly and over her mound, rubbing the heel of his hand against her clit over her leggings and damp panties. "But this spot is my favorite."

"All of you is my favorite," she said on a breathless whisper.

He stilled and looked into her eyes, then he kissed her like he hadn't done so just a second ago, like it had been forever since he touched her.

And right there in the little hallway between the living area and her bedroom, right next to the linen closet, he stripped her clothes away, tore off his, sank to his knees in front of her and nuzzled his nose against her belly. His hands slid up her thighs, over her hips, around to her ass and squeezed as he buried his face in the V of her thighs and loved her with his mouth and that wicked tongue, until her knees buckled and she was lying on the floor, her butt stuck to a magazine, a random spoon poking at her side, and Max's warm body covering hers. His chest pressed to her breasts and he kissed her again and thrust into her. He stopped for a moment to savor the feel of their two bodies joined, then he moved, pulling out, then diving in deep again. She spread her thighs wider, planted her hands on his very fine ass, and pulled him to her again and again.

Max groaned. Their lovemaking became a steady push and pull, until Max broke the kiss, hooked his arm beneath her knee, pulled her leg up and to the side so he had a better angle to rock his hips into hers, creating that sweet friction she needed on her swollen clit. The pleasure coursing through her amplified and exploded, her inner muscles locking onto his long, thick cock, taking him over the edge with her.

He nearly collapsed on top of her, but caught himself on his forearms, keeping his weight off her, so he didn't hurt her ribs, his face in her neck as her legs slid out, pushing several towels that had been tossed out of the linen closet beside them further into the living room. Spent, she held Max in a soft embrace and caressed his back with soft sweeps of her fingers over his smooth skin.

"What were we supposed to be doing?" Max asked, kissing her shoulder.

She responded with the only thing that mattered in life. "Loving each other."

Max rose so he could look down at her, brushed a strand of hair from her cheek, then leaned down and pressed his lips to hers in a kiss so soft and sweet it brought tears to her eyes because of all the love he packed into it. "You are the one who matters most to me."

"I love you so much, Max." It felt right to make one last good memory in the apartment they'd spent so much time in together before their breakup, and for this to be the way they put the past behind them and moved to the ranch that would be their forever home together.

Chapter Thirty-Four

KENNA SAT on the front porch in a rocking chair, resting her sore abdomen and ribs. Max had moved a new dresser into their room yesterday for her. She'd spent the last hour putting away the last of her clothes. To make the room feel more like theirs, she put a few of her favorite things out, like the photos of her and Max and a couple of her family, including one of her and Kyle. She was officially moved in, though most of the boxes from her apartment were still packed and in a spare room. She'd figure out where she wanted to put her other things later, or if she needed them at all.

Right now, she waited for Max to finish work and head up to the house for dinner, excited to spend some alone time with him again later tonight.

Shelby pulled into the drive, just as Chase and Max walked out of the barn. Shelby climbed out, waved to her, then helped Eliza out of the back seat. The little one spotted her daddy and made a run for him. "She wants to see Cupcake. I'm going up to talk to Kenna," Shelby shouted.

Chase scooped up his little one, hugged her, then handed her off to Max, who immediately kissed her on the forehead, settled her on his hip, and took her into the barn to see her favorite pony.

Shelby joined her on the porch and took the rocking chair next to her and sighed with contentment. "It's so good to see you smiling."

Kenna couldn't help herself. "I love that man so much. And I love seeing him with Chase, and his niece. Sitting here, watching them together, seeing you pull up to bring Eliza to see her daddy at work and the horses, it just feels so like family. I feel like I'm right where I'm supposed to be."

"And soon, I hope, we'll be more than friends. You'll be my sister-in-law. Cyn, of course, is already. She married her Wilde man. I got mine. You'll get yours locked up soon. I've never seen Max so happy. When I first met him, he was always a little hungover and kind of sad. He never looked really happy. Or even content. I didn't know him when you were together back in the day. But now I see that without you in his life, he was missing something. You."

Kenna understood that all too well.

Max had expressed how he'd gotten through each day, but he hadn't really been happy. Shelby and his family all saw it.

Kyle had seen the same in her. "I felt the same way. I tried to focus on work and helping my kids. But it wasn't enough to ease the loneliness. I thought about him all the time. I blamed myself for losing him. I thought up ridiculous ways I'd try to bump into him, so that maybe he'd talk to me, but I never followed through."

Shelby grinned. "But now you're together. You're all moved in. You're both looking toward the future. You two should celebrate that all you can. After what Chase and I went through, we don't take a second for granted."

Never again, she silently vowed. "Max and me, we've always been our best when we're with each other."

"That's how Chase and I feel, too. As Cyn would say, 'It's better to be with a Wilde man than without him.'"

They shared a grin and a nod of agreement.

"Damn straight," Kenna added.

Shelby shrugged one shoulder. "And for what it's worth, Max was stupid to let you go. You're awesome."

Kenna laughed under her breath. "Thank you. I think you're pretty cool, too."

Shelby's grin faded, and she stared off toward the barn where Chase had gone. "I was on my own for a long time. Cyn and you, you both lost close siblings. You, me, Cyn, we're sisters now. We're family. I want you to know, I'm here for you, no matter what." Shelby's eyes teared up.

"I feel exactly the same way." Kenna's heart ached for Cyn, who had lost her sister such a short time ago.

Shelby frowned. "I'm sorry about your brother."

Her heart pinched and tears gathered in her eyes, though she fought them back. "Thank you. I'm sorry about Cyn's sister. She and Hunt, they're going to give Lana the most amazing life."

Shelby smiled at Eliza running toward the house,

Chase and Max walking behind her. "We, the Wildes, are going to give all the little ones in our lives the best we can, together as a family."

Kenna's heart overflowed with love and that very heartfelt sentiment from Shelby. She appreciated so much that Shelby included her like she was already a Wilde. Already a member of the family.

She couldn't wait for it to be official.

She hoped it would be soon. Though she and Max had simply slid into the fact that it was coming, they hadn't made any plans. He hadn't asked yet.

But she had no doubt that day was coming soon.

MAX LOVED SEEING Kenna and Shelby rocking on the porch talking like two old friends. Eliza ran up the steps and held her arms out to Kenna, who immediately picked her up and set her on her lap and hugged her close.

Max and Chase stayed at the bottom of the steps looking up at their girls.

"I just got an invitation from Aria to come to the bar. Lyric, Melody, and Jax are all working tonight. Everyone missed you at Hunt's wedding. They can't wait to see you again. Feel like going out with me?" Max hoped she said yes and they could have some fun. He wanted to see her set aside everything they'd been through lately and enjoy herself.

Kenna didn't hesitate. "Yes. Absolutely." She turned to Shelby. "Can you and Chase come with us?"

"Not tonight," Chase said, "I heard this little one

didn't nap today, so she's going down to bed early, which means I have plans with her mama for some quiet time alone."

Shelby stood and picked up Eliza from Kenna's lap. "Now that sounds like heaven to me. Let's go, Wilde man."

Kenna stood and hugged Shelby and Eliza all at once. "I hope I see you soon."

"You will," Shelby assured her.

Max joined Kenna on the porch as they waved goodbye to Chase, Shelby and Eliza, then he turned to Kenna. "You sure about going out?"

Her smile said yes. "Absolutely. It'll be fun. I'm looking forward to seeing your family. And spending time with you is my favorite thing."

He kissed her for being so sweet. "I'll take a quick shower and change."

"I'm sure I can find something cute to wear."

He spun her around and gave her very fine ass a soft pat to get her moving into the house. "Any chance I'll get to see those sexy legs in a dress?"

She glanced over her shoulder and gave him a sexy smile and sultry stare. "You asked for it."

He didn't know exactly what she meant by that until nearly twenty minutes later when he found her downstairs ready to go wearing a little black dress with a deep plunging neckline, nipped in waist, a flirty, flaring skirt that ended mid-thigh, and a pair of fuck-me strappy heels, her toenails painted her favorite fuchsia pink.

But the smile, so confident and sexy and filled with humor and happiness filled his heart with joy. She knew she had his full attention, and that instead of taking her out, he seriously wanted to take her upstairs to bed.

She could still make him want to drop to his knees and beg.

And he let her see it in the sweeping look he gave her because he wanted her to know it.

Because he would beg, but he didn't have to because she wanted him just as much.

And if anyone thought they could take this from them, they had another think coming.

He held his hand out to her and smiled when she immediately took his. The brush of her skin against his electrified him. The grip of her fingers made him feel like she never wanted to let him go.

Tonight, he felt like they'd finally embraced and stepped into the couple they'd be from now on.

He couldn't wait to get to the bar and spend another amazing evening with the woman he loved by his side.

Chapter Thirty-Five

Max HELD the door open to the Dark Horse Dive Bar for Kenna as they entered the packed establishment. He took Kenna's hand and led her to the only table in the room marked RESERVED by Aria after she'd invited them to come and enjoy a blast from their past.

Kenna's cheeks flushed with excitement. "It's been a long time since I've been here." She had to raise her voice over the music to be heard.

He bet she hadn't stepped foot in this place since before they broke up.

"Are you sure this table is for us?"

He pulled out her stool. "Yes. Aria is expecting us."

"How are your cousins?"

"Good. Though I suspect Aria and her boyfriend are having some issues. And Lyric got involved a little while back with some guy in a biker club, who found Cyn's kidnapped niece, and apparently he's still hanging around. Jax doesn't like the look of the guy." Max knew better but he kept that to himself.

"Are they together?"

"Nope. But the guy has a thing for her, even though they hardly ever speak to each other. Apparently he just comes in, orders a drink, and hangs out like everyone else."

"I find it interesting that they're so aware of each other, but they haven't done anything about it. It's sweet he likes her so much but is afraid to approach her."

Max hadn't thought about it like that. "You think he's too shy to ask her out?"

Kenna shrugged. "I mean, I don't know anything about the guy, except he's part of a biker club. That kind of makes me imagine him as a badass, but that doesn't mean he's not shy with women. Or maybe he thinks he's not good enough for her. Who knows? But obviously she and Jax think he likes her."

"I guess so. It'll be interesting to see what happens there." Max knew that to be true.

He spotted his other cousin coming their way. "And then there's Melody, who should be arrested for indecent exposure," he said loud enough for her to hear him as she approached.

"Good thing you came instead of Hunt," she teased and went right in for a hug with Kenna.

"I love that color on you." Kenna always found something nice to say.

The purple dress was a good color on Melody with her dark hair and blue eyes. It outlined every curve. No wonder Jax kept a close eye on Melody in the bar. Every dude in the room had their eyes on her. A few looked like they didn't want to keep their hands to themselves.

"Thank you," Melody said, smiling at Kenna. They'd always gotten along. "I'm happy you two found your way back to each other. I only got the CliffsNotes on how that happened. I want all the deets soon." She elbowed Max in the gut. "I've missed seeing you in here all the time."

"We've got Christmas around the corner. We'll be together for all the family stuff."

Melody smiled. "It's nice there's a lot more of us now. I'd like to see Jax find a woman he can't live without."

"Don't you want a guy . . . or a girl," Kenna tacked on, not wanting to make assumptions, always open to who and what anyone wanted to be, "you can't live without?"

"I'll probably be the last to fall."

Kenna squeezed Melody's hand. "When love comes, it won't let go."

Melody looked out at the crowd. "That's how it should be. You spend enough time in a place like this, you see love come, go, breaking hearts and making them soar."

Max bet she'd seen it all. "You're still young. You've got time."

"No one has time to waste. Not when your number could be up at any time. You two know that firsthand." Melody eyed them. "I want to live each day like it could be my last." Melody scanned the crowd. "But right now, the bar is hopping and I need to make some cash, so what can I get you two? On the house, of course. You're family."

Max didn't even try to argue about paying for the

drinks. He'd been down that road too many times and lost. But he would leave his sweet cousin a big tip.

"What is Aria's drink tonight?" Kenna asked.

Aria picked a drink special every night. Usually something unexpected.

"A peach Bellini. You'll love it. Tastes like spring and summer, even if it is the dead of winter."

"Perfect. I'll have that."

Max gave his usual order, though he bet Melody already knew it. "Beer. Whatever local brew you've got on tap."

Melody closed in and kissed his cheek. "This is the first time you've come in, in a long time, that you actually look happy. It makes me happy to see you smile again."

He hugged her close. "Thanks, cuz." He let her go and caught the content and reassuring look in Kenna's eyes.

"Back in a minute."

Kenna leaned into him. "That was really nice of her."

"They never let me pay."

"No. I mean how concerned she was about you."

"Part of why I changed my ways was because I didn't like seeing my family worried about me. I mean, I knew I wasn't getting anywhere in my life doing what I was doing, but I also made it a habit that I needed to break."

"So you did, and you got to spend more time with them."

"Yeah." He appreciated her continued understanding.

Melody arrived with their drinks and a platter of food.

She set it all on the table. "Lyric is slammed with orders, but she wanted you two to have something to eat."

"This looks amazing." Kenna smiled because they were all their favorites, as Lyric well remembered.

The platter had four barbecue pulled pork sliders with fresh slaw on top, cheddar bacon potato skins, and spicy chicken and cheese flautas with mango chili dipping sauce. No one cooked better than Lyric in the whole state. People came here for the food, just as much as they did to drink, dance, and sing along with a live band on the weekends, though tonight they had a recorded playlist.

Melody bumped her shoulder into his. "Enjoy. Also, there's someone you two know in the second to last booth on the left, behind, and to the side of you. I expect the real show to begin in a few minutes."

"What show?" Max knew nothing about something going on tonight.

The second he spotted Hillary, he cringed. He should have guessed she'd be here tonight. She haunted the bar like ghosts did cemeteries. But he didn't know what Melody meant about a show.

"You'll see." Melody took her tray and went to the next table to take the foursome's drink order.

"What is she talking about?" Kenna asked, taking a big bite of one of the potato skins, one of her favorite treats.

"Uh, I'm not sure." He took a sip of his beer, hoping it settled his nervous stomach and that Kenna didn't see Hillary. He didn't want anything to spoil tonight.

Aria popped up next to him. "Hi, cuz. Kenna," Aria said, giving Kenna a big smile. "I'm so glad you guys came tonight." She slid an arm across Kenna's shoulder and touched the side of her head to Kenna's, avoiding the stitches. "Max told me about what happened to break you two up. I'm really sorry that happened to you. No one should interfere in someone else's relationship." Aria cocked her head toward him. "And besides you, Crazy Lady, who would want Max that bad?"

Kenna laughed, along with him and Aria.

"But seriously. Not cool. Which is why I set up a little gift for both of you, because I believe in love. What you two share is rare and sacred and should be respected. Enjoy the show."

"Aria," Max warned, unsure what she'd done, and afraid of whatever it was jeopardizing what he and Kenna had finally gotten back.

Aria put her hand on his forearm. "Trust me. I only want your happiness. And while you wanted to have fun with Kenna tonight, I wanted that bitch to get what she deserves for fucking with my family. And *me*."

Another alarm went off. "What are you talking about?" Max didn't like the sadness in Aria's eyes. He wanted to hurt whoever hurt her.

She notched her chin up to the table Melody had indicated earlier. "Watch."

Kenna leaned in. "What's going on?"

"You'll see," Aria said and pointed across the room. "Recognize her."

"Hillary." Kenna gasped out the name. "What is she doing here?"

Max sighed. "She's here all the time. She works down the road as a cashier at a gas station minimart."

Aria added, "Yeah, after what she did to you two, her life didn't turn out so hot. She's got a job she hates that barely pays the bills. She lives with two roommates who hate her, because she's inconsiderate and steals their stuff and brings home men at all hours of the night, keeping them up." Aria continued to fill in Hillary's sad life. "She picks up guys who have good jobs, hoping they'll fall for her and take her away from her shit apartment and shower her with love and gifts and give her a better life.

"Some guys fall for it," Aria went on. "But it never lasts more than a couple weeks before she's on the prowl again." Aria glared at Hillary like she had her own vendetta against her.

Kenna frowned. "Sounds like she's stuck in a loop and getting nowhere in life."

"She only cares about herself. Once the people she pulls into her orbit figure that out, they leave, because who wants to be around someone like her?" Aria continued to stare down the woman across the room. "The guy she's with right now . . . She met him last night. He's new to this area. Arrived a few weeks ago to help out his aging grandparents on the little ranch they own nearby. What he doesn't know is that she's been fucking someone else for the past couple weeks."

Max's gut went tight and an alarm went off in his head. "Aria, who are you waiting for to show up?"

She pointed to the man making his way toward Hillary's table.

"Oh shit." Max put his hand over Aria's on the table.

Kenna leaned in. "Who is that?"

"The man who doesn't know that my overprotective brother added extra security cameras around this place because he's worried about his sisters, Lyric in particular, and he got caught cheating. On me." Aria never took her eyes off her boyfriend, now an ex, even if he didn't know it yet, as he approached Hillary's table.

"Aria, I'm so sorry." Kenna put her hand on Aria's forearm right next to Max's hand.

"I'm sure you know exactly how I feel about that woman. And him. He made a commitment. She went after him. He didn't have to cheat, but he did. They're both at fault. But he doesn't know I know about them. He thinks I'm too busy at the bar to notice. He's wrong. On so many levels."

Jax came out of the crowd and approached their table. "Uh, hey, Max and Kenna. Happy to see you back together, but, um, Aria, what's going on over there?"

"That stupid idiot thinks he can cheat on me, in my bar, in front of me and my whole family and get away with it."

"Hell no, he can't." Jax took a menacing step toward Dan.

Aria grabbed her brother's arm. "Let it play out."

And it did. Loudly, because Hillary didn't do anything without making a scene.

"I can see anyone I want." Hillary stood and pointed her finger into Aria's ex's chest. "I'm not the one cheating. You are. You said you'd leave her, but you didn't."

"It's complicated." Dan used that banal statement like it meant something to Hillary or Aria.

"It's really not. You got tired of fucking her and wanted something exciting, so you fucked me on the side."

Max wondered if they realized they were shouting over the music and everyone could hear them. He guessed not, because they kept talking. And making things worse.

"I told you once I had the money, we'd leave Wyoming and go someplace new together." Aria's ex dug his grave deeper.

Jax swore. "If he means the money you've been saving to get married and buy a house together, I'll kill him."

Aria's eyes were glassy with tears, but she didn't let them fall. She stood strong and defiant and courageous in the face of this betrayal.

"It's been weeks and you've done nothing about it. I'm tired of waiting. I found someone new who wants what I want."

The guy who she'd been sitting with stood and held his hands up. "I want nothing to do with this. Or you." He tossed some bills on the table to cover the tab, walked past all the eyes on them, and headed for the door.

"Next time he comes in, his order is on the house," Aria told Jax, who nodded.

"Now look what you've done." Hillary tightened her hands into fists, then her gaze shot over to all of them witnessing her drama. "You've got to be fucking kidding me."

Dan turned and followed Hillary's glaring gaze right to Aria.

Hillary only had eyes for Max and if she could kill him with a look, she would have.

Dan looked like a deer in the headlights but rushed over anyway. "Aria. It's not what it seems."

"It's *not* complicated," she said, using his words against him. "Seems to me I'm free of you."

"You don't mean that." He reached for her.

She stepped back so he couldn't touch her. "Let me make it clear. I never want to see you again. Get out of my bar. Do not ever step foot in here again, or I will have you arrested for trespassing."

Dan turned to Aria's sister, who had joined their circle, and took her hand. "Lyric, help me out here."

Out of nowhere the biker guy intervened and hooked his hand around the ex's upper arm and pulled him away from Lyric and Aria. "Don't ever touch her."

Lyric and Melody stepped back and out of the way.

"Lyric," the ex pleaded, knowing Lyric had a good heart and sweet disposition, and helping others was in her DNA. Just like Kenna.

The biker dude shoved the guy toward the exit. "You don't speak to or look at her ever again."

"You know I love her! She'll listen to you!" Dan tried to get Lyric on his side, hoping the close relationship Lyric had with her sister would help.

All it got him was a smack to the back of the head by the biker guy and shoved out the door.

The patrons in the bar clapped, happy to see the cheater ousted, because everyone loved Aria and didn't want to see her hurt. Plus, it was a great show and a good story for all of them to tell to all their friends and coworkers the next day.

Hillary didn't read the crowd well and tried to approach them.

Aria stood between Max and Hillary. "Don't even think about it. He had nothing to do with this. Like his breakup with Kenna, you instigated all of it. You set this all up because *again* you wanted someone who was already with someone else."

Hillary looked straight at Kenna. "I don't know who is more pathetic. You fell for a lie." She turned back to Aria. "Your man didn't even blink when I came on to him. He was all over me in an instant."

"You're right. He's as pathetic as you. And as alone now as you are and will always be." Aria didn't back down when Hillary took a menacing step toward her. "If you think you can take me, bring it. But I warn you, I fight dirty, in case you didn't notice by the way I set you up tonight."

"You're such a bitch." Hillary turned her sharp gaze back to Kenna. "You're pathetic."

Max stayed close to Kenna and his cousin ready to step in if Hillary took things too far.

Kenna held her own. "If being pathetic means I'm happy and with the man I love, who never wanted you, then I'm okay with that."

"Bitch."

"Jealousy doesn't look good on you. Everyone can see it." Kenna stared past Hillary at all the gazes on them.

Hillary glanced over her shoulder and seemed to catch herself.

Kenna gave Hillary a pitying frown. "At one time, I thought you were a friend. Then I learned you only saw me as a rival and you betrayed me *and* Max. Now I don't care what you think of me or that Max and I are together. We want nothing to do with you. You're nothing to us now."

"Fuck you." Hillary raged.

"Get out." Aria took a step toward Hillary, backing her up a step with the rage rolling off her.

This time the crowd really got into it when Jax started off the chant, "Get out. Get out. Get out."

Hillary huffed out an angry snarl, spun on her toes, and stomped her way to the door and right out it.

"Good riddance." Kenna held her drink up in a toast, then downed half of it.

Aria turned to Kenna. "I'm sorry. I should have warned you."

"It's okay. She's the one who made a fool out of herself. She's just bitter and angry that her life turned out the way it did. I feel sorry for her, going after guys the way she does, in some desperate attempt to make them love her."

"It didn't work with Max. Dan fell for it and went back for seconds and thirds and so on." Beneath the bitter words rang Aria's hurt and pain.

"His loss," Max said. "You're better off without him."

"He doesn't deserve a good woman like you," Kenna agreed.

Jax glared over at a nearby table where Lyric set a beer in front of the biker guy and walked back to the kitchen. "I don't know what is going on with those two, but I appreciate him looking out for my sister."

Max thought the exchange was odd, too. The guy didn't talk to Lyric. She didn't say anything to him. Every once in a while, the guy glanced at her through the pass-through window, then shifted his focus right back to his beer and the guy he was with.

Not once did he look at or acknowledge Max, and Max knew why and kept his mouth shut.

Jax smacked Max on the back. "You two have a good night. I'm taking Aria to the back office to cool down."

Aria kissed Max on the cheek. "She got what she deserved."

"But you didn't. I'm sorry about that asshole." He felt really bad about what happened and that his cousin got hurt the same way he and Kenna had been hurt by Hillary.

Some people were just toxic.

"I'm not sorry at all. I'd rather find out now that he's a liar and a cheater than waste any more of my time on him."

Kenna reached across the table and squeezed Aria's hand. "There's a good guy out there for you."

She shrugged like she wasn't so sure about that. "I'm happy you got yours back. Give Hillary a big f-you and be happy."

"We will," Kenna assured her.

"Enjoy the rest of your night. I'll send Melody back with another round."

Max watched his cousins walk away. "I hope that asshole knows what's good for him and stays away from her."

Kenna eyed him. "Did you know about all this?"

"No. I knew Aria and Dan's relationship seemed strained lately. I never suspected him of cheating. I never saw him with Hillary. If I had, I would have warned him away from her and told Aria to keep an eye on things." Max downed the last sip of his beer. "I guess she didn't need me to warn her."

"She knew about Hillary because of what happened to us."

"Yeah. And now it's done and in the past, and you and I are going to be nothing but happy. We won't let anyone come between us again."

Melody arrived with their drinks. "Sounds like you two should drink to that." She handed over the glasses and took off for the next table.

Max held his beer up.

Kenna tapped her glass to his. "To being happy."

"Amen."

They drank, dove into the food, and smiled at each other. It seemed a weight had been lifted.

"Is it always this busy in here?"

The place was about three-quarters full. Not bad at all for a Thursday night.

"You should see it when they have a live band."

"I'd love to." Kenna gave him another of those pretty smiles, letting him know this was the first of many dates they'd have here again. "If nothing else, it'll be fun to see what happens if that biker and Lyric ever stop circling each other and do something about the attraction between them."

Max eyed the guy. "You think she likes him?"

"I think she can't help herself, even if she is fighting it."

"He doesn't seem to be her type."

"Guys who are kind and protective, but seem like bad boys are every girl's type."

Max chuckled. "What makes you think he's a good guy?"

"The way he looks out for her and those she loves. He didn't have to get involved, but he did because he cares about her."

"I can appreciate that."

"Five bucks says he doesn't wait more than another week to make a move."

Max wasn't so sure, because the guy had secrets, but he went along for old times' sake. "This is probably a sucker bet. You see more than I do about him and her. But you're on."

Kenna laughed. "I think you still owe me five bucks from the last bet we made."

They'd been trading the same five buck bets forever. "I think you owe me."

She eyed him and smirked. "Do you even remember the last bet?"

"Was it about me getting you into bed?"

She chuckled. "Now that's a sure bet. But not it."

Max thought back to the good ol' days and the silly bets that always kept things fun between them. "Was it that you could eat the Mount Everest Sundae at Scoops in ten minutes or less?" He remembered that night. They'd both been stuffed on Peak's Pizza. She proposed they share the sundae. He dared her to eat it all, and they bet on it.

"Yes. And I totally won that bet."

"You had a headache for like three hours and a stomachache for two days."

"I couldn't eat ice cream for weeks." Her smile lit up the dim room. The sound of her amused voice lovelier than the country ballad starting on soft notes and a slow beat.

He held out his hand to her. "Dance with me."

She took it. "I thought you'd never ask."

He led her to the dance floor in front of the raised stage where bands played on the weekend. He took her in his arms, held her close, and just swayed with her while the other couples moved around them.

She smelled exactly how he remembered. Fresh and sweet, like sunshine in a wildflower meadow. She was the same perfect fit against his body.

He'd never wanted a woman the way he wanted her.

He'd never felt for anyone else anything close to what he felt for her.

In that moment, he felt like everything was perfect and couldn't get any better.

But he'd try, because he had plans for them.

Chapter Thirty-Six

KENNA ENJOYED the cozy ride home in the truck with Max, the stars sparkling in the night sky as they drove down the country road. Max held her hand. The songs on the radio all seemed to be her favorites.

Max pulled into the driveway and parked in front of the house.

She stared at it, looking at it for the first time as their home, imagining what it could be in her mind as they made updates to suit them.

With everything going on, they hadn't had time to get the paint for the kitchen or decide on new countertops. In truth, it didn't really matter. What mattered most was that she and Max would make new memories here as a family.

With Christmas coming soon, it would be their first holiday back together. She'd brought her box of decorations she used in her apartment. She'd add them to the Wildes'. Another joining of her life with Max's.

"You okay?" Max squeezed her hand.

She turned to him. "What do you want for Christmas?"

"You."

That warmed her heart. "I'm already yours."

"Then I have everything I need."

She leaned over and kissed him, letting him know how much she appreciated that sweet sentiment.

He answered with a soft, sultry kiss.

Her mind went blank and need took over. She sank into him, holding him close in the confined space. Her elbow hit the steering wheel, but she barely noticed, because the taste of Max sent a wave of desire swirling through her.

Somehow Max managed to open his door and slip out while still kissing her. He gripped her hips and slid her across the seat and right out of the truck until she was standing in front of him, her arms around his shoulders, the kiss spinning out as their tongues entwined and their bodies met in an embrace she didn't want to ever escape.

"We should go inside," Max said against her mouth, his hand dipping low over her hip and covering her ass as he pulled her closer, his thick erection pressed to her belly.

"Mmm-hmm." She was happy to be right here in his arms, even if it was cold as hell out.

"Kenna," he whispered against her lips.

She broke the kiss to scold him. "You talk too much." She dove in for more.

He gave in to the kiss for another moment, then kissed his way to her ear. "It's cold out here. And you're wearing too many clothes," he grumbled back.

"You should fix that." She gave him a sexy smile,

turned in his arms, and felt his hands slide across her hips as she sauntered toward the house.

"Damn. I love that dress. Those legs. That ass."

She glanced over her shoulder.

He hadn't moved, just stood there watching her walk away.

"Come and get them," she ordered with a grin and kept on walking.

Max quickly closed the truck door, locked it, and caught up and took her by the hips, pulling her ass into his thighs as he kissed her neck. Then they made a mad dash, hand in hand, inside the house, up the stairs, and into their room.

Max closed the door and stalked her toward the bed.

The back of her legs hit the mattress, but she didn't sit down. "Thank you for tonight. I enjoyed seeing your cousins again. I especially loved dancing with you."

He narrowed his gaze on her delectable body. "Let's dance some more."

She knew he didn't mean standing up and reached for his jacket, peeling it down his arms, then dropping it to the floor. He did the same with hers. Then he spun her around, put his wide hand flat on her belly to hold her hips snug against his thighs, as he kissed her neck again and undid her hair, letting it fall past her shoulders. He released her and slowly slid the zipper down her back, kissing her spine as he went. His fingertips brushed across her shoulders, slipping beneath the material as he pushed the sleeves down her arms and the dress fell and puddled at her feet.

Max trailed kisses from the outside of her shoulder, along the length of it to her neck and up to her ear. "God, you're beautiful." His hand slid around her hip, down her belly, and dipped between her thighs. He rubbed his fingers over her soft folds. She rocked into his hand, riding the wave of sensations he built inside her.

She reached back between them and covered his hard cock with her hand and stroked him over his jeans, making him groan with pleasure. "You're still wearing too many clothes."

He kissed her neck again, kept rubbing at her clit, and undid her bra. She hated that he pulled his hand free from her, but when he spun her around, pulled the bra off her arms, and bent and took her hard nipple in his mouth, she didn't complain. Mostly because she was too busy moaning out her pleasure and sliding her fingers into his hair and holding him close.

"Max." His name came out a prayer and a plea.

He answered it by sliding her panties down over her hips so they fell down her legs to her ankles.

She kicked them off.

Max let loose her breast and attacked his jeans and the rest of his clothes while she undid her heels and tossed them.

She crawled up the bed, but before she could turn to him, he came up behind her, pulled her up and onto his lap as he sat on his heels, her legs and feet on the outside of his, spreading her thighs wide so he could play with her with those talented fingers of his.

"Does this hurt your ribs?"

She leaned back against his warm body, rolled her hips against his thick erection pressed against her ass, and his fingers sliding over her slick folds. "You feel so good."

Max slid one finger deep inside her over and over again, then two as his other hand cupped her breast and he plucked and played with her hard nipple. The dual sensations coiled her insides into a ball of vibrating pleasure, so that when he sank those fingers deep again and brushed his thumb against her clit, the orgasm exploded through her in waves until she slumped back against Max's strong body. He kept the intimacy going with soft sweeps of his hand up and down her thigh, his other hand on her breast, squeezing and caressing, so she was wholly aware of how much he wanted her.

And she wanted him. "Max, that was—"

"Just the beginning." He helped her move onto the bed, but when he would have laid her back on the pillow, she nudged his shoulder and sent him onto his back.

She straddled his hips and rubbed her wet center over his hard cock, leaned down, and kissed him softly. "My turn to have my way with you."

The grin he gave her was filled with agreement and desire.

She sank back onto his hard shaft, taking him deep.

His eyes rolled back in his head with the sheer pleasure she gave him.

It made her feel powerful and so happy to make him feel that good, so she rose up and sank back down on him again and again, keeping the pace slow and sultry, like she could do this all night, the soreness in her body nothing but background noise as the pleasure coursing through her built and made it fade away.

He used his hands, his mouth on her breasts, amplifying her pleasure. She lost herself in the way he loved her as she moved over him, until the pleasure overtook them again and Max's head fell back deep into the pillow, his hands clamped on her hips, helping her ride him harder and faster as he picked up his hips from the mattress, making him go deeper, and they both shattered with the sheer ecstasy they gave each other.

She gently lowered herself onto his heaving chest, bracing herself on her forearms so she didn't hurt her ribs. Her breath sawed in and out at his throat. His arms wrapped around her and held her close.

Her ribs ached with the deep breaths, but it didn't matter. All that mattered was being in his arms, feeling this intense connection to him, and knowing in this moment, they were as close as they'd ever been.

Max brushed his fingers through her hair in soft caresses, prolonging the intimacy and pampering her with more soft strokes, showering her with his love.

She kissed his shoulder, then his neck, then rose just enough to share a sultry kiss, her lips locked with his. "That was amazing."

Max looked up at her. "With you, it always feels that way. With you, my whole world feels right."

Touched beyond words, she kissed him again, then settled back in his arms.

They cuddled close, their love a warmth and peace that surrounded them.

And right before she fell asleep, she spoke a truth that she'd known for a long time and now knew he felt the same way. "I'm home again." Right here, in his arms.

Max kissed her on the head, hugged her close, and whispered, "Everything is finally right again."

Chapter Thirty-Seven

MAX AND Kenna were sitting at the kitchen table locked in a kiss when his dad came in and cleared his throat. Max kissed Kenna one last time, put her coffee in her hand, enjoyed seeing the blush on her cheeks and the lust in her eyes before he turned to his dad. "Morning."

"Morning, you two." Amusement filled his dad's voice. "What's with all the boxes in the living room?"

Max sat back in his seat. "Kenna and I are headed out to chop down a tree to decorate for Christmas."

"It's been so busy around here, I wasn't sure we'd get to it in time." His dad poured himself a cup of coffee.

"We've done the tree every year, but we haven't decorated in the way Mom liked to do."

His dad grinned at Kenna. "I knew having you here would be a good thing."

Kenna's eyes filled with surprise and warmth. "Thank you."

His dad held his mug out toward Max. "He's happy. I'm happy. But the changes you two are talking about making, for the house and celebrating the holiday, it's all breathing life back into this place. It feels like a home again."

Max appreciated how his dad made Kenna feel welcome. But this was so much more and it warmed his heart to see this softer, gentler, open side to his dad. He'd changed since Mom died and he had a health scare. Max didn't like what brought it on, but he appreciated that it had brought them all closer together.

"How was your date last night?" His dad took a seat at the table. "How are all the Wilde cousins?"

"We had a lot of fun. But it was an interesting night." Kenna's understatement made Max grin.

"What happened?" his dad asked.

"Hillary was there." Max sipped his coffee.

His dad scowled. "I hope that didn't ruin your night."

"Not at all." Kenna waved that away. "Max and I won't let her ruin anything between us ever again. But it was nice to see Aria put Hillary in her place."

"I think you better tell me what happened?" Dad's gaze turned sharp and alert.

Max told him about Hillary and Dan and the whole scene last night.

His dad shook his head. "That girl Hillary sure has caused some trouble in this family."

"Well, she won't anymore," Max said. "Aria banned her from the bar. Kenna and I know what really happened back in the day and are back together. Nothing is going to tear us apart again. And Aria . . . She's smart and better than any man deserves, especially that piece of shit Dan. She'll find someone new who comes close to being good enough for her."

His dad raised a mug to that. "I spoke with your uncle day before yesterday. He said there's some trouble around Lyric."

Max easily guessed what the trouble was. "If you're talking about the biker guy who comes into the bar, I don't think he's as much trouble as people think. He likes her. More than that, I think he wants her. He protected her last night when Dan tried to get Lyric on his side."

"Like she'd defend a guy who cheated on her sister." Dad scoffed.

"Exactly."

Dad shook his head. "Not that guy. Someone else has been making a nuisance of himself. She's only said something to her dad and asked him to talk to Hunt about running a background check on the guy."

Max folded his arms over his chest. "Did Hunt do it?"

"He's working on it."

"Good." Max unfolded his arms. "Let me know what Hunt finds out. If Lyric needs help with anything, I'm in."

His dad nodded.

Max turned his attention to Kenna. "You ready to go?"

She stood. "Yep. I've never cut down my own tree. We always got one from a lot in town. Since my place was so small, I could only get a little one. Still, it was cute and festive."

"We'll find a big one for the living room. We'll

need lots of room for presents now that the family is so big."

His dad grinned. "Lana is too little to appreciate Christmas just yet, but I can't wait to see Eliza opening her gifts."

Max looked up at Kenna. "I can't wait until it's our little one doing the same."

Kenna leaned down and kissed him softly, then looked him in the eye, her beautiful face a couple inches from his. "We'll make it our New Year's resolution to make a baby."

He took her hand and held her in place. "Do you mean that?"

"Yes. We go after what we want from now on."

He stood, took her in his arms, and kissed her again, so grateful and thankful that she wanted a family as much as he did. "I can't wait."

"I have an appointment to get my stitches removed just before the holiday and I'll take care of getting ready to have a baby." She meant to have her IUD removed. She'd asked for a couple months to let her body get back on track, but that still meant that sometime next year, if all went well, they'd be pregnant.

This was really going to happen.

He couldn't be more excited.

Lucky for him, he already had plans to make her his wife.

Waiting now seemed hard, but also gave him a ton of enthusiasm and anticipation for what he had planned for the proposal.

"I'll keep the baby stuff to myself," his dad said, grinning.

Max hadn't told anyone about his upcoming proposal. Not yet anyway.

But everyone, including Kenna, knew it was coming.

In fact, Kenna probably suspected it would come on Christmas Day.

That was too obvious. He wanted her to be really surprised.

Chapter Thirty-Eight

❧

Kᴇɴɴᴀ sᴛᴏᴏᴅ in the living room staring at the beautiful Christmas tree all lit up and decorated, presents stacked and clustered underneath for everyone in the family. She loved the holidays, but this one felt even more special because the entire Wilde family and her parents would be here tomorrow to celebrate together.

Except one person would be missing. Kyle. She thought about him all the time. She missed him. But life went on, and she couldn't be happier than to be here in her new home with Max.

"Hey, I thought you were going to go upstairs so I can fill your stocking."

Because Max was busy on the ranch and she was still recuperating from her injuries, though she was much better now and looking forward to returning to her classroom after winter break, she'd put together all the goodies for the stockings, leaving hers the only one Max needed to fill.

She didn't turn to him, but closed her eyes. "I won't look. I promise."

Max grumbled behind her, but she heard him move to the hearth and fill her stocking with whatever goodies he'd gotten her.

They were alone in the quiet room, nothing but the last embers of the fire crackling in the fireplace, the glow of the Christmas tree lights making the room feel warm and inviting.

Max's hands settled on her shoulders. "You can open them now."

She turned and spotted her stocking, fat to nearly bursting with gifts. "You're sweet."

"It was Santa." The smile on his face showed his utter happiness. He looked around the room, at the tree they'd chopped down and decorated with his family ornaments and the ones she'd added from her collection, back to the mantel where all the stockings were hung beneath the garlands she'd made. They'd even strung lights and garlands up the stairs' balustrade.

Max sighed. "It turned out better than I expected. It's everything I ever wanted."

She turned and faced him. "I know exactly what you mean."

"It's late. Everyone will be here early tomorrow."

She gave him a coaxing smile. "Can I open a present early?"

"Nope."

She tickled his ribs. "You're no fun."

He chuckled. "You know I am." Max gave her a sultry look, then swooped in and picked her up right off her feet and held her close to his chest, cradled in his strong arms.

"You're crazy."

"You're beautiful." He kissed her, long and deep.

She didn't want him to stop. Ever.

She pulled back, breaking the kiss but giving him a sexy grin. "Remember how we used to be like this."

"Used to?" He headed for the stairs. "Don't you mean you love it that we're still hot for each other?"

He hit the landing at the top of the stairs in record time, even carrying her.

"It's so much more than just that now."

He stopped outside their bedroom door and looked her deep in the eyes. "It's always been more than lust, Kenna. I am drawn to you, and you to me."

She kissed him again. "I need you so much."

He set her back on her feet in front of him and cupped her face. "I feel the same. And right now, I'm going to show you. All you're going to feel is me and my love for you." He kissed her at the same time he backed her into their room. The second he cleared the door and kicked it shut, he pulled her top up and over her head. She went for his shirt, too, then the button and fly on his jeans as he slipped her bra down her arms. He stared at her bare breasts, hunger building in his eyes, as he cupped them and swept his thumbs over her hard nipples. "I want you naked and under me right now."

Clothes went flying. Max grabbed a condom from the drawer and rolled it on. She was as desperate for him as he was for her. And when she lay back on their bed and he followed her, covering her body with his, he kissed her again, erasing all the thoughts in her head but one. More.

Of him. Of them taking this time to be together and let the world go on without them for a while.

Lost in his sweet kiss, the feel of his hands moving over her, the taste of him on her lips and tongue, she clung to him. He slid his hand up her thigh, over her mound, slipping his finger over her soft folds and deep into her wet core. She moaned against his mouth and rocked her hips into his hand. He stroked her, his thumb pressed against her clit, rubbing softly until she came hard and fast, her body trembling below his.

She didn't wait to recover, she wanted him too desperately still and pushed on his shoulder and sent him falling to his back beside her. She straddled his lap and rubbed herself along his hard cock as she leaned down and kissed him, her tongue tangling with his. He clamped his hands on her hips and guided her down his thick shaft. She took him deep and rolled against him, a soft moan escaping her lips. He swallowed it down on another searing kiss.

She moved against him. He thrust into her. Over and over again they rocked and rolled, their bodies moving together in a rhythm that amplified their pleasure until they were so in tune they crashed over the edge of ecstasy, clinging to each other.

Completely blissed out and snuggled close to him, she barely moved when he got up for the condom cleanup and slipped back into bed, taking her right back into his arms and kissing her on the head. He hugged her close and whispered, "Best, most beautiful gift in my life, ever."

His sweet words, his love wrapped around her and glowing in her heart, went with her into sleep and made her smile when she woke up to a snowy Christmas morning.

Max wasn't in bed, but he had opened the shade so she woke up to see they'd celebrate a white Christmas.

She immediately found the pen and paper he'd left on his pillow. She picked it up and grinned.

Solve for i. Love, Max
$$9x-7i > 3(3x-7u)$$

Kenna couldn't help but chuckle. But the note also made her think of the games she played with Kyle and appreciate Max all the more for this sweet reminder of her brother, today, done in Max's way and with all his love.

So she solved for i and easily came to the answer in her head, but because she wanted it in ink on paper she wrote it out . . .

$$9x-7i > 9x-21u$$

She subtracted out the x variable . . .

$$-7i > -21u$$

Then she divided by -7 and flipped the > to < and got . . .

i < 3 u

I love you.

She pressed the paper to her heart and let the silent tears fall, thinking about how lucky she was to be loved by Max, hopeful and excited that she got to spend the rest of her life with him.

She remembered the spare frame she'd unpacked and put in the nightstand, thinking she'd use it for a picture of her and Max sometime in the future. Instead, she pulled it out, folded and tore the paper down to size, and framed the note. She positioned it on the nightstand right behind Max's watch so every night she went to sleep, every morning she woke up, she'd see it right there.

Filled with a need to see her Wilde man, like Cyn liked to call Hunt and Shelby called Chase, she threw the covers aside, pulled on the red flannel pajamas she'd picked out just for today, and ran down the stairs to kiss Max.

MAX WAS SITTING on the couch, drinking a cup of coffee, enjoying the Christmas tree lights, the blazing fire he'd set, and the Christmas music he had on low, thinking about Kenna asleep in their bed upstairs.

They'd been through so much to get to today.

He heard her rushing down the stairs before he saw her, but he was already smiling and setting aside his coffee when she came around the couch, straddled his lap, cupped his face, and kissed him soundly.

"I love you, too."

He chuckled. "You liked the note."

"I loved it."

He knew she would. He also knew it would remind her of Kyle. "I have to confess, I'm not as good as your brother at the whole code thing. I found that love equation on the internet."

"I don't care. It's the thought and love behind it that matters to me. Thank you." She kissed him again.

He pulled the present out from under the pillow beside him and held it up to her.

She stared at the green wrapped package with the bright red bow like she didn't know what to do with it.

"Last night you asked if you could open a present early. Well, it's Christmas Day and I'd like you to have this and wear it today."

She took the little gift and unwrapped it, revealing the velvet jewelry box. She grinned at him, then flipped the box open. Nothing but pure joy filled her eyes, along with some tears. "Max, it's gorgeous. I love it."

He took the box, pulled out the necklace, undid the clasp, then wrapped the gold chain around her neck, and clasped it again.

Kenna picked up the diamond heart-shaped necklace and stared at it again, the stones sparkling in the light. "It's beautiful."

He raised a brow. "You weren't expecting something else?"

She grinned. "Maybe for a second."

He put her mind at ease that he wasn't taunting her or holding back. "There's nothing I want more than for you to be my wife. I just want the proposal to be special. Ours. A day we'll remember simply as the day I asked you and you said yes."

She leaned in and kissed him softly. "I completely understand and agree. I know you love me. I know what you want is the same as what I want. So today we'll celebrate the holiday as a family. Yours. Mine. Ours together. And someday soon, we'll have something else to celebrate with them, too."

"And today, you'll wear that and know I love you and that will never change."

"That's all I need." She kissed him again. "Best boyfriend ever."

He brushed his fingers along the side of her face. "Luckiest man alive."

Her eyes teared up. "Max. I don't know what to say, except that's really sweet and I love you."

He took her back upstairs and immediately saw how she'd framed the note and put it by their bed. "You did like it." He thought she'd just been humoring him.

"I wouldn't lie to you."

He kissed her softly. "I never thought you did. I just didn't expect you to keep it."

"Sometimes it's the little things that make the best memories and mean the most." She glanced at the note, then touched her fingers to the diamond heart on her chest. "You love me the way I want to be loved."

He slipped his hand under her hair at the back of her neck and pulled her in for a kiss. "Love me, the way I want to be loved right now."

She grinned. "You have the best ideas."

He didn't know any better way to spend a snowy Christmas morning than making love to Kenna, taking it slow and easy and lavishing her with all his love as she poured all of hers into him. They took their time, then spent a half hour just lying in bed talking about this and that and nothing in each other's arms.

They showered, changed, and made it downstairs in time to welcome their family into the house.

The laughter and love were so abundant they filled the house with raucous joy.

They ate, drank, sang along to the Christmas carols playing, and he, Chase, and Hunt put together several toys for the little ones.

And before Kenna's parents left that evening, he pulled them aside, while Cyn and Shelby kept Kenna distracted, and told Kenna's parents about his plan to ask Kenna to marry him and asked for their blessing.

It wasn't the first Christmas they'd spent together. It wouldn't be their last. But it was the last one they'd spend as boyfriend and girlfriend and not husband and wife.

He fell asleep that night with Kenna in his arms and his heart overflowing with love and excitement, knowing it was only a matter of days before he secured the yes he wanted from the only woman he'd ever loved.

Chapter Thirty-Nine

MAX COULDN'T believe this day had finally come. It required quite a bit of planning, but he was confident he had everything set up and in place.

Kenna walked into the kitchen wearing the dress he'd subtly suggested she put on this morning because he liked staring at her legs and would like to take it off her with his teeth that night.

Maybe not so subtle after all.

Plus she'd look great in the proposal video and pictures their family would take later.

After his comment to her about how he'd undress her later, she'd teased him by dropping her towel and taking an achingly long time to slide her panties on, then a sexy black bra, and finally the cranberry wrap dress, all while he salivated and restrained himself from stripping her bare again and taking her back to bed.

"You look lovely," his dad said, toasting her with his coffee mug.

"Thank you, Wayne." She'd added a simple white cardigan to keep her warm.

It was early January and freezing outside, the ground dusted with fresh snow from last night.

She pulled her new favorite mug from the strainer and filled it with coffee. The mug belonged to her brother. She'd kept a few things after she and her parents cleaned out his place. A picture of her and Kyle as kids sitting on the hearth at their childhood home now sat on the mantel in their living room. The other photos and mementoes she'd kept were up in their room, waiting to be put out after the renovation they had scheduled to start next month.

"Max? You okay?"

He glanced up at her from his seat at the table, where one of her plants sat center stage. "I'm great, sweetheart. Just thinking about all the packing we need to do in here so the contractor can redo the kitchen in a few weeks."

"It won't take that long, though it will be hard to be without the kitchen for a while. We can set up the necessities in the dining room until it's done and make do the best we can."

He smiled, loving that nothing ever seemed insurmountable to her. It was just a problem to be solved.

"Are you excited to be back in the classroom today?" his dad asked.

Kenna put her hand on her stomach. "I don't know why, but I've got butterflies."

"You're just excited," his dad guessed.

Kenna grabbed her bag and purse and held her mug out to the side while she kissed him. "I'm off to school." She said it with such a sweet and enthusiastic smile he couldn't help smiling back at her. "Thank you for waking me up this morning." Since his dad was behind her, he didn't see the sexy smile and sultry look in her eyes, because that thank-you was for *how* he'd woken her up this morning.

"Happy to do it every morning, sweetheart."

"Who needs an alarm, when I have you?"

"You claimed that one's heart a long time ago," his dad chimed in.

She looked over her shoulder. "And I'm keeping him." She turned back, kissed Max again, and off she went to school.

He and his dad waited until they heard the front door open and close again.

Max took off the flannel he'd put on over a T-shirt and pulled on the white dress shirt he'd left on the back of his dad's chair.

Kenna, luckily, hadn't even noticed.

He buttoned it and tucked it in, then patted his front pocket just to be sure he had everything he needed.

His dad grinned like a lunatic. "How long do we wait before we follow her to town?"

"We'll give it ten minutes, so there's no chance we catch up to her on the road and she sees us."

"She's going to love this. You two . . . you were made for each other."

Max knew it. "She seems really happy."

"Today feels like she's back to her normal life, I bet."

"Then it's the perfect day for what I have planned."

"Then let's go. I want to make sure I get a good seat."

Chapter Forty

~~~~~~

Kenna waved to students and said hello as she made her way to her classroom.

"Hi, Miss Baker. Welcome back," one of her Algebra II students, Paula, called out, the other girls from the cheer squad with her smiling in greeting as she passed them in the hall.

It seemed odd to see the cheerleaders in uniform on a Monday. She'd figure out what was going on once she got caught up with the students in her first period class.

Patrice stood outside Kenna's classroom door. "I was just delivering something to your class. How are you? You look absolutely beautiful."

Kenna had picked the dress because it made her feel confident and pretty. She wanted her students to see her looking good and feeling well. Plus, Max liked it. "I'm excited to be back at school and to see my students. I hope my absence didn't cause too much trouble for them or you."

Patrice walked into the classroom ahead of her. "The

substitute did a wonderful job keeping the students on track. But I know they're all excited to have you back."

Kenna followed and dropped her stuff on her chair, smiling at the red roses in a vase on the center of her desk. She knew who they were from, but plucked the card free and opened it.

For the best teacher in the world.
I love you.

Max

"Max," Patrice guessed, smiling knowingly.

"Yes. He's so sweet."

"Very."

Kenna wondered about the knowing smile Patrice gave her this time and chalked it up to Patrice being a romantic.

"Well, I'll let you get settled. First bell is in five minutes." Patrice headed for the door, waving over her shoulder.

Kenna put her things away, but grabbed her phone from her purse to send a quick text to Max.

KENNA: Thank you for the beautiful flowers. I love them. And you!

KENNA: Getting ready for class to start. Missing you. ♥

She set her phone on her desk, not expecting a reply. Max was probably already out working on the ranch. Some of the huge property didn't have cell coverage.

A moment later, her cell pinged with an incoming text.

MAX: Miss you too
MAX: Hope your group is better behaved than mine

She smiled at the picture that popped up a moment later of a herd of black cows surrounding the back end of a truck filled with hay.

KENNA: At least they don't talk back and roll their eyes at you.
MAX: That's what you think ;)
MAX: Love you
KENNA: Love you back

She smiled. They used to end all their texts and conversations just like that. It felt so natural and comforting to fall right back into their routine.

She needed to hurry before the bell rang. She took a seat at her desk and read the notes the substitute left her, along with the graded assignments the students completed last week. She logged into her computer, checked the students' grades to see how they'd done before leaving for the winter break. She heard the bell, but finished reading the sub's notes to be sure she knew where she needed to pick up the lessons in each period.

"Miss Baker," Paula called from the doorway.

Kenna set the notes aside and looked up, not at all prepared to see the entire cheer squad line up in front of her. "Hello, girls. What's all this?"

"We have a surprise for you. Follow us."

She grinned, happy the students and faculty had set up some kind of special welcome back for her. She glanced at the beautiful roses Max sent her and wondered how she got so lucky to have a man like him, students like these, and friends who'd do something so sweet.

She stood. "Lead the way."

Eight of the girls walked ahead in a straight line. The other two flanked her. There were no other students in the hall as they headed out of the building to the gym.

"Don't worry, Miss Baker. It's a good surprise," Paula said, her cheeks flushed with excitement.

The cheerleaders up front opened the gym doors and raucous cheering and stomping in the bleachers spilled out. The cheers grew to a roar when Kenna walked in. Overwhelmed by the noise and the crowd filling the bleachers, all she could do was smile and wave at the students. But then she realized the entire Wilde family, including the cousins and aunt and uncle from Blackrock Falls were all seated in the first row, along with her parents and her aunt and uncle from Idaho.

The cheerleaders let out a bunch of shouts and held up letters spelling out Welcome Back.

And in the center of the gym in front of everyone, Max stood in a heart made out of red rose petals, wearing black jeans, a white dress shirt, and a nervous, but gleeful smile.

She went to him, getting a sense of what was really going on here.

The second she got close enough to him, he took her hand. "Welcome back to school, sweetheart."

She realized he was wearing a small microphone from the drama class so everyone could hear him. "I thought you were at the ranch with your rowdy cows."

He chuckled. "I wanted to surprise you."

"You set this all up?"

"I wanted your first day back to be spectacular."

She looked at the crowd. "You invited our families."

"I wanted everyone we care about to be here for this. We've waited a long time. Though it wasn't always easy, it was worth it to finally get to do this." He dropped to one knee and the crowd went wild. Max kissed the back of her hand, then looked at everyone, put his finger to his lips, and shushed them with a grin. The gym went quiet and Max looked up at her.

She hadn't taken her eyes off him. She wanted to remember every second of this moment.

"It was at this very school where I fell in love with you for the first time. And every day I'm with you, I fall in love with you all over again. And that love gets stronger each and every day. I can't promise that all the challenging times are behind us. What I can promise is that I will spend every day of the rest of my life wholly, completely in love with you. I will be by your side, cheering you on, lifting you up, loving you through everything. I'm already the luckiest man alive to have you in my life, but I'd be even happier if you agreed to be my wife."

The cheerleaders lined up behind Max rolled out a

banner that asked the very question Max spoke to her now, even though she was already nodding.

"Kenna, will you marry me?" He pulled a ring from his shirt pocket and held it up to her.

"Yes. Absolutely yes!"

The crowd cheered so loud it was deafening.

Max pulled the tiny microphone off his ear and let it dangle down his back. He kissed the back of her hand, slid the gorgeous diamond ring on her finger, rose and kissed her again like no one was watching them.

She wrapped her arms around his neck and he picked her right up off her feet and spun her around. She broke the kiss and pressed her cheek to his.

"I'm so damn happy."

She leaned back and looked him right in the eyes. "Me too. This was the best surprise."

"You knew it was coming."

"Not today. Not like this. It was perfect."

"Your kids will have to stop calling you Miss Baker and start calling you Mrs. Wilde soon."

"How long until I can claim you as mine forever?"

"You did that a long time ago, sweetheart, but we'll set a date that is sooner rather than later."

"Perfect. Because I want to be your wife more than anything."

He touched his forehead to hers and they shared a long look that said so much without them saying anything.

Their families surrounded them, offering congratulations. Another cheer went up from all the students led

by Patrice before she announced it was time for all the
students to head to class.

Patrice came up beside her as Kenna picked up little
Eliza. "I'll give you a few minutes with your family and
keep an eye on your class until you return."

"Thank you for helping Max pull this off."

Patrice put her hand on Kenna's arm. "You've been
through a lot. You deserved something wonderful. I'm
so happy for you and Max. I hope you have a long and
happy life together." Patrice headed out to her classroom.

The din in the gym ebbed and it was only her, Max,
and their families. Everyone hugged them, offered their
congratulations, and told Max he'd done a great job on
the proposal. She loved being surrounded by all of her
family and the love they showered on her and Max.

Everyone was happy for them.

Especially her parents, who were still grieving Kyle,
but found joy in Kenna's engagement.

"You're going to be a beautiful bride," her father
gushed, a tear in his eye.

"I can't wait to start planning," her mom said, looking to Shelby and Cyn for support in that effort.

"We're in," Shelby assured her.

Cyn beamed. "I'll do your hair. Some kind of twist in
the back to set off your beautiful face."

She beamed at all of them. "I can't wait."

Max broke away from his brothers' and father's congratulations and hooked his arm over her shoulders.
"Are you happy?"

"Ecstatic."

"I'm sorry your brother wasn't here."

"Me, too." She looked at everyone who took the time on a Monday to come here to celebrate with them. "But this is special. This is our family."

"And there will be more to come. More babies. More celebrations. More of everything. And we'll do it all together." Max kissed her. This one soft and promising and filled with love.

He kissed her the same way on their wedding day.

And every day after that.

Including the day their daughter, Kylie, was born, nine months after the I do's.